SHERLOCK HOLMES AND THE NEFARIOUS SEAFARERS

Book #3 in the Confidential Files of Dr. John H. Watson

C.J. LUTTON

Edited by
JOANNA CAMPBELL SLAN

spot on publishing

Sherlock Holmes and the Nefarious Seafarers: Book #3 in the Confidential Files of Dr. John H. Watson conceived and written by C.J. Lutton. Edited by Joanna Campbell Slan

This paperback edition published by JABberwocky Literary Agency, Inc. in coordination with Spot On Publishing.

JABberwocky Literary Agency, Inc.

49 W. 45th Street, Suite #5N

New York, NY 10036

http://awfulagent.com

ebooks@awfulagent.com

Joanna Campbell Slan

Spot On Publishing

9307 SE Olympus Street

Hobe Sound, FL 33455 / USA

http://www.SpotOnPublishing.org

http://www.JoannaSlan.com

http://www.theSherlockStories.com

Cover by Dar Albert, Wicked Smart Designs

http://www.WickedSmartDesigns.com

Revised 09/25/2024

ISBN 9781625677471

Sherlock Holmes and the Nefarious Seafarers: Book #3 in the Confidential Files of Dr. John H. Watson conceived and written by C.J. Lutton. Edited by Joanna Campbell Slan

CONTENTS

Dedicated to Rita Lutton –

She and I together - her son, my husband – she loved him, he loved her – he loved me, and I loved him. Our bond was the love and faith we had in CJ. We encouraged him to finish these books because they were where his heart was.

PUBLISHER'S NOTE

In accordance with the previous work by Sir Arthur Conan Doyle, we've made every attempt to use British spelling and vocabulary throughout. Also, the Bethlehem Hospital was pronounced as "Bedlam" when spoken, but written "Bethlehem." Hence the nickname "bedlam," meaning madness.

PREFACE

FROM THE JOURNALS OF DR. JOHN H. WATSON—

To those so inclined, my long association with the great Sherlock Holmes may appear, at first blush, an incredible journey through life. We were valiant knights on a quest to rid the world of evildoers with the occasional slaying of a dragon along the way. This might seem to be a romantic's ideal. After all, what child hasn't dreamt of curing the world's ills and ridding the populace of its least desirable elements?

Of that mythology, I can say this: Rooming with one of the most remarkable minds of our time afforded me the privilege of chronicling many of our exciting adventures. But as many of my readers are well aware, Holmes could be churlish and disagreeable when there were no cases to challenge his keen mind.

Once a puzzle presents itself, Holmes is dogged in his pursuit of the solution. No challenge along the way can pose an insurmountable impediment. I originally thought of his single-mindedness as courage, but upon reflection, courage takes a second-row seat to his focused willpower. Often he performs feats of unimaginable strength; multiple times he puts his life at extreme risk, and usually he deprives his body of the nourishment most of us crave. There is a driving force within him that compels the man past the limitations of human endurance when he seeks to right a wrong.

Another odd dichotomy is Holmes' relationship with the Crown. He comes from a family of staunch royalists, and of course, his brother Mycroft is a protector of all the hereditary rights and respect due to the royal family. But Sherlock Holmes is not in awe of anyone, no matter what title or position that person might hold. Naturally, he is pleased when the Crown turns to him for assistance, but he does not seek self-promotion. In fact, he would rather operate as he puts it "in the shadows" because that hidden place allows him the most freedom to do what he must do to solve a crime.

I have never seen in Holmes any sort of prejudice against other people whether they differ in skin color or national origin. Admittedly, he sees most women as less capable than men, but he is observant enough to note there are exceptions to this sweeping generalization. Also, Holmes understands that the same social customs that have been put in place to protect women actually serve to trap them, forcing them into roles that deny them full exercise of their intellectual ability.

Indeed, Holmes is an admirer of science, praising it as a twin to intellect, because without the scientific method of inquiry, no progress will ever be made. "Logic is the language of science," he has often said. "Logic is a byproduct of looking at those rules that underpin the functioning of the universe. When we approach that which is without logic, we see a deleterious waste of time, jumbled thinking, and wrongful expenditure of energy that get us nowhere."

I share these observations on Holmes' personality here, at the beginning of a new adventure, because I believe them to be pertinent. They go a long way in explaining behavior that at first blush might seem extreme or even preposterous. For during this case, we were called upon to enter environments totally beyond the bounds of our personal experience or expertise.

I leave it to our readers to decide whether what we did came down on the side of the angels or blackened our names forever.

— Preface by Dr. John H. Watson

I

In my experience, two extremes of weather conspire to keep the criminal population of London off the streets, and thus these extremes provoke equally intemperate behavior in the great Consulting Detective. Summer, with its broiling heat, its stink, and its unwholesome atmosphere, caused Holmes to act in a fretful manner that tried my patience. The depths of winter when frigid weather conjoined with ice and snow also gave my friend a plethora of reasons for bemoaning his fate. This week had been particularly cruel to him, as fresh snow added another layer of mischief to the streets.

"My mind must be stimulated!" Holmes grumbled. "Give me a problem to solve. A cipher to wrestle into clarity. A clue to follow! But do not force me to go without. This will not do, Watson."

He punctuated with a jab of the fireplace poker, an action fraught with such intensity that the log he attacked spat sparks all over Mrs. Hudson's carpet. Most of the sparks extinguished themselves as quickly as they appeared, but two were more lively than the rest and flared up as they discovered the combustible wool floor covering.

"Good heavens, Holmes." I jumped to my feet. Tearing the shawl off my shoulders, I beat the tiny fires until they were no more. "It is one thing to be melancholy and ill-tempered, but quite another to set the rooms on fire. Steady, man. This cold cannot persist forever. Have you read today's paper? Are you sure there are no cries for help in the columns of the Times?"

"Perhaps." Holmes cocked his head at an odd angle. Before he could expand on this paltry admission, he cried out, "Come in, Mrs. Hudson!"

Our landlady entered and handed Holmes an envelope. "A street urchin brought this. He said it was urgent, Mr. Holmes."

"Thank you, Mrs. Hudson!" Holmes answered, loudly.

"Whatever happened here?" she scolded, looking at the charred spots on the carpet. "I thought I smelled wool burning!"

"My dear Mrs. Hudson, I told Dr. Watson that you would be most angry at his lack of care. As you can see, he tends the fire with little regard for the harm a stray spark can do! Rest assured, I have chastised him violently on this bad habit. I fear that I shall have to keep my eye on him every second lest he act so foolishly again. Good day to you, dear lady. " Holmes rose to his feet and ushered a flustered Mrs. Hudson out, but not before she had the opportunity to glance back over her shoulder and cluck disapprovingly in my direction.

"I-I-I-I did no such—" But before I could mount a defense, Holmes had closed the door behind our landlady.

Holding himself upright by dint of resting his palms on his thighs, my friend bent at the waist and laughed uproariously. Wiping his eyes, he hugged his torso as he struggled not to topple over. "Ho! That was rich indeed."

"Holmes!" I protested, embarrassed by his playful lie.

"Oh, Watson, I'm sure she knows who made the mess. Your reputation shall remain pure. Now, what could be so urgent?" he asked, tearing open the envelope and unfolding the note inside. "Short and direct!" he remarked, reading its contents.

"What does it say, Holmes?"

"We have a missing husband," came the reply.

This time, I clucked disapprovingly. "What sort of fool would go out in weather such as this? Perhaps the man deserves to be lost! And more to the point, perhaps that note is from an hysterical woman who drove her husband from their home into the frigid air. I, for one, am sympathetic to the plight of a person living in close quarters with a madman."

Holmes ignored my taunt. "Do not be so quick to dismiss this as the rantings of an hysterical woman. Perhaps this letter will be of some interest to you." Holmes handed me the note.

I read the letter to myself: *Husband Jeremy Morel missing, three weeks. Require your services, immediately! Will await your arrival. Please come. –Mrs. Maria Morel*

It showed an address in Kennington. In fact, I knew the very street as I had cause to admire the homes there on more than one occasion. This was the sort of case that would no doubt command a handsome fee, an exorbitant one if my friend had not settled on fixed fees. The invitation was timely as we'd had the last of the bottle of whiskey last evening and purchasing more would be a considerable financial hardship on us both.

Taking long strides across the sitting room, Holmes moved to one of our two windows with alacrity. Throwing it open, and ignoring the blast of cold air that intruded, he put both fingers in his mouth and whistled an ear-splitting blast. This was his tried-and-true method for summoning the Baker Street Irregulars, as this shrill ejaculation carried for an incredible distance. Today would be no exception. Indeed, given the dearth of traffic on the streets, our environment was conducive to that whistle traveling farther than normal. Even so, I hated the idea of forcing one of Holmes' young confederates to leave whatever warmth they could muster and race around the numbingly cold world that was London on this date in 1897.

I could not help but chastise my friend. "Don't be ridiculous, Holmes. Those unruly children you use to run your errands will not venture out in such miserable weather. It's too much for you to expect of them. In fact, I think it rather heartless—" and again I was interrupted. This time the knock on the door came at a level closer to the floor that a typical salutation.

"Get that, please, Watson." Holmes slammed the window down, hard. A large chunk of ice cracked and fell from the architrave.

I opened the door to a creature so bundled up that I could scarce perceive any signs of humanity. Bouncing past me, the mite ran over and bowed in front of Holmes.

"Sir? You was wanting me?"

"Evans?" I asked with more than a little astonishment. "Is that you?"

"Who else would it be, Doctor?" The swaddled figure turned my way. Pulling a scrap of fabric serving as a muffler down to expose his eyes, he glared at me. Evans had replaced Wiggins as the leader of Holmes' gang of street urchins who served as auxiliary eyes and ears for the world's first consulting detective. In his own ingenious way, Holmes had seen the group's leadership handed from one capable young person to the next. In short, he had tasked each leader with every aspect of grooming the next leader in line so that the responsibility for finding a new person as skilled, loyal, and trustworthy as the old remained a sacred trust. Of all the BSI leaders I'd known, Evans was undoubtedly one of the most intelligent. He was younger than some, and he normally wore such an expression of natural guilelessness that understandably he slipped in and out of situations where a less innocent-looking youngster would be detained.

"Evans, I want you to go to this address in Kennington. You will not need to take a note. Simply knock on the door, ask for Mrs. Morel, and tell her I shall come and see her this evening around half past seven." Holmes spoke briskly, handing Evans a slip of paper on which he'd written the address in pencil. I believe there was also a coin folded into the note. While Evans committed the address to memory, Holmes reached for his black pipe, the one he called "that little black devil." An imaginative illustrator of my tales took the liberty of giving my friend a calabash. The publisher and I went round and round about the inaccuracy of such a representation. Eventually, I threw up my hands in disgust and gave in.

Of course, Holmes had no use for such a large piece of gear as a calabash. An expensive and intricate pipe would be impractical for carrying around in one's coat. The little black devil fit perfectly into those long, artistic fingers and could be hidden in a coat pocket. I dare say the pipe was not expensive and would be easy to replace, making it ideal for the sort of gymnastics that Holmes often endured. Indeed, buying a new "little black devil" would take hardly any effort at all.

"You got it, sir," said Evans, crumpling and then tossing the paper into the fire. Turning on his heel, the boy ran out of the room. His light footfalls echoed as he galloped down the stairs.

"You were saying, Watson? Something about the weather being too cold for my Baker Street Irregulars? Hmm?"

Even the thought of moving about in that frozen diorama that spread beyond our cozy rooms sent a chill through the core of my being. "Really, Holmes, you are cruel to that boy. He's little more than a child."

"Watson, I am all that stands between that boy and a short, wretched life in the poorhouse. Evans knows full well that he can refuse my commissions at any time. If you think I am careless with the Baker Street Irregulars, think again. Remember that Wiggins has grown into a fine young man with a bright future. No, I would never take the welfare of the Irregulars lightly. They are an invaluable resource to me and to the Crown. In that spirit, I slipped Evans an extra coin, enough to feed him and his friends, because I know at this age in life, they are missing the amount of proper victuals necessary to sustain them in this filthy weather."

I would not admit it to Holmes, as I did not want to belabor the point, but his thoughtfulness gratified me to no end. The street urchins of London are a source of ongoing shame to those who have eyes to see and a heart to feel. Holmes had gathered the most extraordinary team of young people that I have ever seen, and they did his bidding with a perky diligence that suggested they valued the relationship from their end.

I went back to working on my journals, scanning the shorthand I invented for the purpose of keeping up with speech. Whilst recitations were fresh in my mind, it behooved me to go over my scrawled abbreviations and expand on them, bringing clarity and a sense of background to them all.

Thus I was fully absorbed when Evans knocked on our door once again. With flushed cheeks, he handed Holmes another thick piece of stationery. "That will be all, Evans," said Holmes. The boy turned to go, but my earlier remarks must have pricked at Holmes' conscience because he asked, "Evans? Is everything all right? How is your tribe?"

"Right as rain, sir. We found ourselves a nice spot with the money you gave me, and we're keeping ourselves warm and toasty in this cold weather." Evans stood as rigid as a soldier while making his report to Holmes.

My friend's philanthropy had helped these homeless children, and that gratified me, for they are the least of us. During times of hardship too many of them must resort to illegal activity to stave off hunger and cold. The poorhouses and workhouses are not much better because the rations are paltry and the environment downright insalubrious.

"So was the reply satisfactory?" I asked Holmes as he tossed this second piece of stationery into the coals on the hearth.

"She wishes to meet us at half past five this afternoon." He took a poker and stirred the fragments of wood timber. A chunk of burned wood rolled out onto the brick hearth where it glowed like the eyes of a demon.

"Half past five o'clock?" I repeated the time because I was confident I had heard him wrong. "That is odd."

Typically one called on visitors between three and five p.m. The better acquainted one was, the later one might call. But a visit after five to someone to whom Holmes had not been properly introduced was exceedingly odd. Furthermore, if a spouse was missing, wouldn't one hope to see the great detective immediately? If the missing person in question had been Mary, I should have beaten down Sherlock Holmes' door and begged for help finding my wife. Yet, Mrs. Morel had sent along a note, received an answer, and decided to content herself by waiting for our help. Astonishing!

"Yes," agreed Holmes. "The hour is rather curious, is it not?

⁂ 2 ⁂

Later that day, we did as instructed and found ourselves standing outside a two-story white house with black shutters and a black door. Holmes lifted the knocker and let it fall twice. The wait for an answer gave me a chance to scrutinize the neighborhood, an elegant residential area where lace curtains shielded the interiors from casual viewers even after the heavy velvet drapes had been drawn. Shivering in my tweed jacket, I hoped we'd be allowed entrance soon, when we were greeted by a parlour maid whose height was nearly that of Holmes', yet another unusual aspect of this strange visit. Most household staff members tend to be small in stature. Often, they have lived their lives on the verge of starvation until coming into service, and this lack of proper nutrition stunts their growth.

This particular servant was wearing the black skirt, white blouse, and white apron so appropriate for her station in life, but unless my eyes deceived me, she had also artfully applied rouge to her cheeks. The distinct fragrance of violets clung to her person. My only qualification for making such judgements, I might add, is that my marriage to Mary opened my eyes to many of the closely guarded secrets of the feminine toilette. Before our wedding, I should never have stopped to ponder whether ruddy cheeks were the end result of nature or of artifice. Mary had also laughingly revealed other sundry trifles that now came back to me when Holmes and I had been welcomed into the home. Thanks to my late wife, I knew that a parlour maid did not wear scent, as this was viewed as putting on airs. Yet the parlour maid at the Morels' home seemed to have missed the rules that Mary had quoted me.

We followed the young woman into the foyer of an immaculate and tastefully furnished home. We relieved ourselves of our topcoats, as the parlour maid had not offered to take them from us. Curiously, she hesitated at the door to the hallway before making up her mind to carry our outer garments up the stairs. Holmes and I stood there in that vestibule and waited to meet our hostess.

Soft footsteps marked the arrival of Maria Morel. The lady took my breath away, and I mean that literally. Her hair was the color of spun gold, and although she had made an effort to tame her locks, a few escaped to curl around her heart-shaped face. Her eyes were an unusual dark brown and framed by lashes so long they dusted her cheeks each time she blinked. Most alluring of all was her porcelain skin, a dermis as smooth and silky as any I have ever seen. The color was the palest pink and the texture flawless. All of this beauty was set off by a pair of delicately arched brows that added a piquant quality to what was already both an intelligent and feminine face. Needless to say, her figure was exquisite and her tiny hands with their thin graceful fingers were absolutely charming.

"You must be Sherlock Holmes," she said, offering her hand to the detective.

"I am, and this is my associate, Dr. Watson."

Her smile was disarming, as was her firm handshake.

"Thank you for coming, gentlemen. I am Maria deMare Morel. Welcome to my home," she said in a slightly breathy voice.

"Please come in and make yourselves comfortable," she said sweetly.

Stepping aside to allow us entry into the sitting room, Mrs. Morel never averted her eyes as her silk skirts swished becomingly. Instead she watched us carefully as she nodded towards two leather-covered armchairs with ottomans that had been painstakingly needlepointed. I took one of the seats; Holmes took the other. A cozy fire was blazing away in the fireplace, imbuing the space with a sense of warmth and comfort. Wisps of steam rose from a recently poured cup of tea that sat untouched on a small side table.

"May I get you some tea?" Mrs. Morel asked breathlessly, as she took what seemed to be her accustomed place on a green damask settee. Her hand paused over the tea cozy. A fragrance of bergamot hung in the air.

"Yes, please, with milk," replied Holmes, settling his long, lanky frame.

I could not help it, but my mouth fell open. I've never known Holmes to take milk in his tea. Gathering my wits, I realised that our lovely hostess was waiting to hear from me.

"The same," I said. Perhaps Holmes knew something about this particular tea that I did not. Mrs. Morel lifted a silver bell and rang it. "Tea for these gentlemen, Linton," she said politely when the maid reappeared.

"Tell us how we may be of assistance." Holmes regarded the lady of the house coolly as he crossed one knee over the other leg. His hands rested loosely in his lap.

"Mr. Holmes and Dr. Watson," she said, while searching our eyes, "I am not normally a nervous woman. My husband has gone on extended trips before, and there have been weeks on end that I would not hear from him. But this feels different. I know that something's amiss, but I do not know what it is."

"Take your time, Mrs. Morel," I remarked, feeling protective. The colorful needlework reminded me of my Mary. How I missed her!

"Thank you, Doctor," Mrs. Morel smiled. Yet her voice trembled as she said, "But it is my husband that should be of concern to you. Perhaps I should not have contacted you, Mr. Holmes. There are those in authority who will become greatly agitated at my indiscretion; but confound them all! It is my husband that I care most about! Not my position!"

Her eyes glowed defiantly and spoke of an immensely strong and competent woman.

Holmes cocked his head and studied her. "Do go on, I beg of you. Time is of the essence, and I must hear everything."

The woman composed herself, folding her hands in her lap. "Yes, of course. I'm sorry, Mr. Holmes. My husband has been retained by the firm of Morrison, Morrison, and Dodd for three years now. Before that, he was a part of the Royal Navy."

"I'm familiar with Morrison, Morrison, and Dodd," Holmes remarked. "They're a highly reputable firm, specializing exclusively in the shipping industry. What's your husband's position with them?"

"He is a lieutenant, and he is one of the naval officers who are responsible for piloting the screw steamships Morrison, Morrison, and Dodd own. Lieutenant Morel is his proper title, and his job is sailing the vessels from Sydney to Liverpool and back again, once a month. Specifically, he's been assigned to the Celestial."

Holmes nodded for her to continue.

She cast her eyes down demurely and played with a linen handkerchief that she must have tucked up one sleeve. "Perhaps I should explain my relationship with my husband. Not only am I his wife, but I am also his confidante. We speak openly to each other about everything. Therefore, Mr. Holmes, I know that something is wrong. I know it. This is not mere suspicion. Nor is it the ramblings of an insecure wife! Rather, my conjecture is the result of piecing together a variety of happenings in a logical manner."

I smiled to myself. Mrs. Morel knew the way to make Holmes sit up and pay attention!

She continued, "Two months ago, my husband was informed that a serious mishap at sea had occurred. He was told this in a very confidential manner by a person who had reason to know. It seems that a ship carrying the usual cargo disappeared off the coast of Portugal. The crew was missing, too. No bodies washed up on the sand. No spars or bits of wood planking. Nothing. The cargo disappeared as well. Nothing was salvaged. The ship was a total loss. My husband wrote off the disappearance as bad luck. He presumed a storm at sea had knocked the ship off course and then they hit a reef. Since the ship would have been heavily laden with cargo, it might have gone straight down. That can happen. I know it does happen. I have not grown inured to the dangers of my husband's profession.

"But I do have tremendous faith in my husband's abilities. Last month, shortly before he was to sail from Liverpool, an old friend visited. He told my husband about another such tragedy. A second ship from another shipping firm went down shortly after passing through the Suez Canal and clearing Port Said.. Only a handful of those men survived, and the stories they told were so clearly fabricated, that my husband's first impulse was to ignore them. However, two such incidents happening so close to each other are highly irregular. I told Mr. Morel that I felt ill at ease about his upcoming voyage. My husband assured me that he'd taken every precaution. The crew was handpicked by him, down to a man. The vessel was one he'd seen being built. He'd sailed that particular ship twice, so he knew it intimately. Yet, my sense of dread was powerful. I could not overcome it. Seeing my agitation, he made me a promise. He swore to me that he would send a message each time the ship stopped at a port. That way I could track their progress as they returned to England."

"And did he keep his word?" Holmes asked.

Mrs. Morel's answer was delayed because the maid had returned. Linton was carrying a walnut tray trimmed with brass. On the tray there was a fresh pot of tea, two teacups, two saucers, and a plate of biscuits. Mrs. Morel poured our tea and Linton walked to the right of me and handed me the cup and saucer. She did the same with Holmes and then sat back in her seat and studied us both.

"Milk?" asked my friend, raising an eyebrow and addressing the maid.

"The milkman must have forgotten our order," Linton said. Adding the quickest bob for a curtsey that I've ever seen, she seemed to recover herself, "Believe me, I'll have words with him. It ain't right. Not at all. Begging your pardon, sir. I did bring biscuits. Hope you like them." With that, she held the plate of biscuits close enough for me to help myself. I did.

However, that first bite told me that I had made a mistake. The biscuit was old and hard as a rock. I did my best to swallow that piece and rested what was left of the wretched pastry next to my tea cup and thanked the stars above that I hadn't broken a tooth.

"As you were saying," Holmes prodded Mrs. Morel. "You received correspondence from each port where your husband's ship docked."

"Yes. However, my husband should have been home by now. In point of fact, he's more than three weeks overdue! He last wrote me from Marseilles, and the last leg of the journey is only three days long at the most." She touched her throat with delicate fingers. From the depths of her dress she withdrew a locket. As her fingers toyed with the chain, the locket twisted and caught the light. From my chair, I could discern golden wisps of hair. Not much more than a curl, actually. Clearly her next comment took a great deal of strength to share, "That was the last I heard from him."

"But surely," I interrupted, hoping to ease her fears, "three weeks is not a very long time to be gone, especially if they must travel to Portugal and remain there for the investigation."

"Normally, I would agree with you, Watson," Holmes remarked. "But Mrs. Morel has more to add—something that has caused her to question her husband's whereabouts and safety. Is that not so, Mrs. Morel?"

"Why, yes. I'll get them." With grace, she rose to her feet.

Holmes' eyes followed Mrs. Morel as she left the room. Anger flashed when he turned in my direction. His expression shelved any possibility for us to have a civil conversation, and I sank back into my chair and kept silent.

What next? I thought, disgustedly. The room suddenly grew hot and uncomfortable.

A few moments later, Mrs. Morel returned. Her delicate fingers held a folder overflowing with papers. "This is everything concerning this voyage, Mr. Holmes. My husband is a very precise and practical man and has taken on the habit, as of late, to make duplicate records. I believe this is what you might need to trace his journey."

Sitting back, her face manifested a myriad of emotions. Most notably, she displayed a look of concern. After a brief pause, she added, "There is one more thing, Mr. Holmes. It is nothing that is written in those sheets of paper, but my husband did mention it to me on more than one occasion. He said that if anything should anything ever happen to him, I should seek you out and ask you to speak with someone called the Bard. That's all I can say, as my husband provided me with no further information. Do you know of this person? Is that name familiar to you?"

"No." Holmes shook his head glumly. "But I will tell you this, madam. In time, I will know all that there is to know about him." Holmes spread the small amount of paper out on the table that stood between us and Mrs. Morel. He studied them for a minute. She nervously bit into her lower lip. But she was a strong woman indeed, and watched Holmes in silence.

I sat back and waited for Holmes to complete his reading. Mrs. Morel did the same. From time to time, she would nervously sip her tea. When she wasn't drinking from her china cup, she sat with her head bowed. She kept her gaze down, aimed at her hands. I fully expected to watch the tears flow. However, when she raised her eyes to meet mine, her face startled me because it held no emotion at all. That calm visage changed suddenly, or so it appeared to me, when she became aware that I was watching her. Her face grew rapidly worried and concerned. *A remarkable woman*! I thought.

"We may take these?" Holmes asked, snapping the folder shut and already stashing it in his coat. "Of course, they'll be returned. Do you have any photographs of your husband? Obviously, the process of finding him would be greatly enhanced if I knew how to recognise the man."

She colored. "No, sadly, I do not. Mr. Morel is averse to seeing his own image. My husband believes his features to be rather coarse. I see him through the eyes of love, and to me, he is the most handsome man in the world."

What a pleasure it was to hear a woman speak of her husband with such love! The tilt of her head, the genteel way she compensated for his rough looks, were altogether a compliment of the highest rank.

"Could you describe him to us? How tall is he? Is he fair or dark? Portly or thin? Clean-shaven or not?" Holmes pressed on. I noticed my friend's eyes had narrowed, and I calculated that he was unmoved by her profession of love.

Our hostess's glance flitted to the ceiling and then down to her hands, clasped as they were in her lap. Her grip tightened as if the effort of recalling a person so familiar was difficult. After all, once we love, do we continue to assess? No, we accept and are accepted.

"I would have to say my husband is average in all respects, except of course, the regard he holds for me. His temperament and his mind are those aspects that set him apart from the vast sea of men. One could not look upon him and discern a particular appealing trait in his person. Rather it is the man's inner life that I have found so admirable."

Holmes eyed her thoughtfully. "Tell me, Mrs. Morel, did your husband have any distinctive marks on his person? Sailors are exceedingly fond of tattoos. Did Mr. Morel have one?"

"Y-Y-Yes," she said with ladylike hesitancy. "I do not like to speak of it because I do not find it attractive. When my husband first presented it to me, I could not hide my disgust. Over time, I've learned to accept that such adornments are part and parcel of his trade."

"And could you describe that adornment to me?" Holmes pressed.

"Very well. He has a version of my name inscribed on his forearm," she said in a voice not more than a whisper. "Here." Gently she unbuttoned the cuff on the sleeve of her blouse and rolled the fabric up to expose creamy, unblemished skin. Slowly, she let her fingertips play over the porcelain flesh.

"I see," Holmes sounded gruff. "But Mrs. Morel, you are not

giving me much help. I am confident that almost any sailor I might find could show me a tattoo in that spot. What I need is a fulsome description of the image. Give me every detail you can."

She pouted and rolled down her sleeve. "I do not like to speak of this. It is indelicate. However, since you insist—"

"I do," Holmes rejoined.

"He had the letters L. I. V. inscribed there inside a heart-shaped frame."

I was thoroughly puzzled and could not contain my exasperation. "How does one start with Maria and conjure up that combination of letters? It makes no sense. None at all."

She gave me a shy smile. "My middle name is Olivia. He liked to call me Livvy. I can only guess that Liv fit better on his arm. You see, Doctor, it was a silly pet name. The sort of tomfoolery two lovers oft engage in. Only he took it to—" and she gasped as if a sharp pain coursed through her body. "He took it to his body as a way of saying we would never be parted. Ever! And yet here I am! Bereft of him! And worse, I have no body to mourn. I cannot rightly call myself a widow. I cannot honestly put on black. It is too, too hard."

She burst into noisy tears. "Forgive me, I am overcome with grief. I cannot live without dear Jeremy."

"Jeremy?" Holmes pressed her. "How did you come to call him Jonas in your note to me?'

"Oh!" and those delicate hands of hers flew to her mouth. "How silly of me. You see, Mr. Holmes, my husband's given name is Jeremy, the same as his father, but he is known to all as Jonas, which is his middle name. At the time that I penned the note that summoned you here, I was worried about sharing this news with his father, and quite naturally, I confused their names."

"I see," said Holmes, pressing his lips together tightly. "Is it possible your husband's father knows where to find his son?

Where does his father live? Could Mr. Morel have diverted his route home and stopped to see his father? Is it possible that a message affirming such was never sent and therefore caused you to worry without cause?"

Her shoulders drooped and those lovely features fell. The sadness portrayed by her body moved me beyond what I can say here. "Mr. Jeremy Morel Senior does not approve of our marriage. I regret the censure more than I can say. That is an ongoing source of pain for my dear husband. And therefore for me, of course. Currently his father is running a plantation in Jamaica. I seriously doubt that Jonas could be there with his father. He would never abandon his responsibilities to his captain or his crew. On this point I am abundantly certain."

"One more thing, Mrs. Morel," Holmes said, raising his voice slightly. "You are expecting to entertain other people this evening?"

She seemed surprised by my friend's question. "Why no, Mr. Holmes. I have only been expecting you and Dr. Watson."

Holmes stared at the woman, questioningly, and narrowed his eyes. "Are you quite certain?"

"I am entirely certain," she said with a tinge of defiance that brought a lovely shade of pink to her cheeks.

3

Linton brought us our winter coats and helped us slip into them before we stepped out into the blustery frigid weather. After the cozy warmth of the fireplace, this miserable cold snap felt like an assault on our physical being, although I shall admit the shifting temperatures did seem to sharpen my thought processes. Luckily, we quickly hailed a carriage. As Holmes banged on the roof for the driver to start, I suffered a sense of unease that I couldn't shake off. Something was wrong. Over the years, I've been accustomed to accompanying my friend as he pursues his investigations, and rarely do I feel discouraged, but now I did and the feeling was unwelcome.

"What is happening, Holmes? This is rather queer, but I sense things are not as they should be."

"How very prescient of you, Watson! And here I was, convinced that you were beguiled by our hostess. I worried that, just like the sirens of old, she had enchanted you. Good to know that you have kept some semblance of your wits about you. All will be made clear in good time, my friend," said Holmes. "Tomorrow, we shall go to the docks and see if the ship has been sighted. If the Celestial is there at anchor, then we will know that Jonas Morel is not missing because his vessel came to harm. I recognise such a docking is unlikely, but I think it worth taking a look. Don't you agree?"

I nodded and since the cab was dark, I added. "Of course. That poor, poor woman."

"What makes you say that?" asked Holmes.

"What makes me say that? Why, isn't it obvious? She is, for all intents and purposes, a widow. I hope her husband has set aside money for her. Elsewise, she will have to give up that lovely home in that gracious neighborhood."

Holmes chuckled. "And what if I were to tell you that isn't her home? In fact, I would wager you a half crown that she'd never been inside that house until today. I would further suggest that the woman playing the part of her maid was also a newcomer to the house."

"Ha!" I scoffed. "Don't be preposterous, Holmes. You can be exceedingly strange at times."

"Really?" As he said this, I swear I could imagine his eyebrow lifting. "Then explain to me why her maid had no idea what to do with our coats."

"The poor girl was flummoxed. Meeting the great Sherlock Holmes was the highlight of her evening. Do not endeavor to make a mountain out of the proverbial molehill."

"All right," and Holmes leaned closer to me. "Tell me why there was no fresh milk in the house."

"You heard the explanation, Holmes. The milkman was derelict in his duties. When on earth did that matter to you? I have never known you to require milk to add to your tea."

"My purpose was sound. I wanted to know how long Mrs. Morel and Linton had occupied the house."

"I don't follow." There are times when he confounds me, and this was one of them.

Holmes sighed in the manner of a man who has been disappointed. "If the women took the house last night or very early this morning, they could have set out a note for the milk delivery man. They would have had milk for their guests. But they had none. Did you notice the biscuits? They were stale. And did you notice that Linton, or whoever she really is, served us both from the right? No well-trained servant would do that! Also, the hem of Mrs. Morel's dress was wet and dirty, as if she'd been outside in it—and no lady from such lofty circumstances would have worn a gown like that for making calls. No, Watson, those two women were definitely playing parts. From these facts we can deduce that Linton and Mrs. Morel, or whatever their names are, arrived at that house only a short time before we did."

"To what end?" I cried. "You are proposing a charade of complexity and large proportions. But you have not suggested a motive for these rash actions."

"Then perhaps it is time that we cleared some of this mystery up for you," said Holmes. Leaning his head out the window, he called up to the cabman, "Covent Garden."

4

London is a lively town after the sun goes down, and no place is more festive, more crammed cheek-to-jowl with people, and more varied in its aspect than Covent Garden. The theatres are worlds unto themselves, but the streets are nonetheless as busy and as entertaining. Our cabman let us off at a corner where an old man with a flat cap pulled low on his head sat on an overturned bucket and roasted chestnuts on a small black metal brazier. Their nutty fragrance scented the air. The heat those coals gave off was eagerly absorbed by a tiny monkey with a chain attached to a bracelet on his foot. The little scamp would warm his hands over the hot coals in a most amusing way.

When his owner picked up his old accordion and played a happy polka, the small performer danced about and did a number of athletic feats. He timed a gentleman's bow with the end of the song and subsequently grabbed a small metal cup. This he thrust at passersby while his free hand tugged on pants legs and skirt hems.

Nor were these the only poor souls hoping for a coin or two.

The daytime posy sellers had exchanged their floral offerings for sprigs of fragrant balsam and pinecones dipped in wax. In an alcove, observing all of this industry, stood a man leaning on crutches. He wore a sign, hanging around his neck from a lanyard of twine. The placard introduced the beggar as a soldier who'd lost his leg at Trafalgar.

"Why are we here?" I asked Holmes. The cold was quick to penetrate my coat.

"We are doing reconnaissance," he explained, "and we are also clearing up a variety of mysteries that you claim are confounding you."

"Really, Holmes," I said in a peevish voice, "it's too cold for us to wander the streets at night. If you have a point to prove, do so and let us find a public house where we can eat our supper."

"Not so fast, my friend. All will be revealed in the fullness of time. Rather than a public house, I see a pasty seller at the next corner. Let's buy a couple of their hot meat pies for our supper. They'll do us double duty by warming our hands. We still have a way to go before we reach our destination."

As promised by the seller as she reached inside a metal pail, the pasty was piping hot. The meat and potatoes inside had been spiced perfectly with a liberal touch of pepper. Given the cold air nipping at us, I was ever so pleased to bite into the flaky crust and enjoy my food. Half of the pasty was still uneaten when we found ourselves in front of a music hall advertising the city's best entertainment. Holmes put down two coins to buy us entry. Wrapping the remainder of my meal my linen handkerchief, I stuffed it into my coat pocket. Holmes noticed and said, "We'll get a beverage once we're seated."

The music hall was packed with patrons, most of whom were already inebriated. A cheerful serving girl brought us two mugs of an agreeable ale. Not what Holmes typically drank, but under the circumstances, it was satisfactory. She'd no more than swept Holmes' coins off the table and pocketed them when a drumroll commanded the audience's attention. The gaslights dimmed and the curtain swept back to reveal a delightful tableau on the gaslit stage in front of us. Six young women were posed to create a striking scene. They each wore a dress that exposed a generous amount of décolleté, as well as bare arms, and well-turned ankles. The band struck up a lively tune, and the chorus girls launched into a cheerful ditty filled with double meanings that made me blush.

In the midst of their second number, the six performers joined hands and after breaking into two groups of three, they moved as a unit, swinging out like a garden gate. A woman whose face was shielded by a parasol strode into the center of the stage. The chorus reached a climax as the star spun the parasol faster and faster. Finally she let it dip to reveal her lovely face, the face of the woman we'd met earlier who called herself Mrs. Morel.

"Oh!" I said. I could not help myself. A sidewise glance at Holmes told me he was amused by my surprise.

"You knew this all along?" I asked him when the curtain came down to thunderous applause. "You knew she was an actress? What was it on the billboard outside? A performer who uses the name Jewel DeMare?"

Holmes pursed his lips. "Really, Watson, you act surprised and yet you, of all people, are well-versed in my methodology. It is always prudent for me to know everything I can about my clients. To be a successful consulting detective, it is of the utmost importance to know with whom one is dealing. Are you terribly disappointed that Mrs. Morel is actually an entertainer?"

"Well," I began and let the matter drop. I could not lie to Holmes; I had enjoyed the performance. Fortunately, I did not have to dig around for a suitable reaction. Holmes was on his feet. "Shall we beard the lioness in her den?"

5

Weaving our way through the crowd, we muscled our way into a hallway that led to the entertainers' dressing rooms. There our path was blocked by an intimidating man who glared at us. Speaking in rough tones, he barked, "Performers only!"

Holmes nodded. "And employees of those performers, I assume? I am in the employ of Mrs. Morel. I believe you know her as Jewel DeMare."

The fact that Holmes knew the woman's married name made an impression on the thug. But it was not enough to gain us entry. Holmes added, "My name is Sherlock Holmes, and I'm a consulting detective. I have—"

"Sherlock Holmes?" the man asked. His surly expression changed to one of wonder. "The man who fought Moriarty at Reichenbach Falls? The one who solved the murders in that story, *A Study in Scarlet?* The very one?"

I stepped forwards. "Indeed, he is and I am Dr. John Watson, his biographer."

"What a singular thrill this is!" said the man. "I've read everything you've ever written, Dr. Watson. Oh, my! Wait until I tell the missus. Go on back, gents. I bet you're working a big case now, eh?"

Rather than answer, we slipped past the man and found ourselves outside a dressing room assigned to Mrs. Morel – that is, Jewel DeMare. Holmes rapped sharply on the door, and neither of us was very surprised when Linton opened it.

"I need to speak to Mrs. Morel," said Holmes.

Linton scowled as she recognized us. "I don't know that she'll see you. She's already wasted too much time with the both of you. She's very tired after her performance, and she's got lots more important fellows who are hoping to talk to her than you!"

This rather took me aback. Linton's reversal from meek parlour maid to harridan was unexpected. Holmes was not amused. "Either she sees us or I refuse to take her on as a client."

Linton muttered dark remarks under her breath and said, "Stay here," before slamming the door in Holmes' face.

My friend took his little black devil out of his coat pocket and chewed on the stem. I ventured an opinion, "This does not mean she isn't married to a man who is missing, Holmes. Jeremy or Jonas Morel could be a lieutenant as she says and he could be in some sort of—"

Before I could finish, the door opened and Linton said, "You've got two minutes with her. That's all. You might *think* you're important, but you're just another couple of blokes to her. Believe you me, she's got a string of them lined up outside, begging to come in, and all of those fellows are smart enough to send a coin or two my way."

Linton moved to allow us entry. The dressing room was small. A rack stuffed with frilly dresses took up much of the space on the right side. To the left was a dressing table and an enormous round mirror. Straight ahead was a dressing screen and over it had been tossed a number of delicate undergarments. But what took up the most space in the room was an extraordinary number of floral tributes. I recognised roses and lilies, but most of the flowers were too exotic for me to name. At length, I saw what I assumed were orchids, as I once went to an exhibition of them with Mary. In pride of place, there was one huge floral tribute with white ostrich feathers among the blossoms. Holmes saw it about the same time as I did. He wandered closer and was gazing at the signed card when Mrs. Morel came out from behind the screen and said, "That is none of your business, Mr. Holmes."

"Really?" he said, raising his eyebrows. "I should think that the fact you have admirers is very much my business, as it may well explain what has happened to your husband. Is it not possible that one of your many admirers saw the voyage on the Celestial as an opportunity to brush your husband aside?"

Rather than answer him, Mrs. Morel burst into noisy sobs.

6

Mrs. Morel's overwrought emotional response made an interview with her extremely difficult. Linton came over to her mistress and patted Mrs. Morel on the shoulder while murmuring comforting remarks. Holmes was unmoved, the way he often is when confronted by excess. He once told me, "Emotions cloud the faculty of reason. They solve nothing. They only make answers more obscure."

After a small taste of these feminine dramatics, a jerk of Holmes' head suggested we leave. I was all too glad to go.

In the hansom on our way back to Baker Street, I asked, "How did you know she was an actress?"

I could scarcely see his face in the dark, but an occasional glimpse by streetlamp suggested the hint of a smile. "Several clues. I believe you saw them also, but perhaps you did not place them in their proper context. Firstly, the timing of our appointment at her house was exceedingly odd. She assured me she was not expecting guests, so I deduced that she had an appointment herself. Then there was the distinctive imprint of her lips on her teacup. Ladies of quality do not rouge their lips, and yet Mrs. Morel was perched on an expensive sofa in an expensive house in an exclusive neighborhood. That led me to wonder why. But the aspect of our visit that put it all into focus was the way she walked when she accompanied us to the front door. Unconsciously, she adopted a pose from ballet. Fifth position. That references the way in which she positioned her feet and the slight bend of her arms. You might also have recognised, as a medical man, that she rolled her shoulders back and lifted her rib cage up when she sat down. Another sign of theatrical training."

Over the years, I had thought Holmes could no longer stun me with his surprising breadth of knowledge. Yet once again, he had proven himself to be a connoisseur of the unusual and exotic.

"Are you very much disappointed, Watson?" my old friend asked.

I sighed. "Not really. It's more that I am missing Mary. The grief sneaks up on me and catches me unaware. I think that I have recovered, only to be struck down again."

Holmes only nodded. I was glad he did not try to comfort me. It was not comfort that I wanted: it was Mary.

7

The next morning, I awakened to what seemed like unnatural silence. But even as I finished my toilette, I discerned another noise, a whisper-like turning of pages. Or the thin fluttering of paper. I could not clearly tell which. I stepped out of my bedroom full of curiosity for what adventures lay ahead!

Holmes was sitting in the midst of a large, disorderly pile of old newspapers. Like his brother, Mycroft, he is terrified of ever turning loose of papers that could hold valuable information. Unlike Mycroft, he does not have a staff to index and store his papers, but Holmes does have Mrs. Hudson, bless her. She keeps crates in the back room and lets my friend store *The Times* there in a rough semblance of order.

"Hmm," Holmes hummed to himself. I did not think he even noticed my approach.

I sat down at the table and availed myself of a piece of cold toast in the silver toast rack. The butter had melted, thanks to the heat from the fire in the hearth, so I easily spread that and added strawberry jam.

"Watson? Why not ring for a pot of coffee?" asked Holmes, without looking up from the mess he'd made.

"A capital idea." I rang and very quickly Bryony carried in a tray with a fresh pot of steaming coffee. I thanked the young woman and she offered me a timid smile.

"What are you looking for?" I asked my friend.

"Word about those ships. The two that Mrs. Morel told us sank."

"And have you found reports? Surely such tragedies would make the front page. An entire ship? That would mean many lives and much merchandise."

Holmes slowly turned to meet my eyes. "That's the curious part, Watson. I have found nothing. Not even a hint. And I am almost through with every newspaper from the past twelvemonth."

I set my cup down with a clatter. "Are you sure? Have you checked the dates of the papers? Perhaps Mrs. Hudson tossed out the specific months you are in need of."

"No," said Holmes. "Observe." Unfolding his thin frame, he rose to his feet. "I first designated spots on the floor. One for each month of the year. As you can see, we have November through November. I even have the following December and a portion of January."

"But the dates," I persisted. "Perhaps you missed a week or two."

"No. Again, I did not approach this task willy-nilly. If you'd care to check, these newspapers are in date order. Not a single day is missing." He stood with his fists on his hips as he bent his head and surveyed the mess.

"Then perhaps you are missing the correct section. Perhaps the crew was foreign, and therefore, the reporters did not explore their lives. Maybe they concentrated on the cargo rather than the crew." My voice sounded increasingly unsure, even to my own ears.

"I hope you are right. I hope that I've overlooked an article. Please exchange places with me. I'll have another cup of coffee whilst you critique my efforts.

As he requested, I exchanged places with him and got down on my hands and knees so I could crawl from stack to stack. After making a circuit of the months of the years, I sat back down on my heels and delivered the gloomy news. "I cannot find a flaw in your methodology. I could spot-check the papers."

"No," he said, waving off my suggestion in a disheartened way. "Think of it, Watson. Two naval calamities. Two entire crews missing. Two cargoes gone. And both are English ships. We're the dominant military force in the world, and yet there has been no national alarm. These brave men died and no one cared. Of all the crimes committed, perhaps that is the one that best resembles a mortal sin."

I thought he'd come to terms with the missing information, but Holmes had researched, considered, and now he could announce where all of this led his thinking. "Watson? If a calamity such as this never makes the papers, we must ask ourselves why."

I considered this. "Because it never happened?"

He sighed, sounding a wee bit exasperated. "No, no, no. Only a fool would make up the sinking of not one, but two, cargo ships! Mrs. Morel had to know I would check out her story. And yet she persisted in telling us that two ships had been destroyed. Why? Why would she make a claim that could be so easily disputed? Why make a claim about a sinking at all? The story has enough substance without all this superfluous detail. She was careful. She was deliberate. And she was well-prepared, so what was her reason for telling us? For alerting us to a pair of sinkings that never happened?"

"Maybe they did," I said. "Maybe that is the point. These tragedies happened and for whatever reason, they were hidden. They were not brought to public attention. They were not shared with reporters. None of that." I paused and considered this development. "There is another way to find out what you need. I suggest we avail ourselves of the ledgers at the registry office. After all, if the ships sank, their owners would have clamoured to be compensated."

"Watson?" Holmes jumped to his feet. "There are times when I think you are a genius. Honestly, I do. Under that unassuming exterior is a keen mind. Untrained and unfocused, but keen nevertheless. I had been doggedly following one path with singularity of purpose, and as you point out...there is another possibility. Perhaps even two! Grab your coat. We're going to the docks."

I raced into my bedroom to bundle up. As I pulled a warm jumper over my head, I thought I heard Holmes' whistle, but I couldn't be sure. I finished piling on all my outerwear and joined him as he fairly hopped from one foot to another.

"There's no time to waste!" he shouted. I followed, hot on his heels, down the stairs and out the door. The cold slapped us in the face like an angry hussy. A cabman waited at the kerb. Holmes and I piled into the conveyance. "To the docks!" my friend yelled up at the man, before slamming the door behind him.

The bitter cold made every bump along the way much more keen and painful. A sway and dip suggested someone had jumped on the back and joined us, but that is hardly surprising, as London is full of souls without a cent in their pockets who need conveyance. Hopping on and off of hansoms is a sport the young and poor learn as soon as they are tall enough to reach up and hang on! I could have sworn the cabman shouted, "Get off! Get down!" Indeed, I gave it no thought at all. What did it matter?

Soon enough we came to Wapping, a place synonymous with the lowest form of human justice, hangings designed to titillate the crowd more than to mete out deserved punishment. For here it was, at the Execution Dock, that pirates and other criminals of the seas would follow the Admiralty Marshal as he carried his silver oar, emblematic of his authority over all aspects of nautical life. The condemned were given one small kindness, a last quart of ale, supposedly to "take the edge off," but as a medical man, I can attest the drink would hardly have made a difference to those who were hanged with a short rope. Unlike a long rope that snaps the neck and can be argued therefore to be humane, the short rope simply strangles a man, slowly, ever so slowly. His body, thus deprived of oxygen, goes into a series of spasms that onlookers nicknamed the marshal's dance. Not even after death did the barbarity end. Three tides had to pass over the body before it could be moved. Then it was covered in tar and locked inside a metal cage, a gibbet, and displayed there in the Thames estuary.

I shudder as I think of this, and Holmes noticed, as he is wont to do. "The weather will turn soon enough, Watson, and as for today, much of our work will be indoors."

I nodded. The Ships Registry was a large, long building with windows running the length of it. Empty wine barrels had been arranged as a sort of barricade around the front of the building. Possibly they held flowers in the summer. Their bulk was imposing but the level of security they provided was feeble. "The original building was half this size," explained Holmes, as he grasped the door handle, "but the growth of her Majesty's fleet has caused there to be more ships built and registered than ever before. This edifice has been added onto."

Inside, we waited for what seemed like an unreasonable

length of time at a counter that jutted out at a right angle from the wall. There was no bell to ring. Finally, a clerk hurried out of the back. He looked surprised by our presence, as though he'd never encountered a visitor before. Close up, I was able to tell the clerk wasn't more than sixteen and scared as a rabbit that has caught the scent of a pack of hounds. Nervously, he drummed his fingers on the counter. "Yes?" He finally managed that one-word question.

"We have business with the Registrar," said Holmes.

Shuffling off, the young man fled back the way he'd come. Moving to the left and then to the right, I could see that doorways opened onto a main hall. The clerk bypassed the first three and ducked into the fourth. A hushed whisper reached up, but was too muffled to make sense.

The clerk hurried towards us again, as a man in a loose blouse slipped out of that third room and into the first room on the right.

"Do you have an appointment?" asked the clerk. Never was a man so tortured by a simple question!

"No," said Holmes.

That was all. Just plain no. The singular word hung out there in the air, like a sign unattached to a fingerpost.

"Um, I suspect that the Registrar is busy," said the clerk.

"I suspect he can make time for us. I rather doubt he gets a lot of visitors on any given day." Holmes paused and added, "Does he?"

"I wouldn't know, sir. I started here not that long ago." His cuffs were frayed and his sleeves too long. His vest was missing a top button. All in all, he looked like a schoolboy who was pretending to have a position with a bit of responsibility.

"I see. Well, I suggest that you go into the Registrar's office and tell him he has two important visitors. Explain that we are here in service of a murder inquiry. Have you got that? Tell him we are impatient and have other work to attend to, so we'd like to speak with him, posthaste."

"Right." The clerk blinked rapidly. One could almost tell that the young man was digesting all of this, trying to shove a square peg into a round hole. Slowly, he turned and walked back into the office of the Registrar.

Another round of loud talking followed. At length, there was the sound of a squeaking chair moved to one side. The clerk came forwards, and announced with great formality, "Mr. Reginald Barlow-Smythe the Third is willing to make time in his busy day to meet with you. Please come this way."

We followed the clerk into a large, brightly lit office with a huge fireplace sending hot air into the atmosphere. To one side was a mahogany table with intricate woodwork. The surface of the desk might or might not have been much used, because a desktop calendar covered most of it. Reginald Barlow-Smythe the Third, for such was how he introduced himself, was not what I had expected. The Registrar did not invite us to sit down. Nor did he stand to greet us. Instead he perched on a wheeled stool with a swiveling, backless seat. A most unusual set-up for an office worker. Barlow-Smythe glared at us. Curiously, the man did not wear a jacket. Instead, he wore a loose blouse that appeared far too large for his frame. It bagged around his shoulders and his torso. His hair gleamed with oils. His moustache was waxed and curled tightly at each end. His tiny piggy eyes were red and raw under girlish brows.

"You do not have an appointment, and I have no time for you. Present your case and begone!"

Holmes introduced himself and me. Barlow-Smythe cut my friend short. "You say your name is Holmes? Sherlock Holmes? And that is Dr. Watson? Why should I care?"

I cleared my throat. "See here! Sherlock Holmes is the world's greatest consulting detective, and we have come to you because he is in service of a poor woman who has lost her husband, a sailor. We have exhausted all other options in tracking the man down and hope to find helpful information in your records. After all, you exist to serve the public, do you not?"

Barlow-Smythe curled his lip. "The great Sherlock Holmes? Ho! I have read the sensational accounts of your exploits as chronicled by Dr. Watson. What a load of poppycock. And again, I ask, why should I care about you and your project?"

"I do not ask you to care," said Holmes. "I only ask you to do your job. In this case, I wish to see copies of ships' registries."

"Perhaps it is *you* who should do your job. I've read how you set such great store by your vaunted analytical abilities. Why would you need my help? Surely, if there is a challenge or a problem, you can solve it yourself. The great Sherlock Holmes, eh? As I said, that's nothing more than a load of rubbish."

Holmes shook his head with disgust. "My dear, sir. You are too easy to read by half. Yes, you have learned nothing from your trials, have you? Did it not occur to you that your uncivil manner caused the crew to turn against you?"

Barton-Smythe's face turned scarlet. "I don't know what you're talking about. Harrington! Harrington, get in here."

When the clerk appeared in the doorway, Barlow-Smythe took a struggling step towards the other man. "Get rid of this man. He's an imposter. He claims to be Sherlock Holmes, and yet he cannot support his assertion."

"Oh, yes, I can," said Holmes in a dry tone. "Let me tell you all about your brief career, Mr. Barlow-Smythe, shall I? You have not always worked in the Ships Registry office. No, this is a job given to you in recompense. It was a bribe to keep you quiet after you infuriated the crew of a ship you were on. Isn't it?"

Barton-Smythe chewed the air. He sputtered but could not

speak coherently. "Y-Y-You don't know what you are talking about."

"Yes, I do. You got into a quarrel with the crew. You also angered the captain. He refused to step in and stop the men when they gave you a checkered shirt for your troubles."

The clerk gasped audibly. "How did you know?"

"Silence!" yelled Barlow-Smythe.

Holmes continued, "You barely escaped with your life, didn't you? Because of your father's influence in certain circles, he arranged to have you compensated, and so you were given the privilege of managing the registries for all of the UK. The pay is good, and best of all, you are somewhat your own master. That is essential because you are incapable of getting along with others. Is that not so? Or shall I ask your clerk? He's fairly new here, right? You probably dismiss a clerk every other week or so."

"Mr. Holmes, apart from your fancy parlour tricks, you are not worth a tinker's dam," Barton-Smythe said. "Now get out of my office. Begone!"

"Not until I have the information I need." Holmes put a scrap of notepaper on the Registrar's desk. "Here are your choices: help me now or defend your actions to my brother, Mycroft Holmes."

The Registrar's face went from florid red to linen white. For a tick, I thought he might topple over in a faint. Instead, he gripped his desk for support and collapsed onto the swivel stool. "Mycroft Holmes is your brother?"

"He is indeed," said Sherlock Holmes. "Now quit wasting my time, Mr. Barlow-Smythe. I require any documents you have relating to those ships and those dates."

"I-I-I have nothing to tell you," said Mr. Barlow-Smythe, in a tone that could only be described as piteous. "I swear to you, sir. All we keep here are the original registrations. As you probably know, Lloyd's copies these documents and compiles them in their yearly ledgers. If the ship is more than one year old, you can look it up in a Lloyd's Book of Registries. Otherwise, you would set a daunting task for yourself, digging through all the paperwork we have, as much of it is unfiled."

Holmes said, "Then at least do us the courtesy of allowing my confederate and I to look over your records. Perhaps your clerk can point us in the right direction."

"Sir! The ship owners would have me keelhauled if I allowed you to make free with the information about their earnings." Barlow-Smythe's voice broke with fright.

"Just so. I'm asking to look at the building records, if you please." Holmes regarded the younger man thoughtfully. "Surely no one could complain about that."

"Harrington, get them the building records, please."

Barton-Smythe cradled his head in his hands and rested his elbows on his desk. I could tell the man was in pain. Grave pain, I would say from the way his hands trembled. Belatedly, I realised that he had used a considerable amount of fortitude to confront us as he did. At this point, the Registrar was spent, utterly and wholly exhausted from the effort he had made to seem intimidating.

I did not know what a checkered shirt was, but I planned to ask Holmes more about it as soon as possible.

Holmes waited until Harrington was halfway down the hall and then he shouted, "Bring me the manifest for those ships, too." Turning to watch, I saw Harrington stop, pivot towards a different direction, and take two steps before Barlow-Smythe screamed, "Not the manifest!"

Harrington corrected his course and entered a doorway to the left.

"But not the manifest. No, sir, you have no right to that," the

Registrar muttered angrily. Harrington carried a heavy book past us. "If you'll come with me, sirs," he said.

We took our leave of Mr. Barlow-Smythe.

Harrington set the heavy book down on a long table in a room empty of all furniture except a trio of chairs. The clerk left us alone. Holmes moved quickly to the nearest window and unlatched it. Next, he raised the sash entirely, testing to see that it would indeed, rise as it should. Once he was satisfied, he lowered the window until it was three inches or so from the casing. Brushing off his hands, Holmes came back to the table where I was standing over the book. Whipping his glass out of his pocket, Holmes flipped through pages and examined several columns with deliberation.

"Write this down, Watson," he said. I copied down measurements for two different boats, the Celestial and the Clarissa. Curiously enough, they were built by the same builder, launched a few days apart, and their dimensions matched almost perfectly. The only difference was the gross tonnage. One ship weighed ever so slightly more than the other. Unfortunately the ledger did not share the names of the owners, the names of the shipping companies, or the types of cargo the ships carried. This was highly unusual, or so it appeared to my eyes, because the other ships' documents were thorough in all of these aspects.

"Thank you, my good sir," said Holmes to me, closing the book.

"Mr. Harrington?" Holmes called down the hallway. As Harrington scurried towards us, Holmes lifted the book and handed it to the young man. "Thank you. I should still like to see the ships' manifest."

"Mr. Barlow-Smythe won't allow it," said Harrington.

"Right," Holmes acceded. "Watson, would you care to join me for a brisk stroll? Sea air is so refreshing."

As it was freezing outside, I wondered if Holmes had lost his mind. The two of us stepped out of the Registrar's office. Holmes spoke to me under his breath, "We needs must pace up and down, Watson, for a spell."

"To what purpose?" I asked.

"Really, Watson. You need me to explain every detail to you? No, I will not. Instead, I invite you to use your eyes and ears and report your findings back to me. If you are still confused when this little escapade is over, I shall make it all clear to you."

We had no more than made our third circuit when the Registrar came roaring out of the office. "See, here!" Barlow-Smythe screamed. "You have no right to march up and down in front of my office. Nor to intimidate me. I gave you what you wanted!"

"Not all of it," said Holmes in a level voice. "Really, sir. All you did was dispatch an errand boy to bring me a book with little to no information. Certainly nothing that was useful or helpful. I'm currently debating with Watson whether or not I should tell my brother."

"How dare you bully me!" Barlow-Smythe screamed before launching into a scurrilous accounting of my friend's flaws.

As the Registrar yelled at Holmes, I glimpsed Evans sneaking around the building. He had hunched over to make himself less noticeable as he moved from shadow to shadow. When he realised I had spotted him, he put a finger to his lips. Out of the corner of my eye, I saw Evans struggle to slide up the window that Holmes had left open. After a might heave-ho, Evans succeeded and with the grace of a cat, the child threw himself over the sill and into the building.

"On the contrary," said Holmes in a very loud voice. "I have two reasons and every right to be here!"

The Registrar continued to rail at Holmes, but Holmes was placid. "If you must, I suggest you call the police. In fact, why don't you?" He poked the Registrar in the chest with his index finger.

"You won't because you are a coward. Aren't you? I bet you cried like a schoolboy when the first mate set the lash to your back..." As Holmes rehashed the making of a checkered shirt in great detail, the Registrar became inchoate with rage, and Evans' head reappeared at yet another window. He dropped a canvas bag to the ground and then feet first slid out of the window. Picking up the bag, the boy disappeared among the luggage and containers that littered the dock.

"Holmes," I said. "That is enough. We are getting nowhere."

Holmes gave me a sidelong glance, a measuring up. I responded with a nod of affirmation. "All right," said my friend. "Come along, Watson."

As soon as we were clear of the building, Evans joined us. He handed the bag to Holmes. My friend opened the canvas sack and looked inside. "Excellent work, Evans. Outstanding," he said.

"Watson?" Holmes continued. "We now have a record of the various manifests of the ships. This information should go a long way towards answering our many questions."

Holmes whistled a lively tune as we searched the street for an unoccupied hansom. I bit my tongue rather than share my thoughts, although I was boiling over with anger. In fact, I did not notice the cold because of my fury. I waited until Holmes and I had both taken seats in the vehicle and the cabman had been given our address.

Once again, the cabman shouted, "Get ye down, ye rascal."

Holmes turned to Watson and smiled. "Evans. He's rather resourceful when it comes to catching a hansom, isn't he?"

"Yes, I noticed him slipping in to do your dirty work. If that boy had been caught—" I glowered. I hated that Holmes used the youth with such little regard to the child's safekeeping. Oft times, my friend became so enmeshed in his adventures, so fervent about his tasks, that he lost all sense of proportion. In particular, he skipped over the problems and concerns that he created for others, whether they be Mrs. Hudson, or me, or Evans. Mrs. Hudson and I can take care of ourselves, I should say, but Evans is but a poor street urchin with no resources to draw on. Given Barlow-Smythe's foul temper, I shivered to think of how he might have punished the boy for removing a book from the registry.

Holmes lifted his chin in that imperious way of his that always irritated me. "But Evans was not caught. He's a masterful thief, and if he were to be apprehended, I should go to my brother and demand Evans' release. Come now, it is too cold and miserable to argue. Let us occupy our minds with other diversions."

8

This argument was getting us nowhere. I decided I should table the subject for now. "All right, tell me how you knew all that about the Registrar."

"It's elementary. What portion baffles you?"

"The checkered shirt."

"The easiest part! Did you not notice that he was wearing a light muslin blouse? What man does that? The fabric was as soft as the down on a hatchling. Applying simple logic, one can deduce that the Registrar's skin was tender where the lash had been applied right to left and then again, left to right. I, for one, cannot imagine the pain associated with a checkered shirt. Can you? As a medical man, it must fill you with horror."

"Too true." I nodded. My colleagues had told me stomach-turning tales regarding such injuries. For example, rubbing salt into the open crevices of tortured flesh was a means of adding to the pain. This practice was barbaric in its cruelty and yet unwittingly an act of kindness. The salt aided the recovery process, a slow healing that might well take years.

"What about the fact that his father has influence?"

"Ho!" Holmes laughed out loud. "Holmes, do you truly see

and hear without understanding? The man introduced himself as Reginald Barlow-Smythe the Third. Only a man who believes he has much to pass along deigns to saddle his son with such a pretentious name. As it happens, I've heard of Reginald Barlow-Smith, Junior, from my brother. He's not so intelligent as he thinks he is, but he's on a fast inside track in the race to win Her Majesty's favour. Mycroft can't abide the man. The fact that he was cognizant of my purported abilities tells me he's not adverse to reading popular fiction. Only a young man of privilege would have the time and money to purchase a complete set of your fantasies."

My cheeks turned florid. "Really, Holmes. Since my so-called fantasies have caused you to be a person freely lauded by the populace, the aristocracy, and the police themselves, one might expect a modicum of appreciation rather than your ongoing attempts to shrink my success down to a size you can manage."

Holmes laughed again. "Touché, Watson. Touché. I believe my shallow words have done their job, have they not?"

"What job is that?" I replied in a huffy tone.

"Given how blasted cold it is, I had hoped that my words would succeed in igniting your anger. I cannot rub two sticks together to build a roaring fire in this cab, so I did the next best thing. I rubbed your ego the wrong way, and thus, I let your emotions heat up your body. It did work, didn't it?"

Cocking my head, I observed my friend. "Holmes? One of these days, I'll forget myself and do you harm."

This time his laughter was explosive.

9

Back at 221B Baker Street, we hopped out of our cab, and Evans jumped off the back of the carriage. Holmes tossed the cabman a coin that covered the cost of our trip, and this time he also paid for the ride that Evans had purloined. The lad skipped up the stairs ahead of us and opened our locked door with the greatest of ease. I turned to Holmes with the plan of remarking on this breach of privacy, but my friend only shrugged. "If Evans were not so good at what he does, I should have no use for him, Doctor. His bad habits serve to remind me how truly talented the child is."

After Holmes set the book on the dining room table, Evans darted around the room like a terrier in search of a rat. Without asking, he put another log on the fire. When he stretched out his small hands, I saw the chilblains, those swollen and red lumps that must have caused him considerable misery. "Young man," I said in my most reassuring voice. "I shall ring for the girl to bring up a pitcher of warm water. Once it arrives, I want you to go into my bedroom and wash your hands thoroughly. Apply the sandalwood soap liberally to all surfaces. Once you are done, I shall apply a salve to your hands, one that will make the itching and burning subside."

"Ain't no need, Doctor," the scamp returned. "I ain't got no gloves. Them fingers of mine will just get cold and itchy all over again."

Nonetheless, I rang the bell and when the maid appeared, I told her what was needed. "Bryony?" I asked, stopping her from making a hasty departure and hoping I had her Christian name right. She had only recently come to work here at 221B Baker Street. As Mrs. Hudson aged, Holmes and I despaired of her climbing the stairs while carrying heavy trays. We'd also noticed that our dear landlady's eyesight was fading, as small tasks were no longer done to her original high standards. Rather than tax that kindly woman further, my friend and I told her that we'd decided to pay for a serving girl to help, and we'd blamed our increasing case load for the work the girl would do. Bryony was immensely suitable for her position, as she could not read but was keen to learn. This, we pointed out to Mrs. Hudson, was a chance for all of us to do a good turn. Working together, we could offer the girl food, shelter, and an education.

"Do you know how to knit?"

She nodded.

"Could you do me a large favour? Would you use this money to purchase yarn and make this young man a pair of gloves or mittens? Is that within your abilities?"

"I could do, sir, I could. Was there something else you was needing?" I instructed her to bring a pitcher of warm water and then I gave her enough coinage to purchase a ball of yarn.

"This is too much, sir," she said, as her face pinked with embarrassment.

"The money is for both the yarn and your labour, Bryony. Thank you for your diligence. You're a good girl."

When she left, Evans examined his hands thoughtfully. "I

ain't never had a pair of gloves nor mittens. Coo. I'll be warm as toast, I will."

During this small domestic exchange, Holmes pored over the large book that was entrusted with manifests of various ships. After flipping pages quickly this way, and then that, he had gone back and forth between one finding and another. His concentration was total. In fact, he'd taken the little black devil out of his coat pocket and put it between his teeth, although he hadn't had the time to light it. A series of satisfied grunts suggested he had found information of some value.

"It is exactly as I had suspected." Holmes slammed shut the most recent volume of *Lloyd's Register of Shipping Vessels.* "We were allowed to see a dummy ledger. You noticed, I am sure, that a great deal of pertinent information was missing. This is the real register. As we noted before, the Celestial and the Clarity are sister ships, nearly twins. Built at the same shipyard. Their registered tonnage is but four tons apart. All their other measurements are the same. In fact, they could be the same ship, save for one detail, of course. The Celestial is owned by the Crown. As one of the navy vessels owned by our dear Queen, she carries no passengers. Her crew is minimal. Her cargo is always the same."

"That is?" I prompted Holmes for an answer.

"Gold, meat, and livestock." My friend shook his head. "The Celestial sets out from Sydney once a month laden with goods from Australia. Do you recall that story in *The Times?* Eighteen years ago, the first ship with a compression refrigerator brought forty-one long tons of frozen beef and mutton from New Zealand to France. After that, William Davidson, the Director of the New Zealand and Australian Land Company, convinced the company to retrofit a ship, the Dunedin, with a refrigeration unit. The ship set sail with a cargo of 4,331 mutton, 598 lamb and 22 pig carcasses, 250 kegs of butter, hare, pheasant, turkey, chicken and 2,226 sheep tongues. Although it later was becalmed in the tropics, after ninety-eight days, the Dunedin docked in London. Inspectors found only one carcass to be spoiled. *The Times* hailed the voyage as a triumph: 'Today we have to record such a triumph over physical difficulties, as would have been incredible, even unimaginable, a very few days ago.'"

"Then the amendment to the vessel was profitable?" I asked.

Holmes smiled. "Even deducting the expenses, the gain was beyond all expectations. Nearly five thousand pounds."

"Five thousand pounds British sterling?" I could not help but gasp.

"Indeed, and that is only the profit realised from a journey one way. Not round trip. Once in London, the ship was emptied for a short hop to Lancashire. There the Dunedin was filled with cotton and wool from our mills. In essence, Watson, we are talking about an immensely profitable venture, this trade between Australia and Mother England."

Evans had washed his hands and I was applying salve to them when footsteps pounded on the staircase. What the devil? I wondered, as I put the cap on the glass jug. "Take this," I urged Evans. "Rub it into your skin. Use it lavishly, as I can easily get you more. The pain and itching should subside."

10

The words were only just out of my mouth when a courier rapped on our door. His knocks were made with a sort of frantic gusto. Holmes let the man in as Bryony slipped past him with the basin of dirty water. The messenger cast his round eyes about our flat, taking in the appointments and the curious vision of me holding Evans' hands in mine. "Mr. Holmes? Mr. Sherlock Holmes? The lady, Mrs. Morel, bids you to come to her place right this minute. She's heard news and she's mad keen for you to hear it, too."

Throwing on our winter garments, we left so quickly that I almost forgot to lock the door behind us. Although I must admit, after witnessing Evans' proud skills in lock picking, I doubted that a deadbolt was much use. Nevertheless, I turned and ran back upstairs to put the key to the lock. We could not chance the book of manifests stolen.

I returned to the cab, huffing and puffing.

"Good job, Watson," Holmes congratulated me. "I should not like to lose that large journal. While it is possible that it shan't be missed, we cannot afford to lose the head start we've gained from our newfound knowledge. With a bit of good luck, we might yet return Mr. Morel to the arms of his loving wife. If such a man really exists."

As happy as I would be to perform such a service for Mrs. Morel, those words "loving wife" settled on me like a heavy robe, dampening my spirits. My own sweet wife, who had died a few months before, had been a source of great comfort and joy to me. I missed her more each day. At times like this, I envied Holmes. His passion seemed reserved for his work. He was a thinking creature, rather than a man of sentiment. In point of fact, he had been trained for the role he played with such élan.

As the second son, his mother did not dote on him. Yes, he was loved, but Mycroft, Sherlock's older brother by seven years, had resolved that age-old question that plagues every dynastic family: Shall we have an heir? The arrival of Mycroft meant that Violet had fulfilled all her maternal duties to the Holmes family. Violet had done all that was required of her, and never again would she submit herself to such indignities. For seven long years, she enjoyed the accolades of the Holmes family as her husband and his kin adored their youngest member. Mycroft was precocious and an "easy" child, in that his chief pleasure in life was food. The promise of a crumpet with jam, a scone with clotted cream, or a biscuit with lemon curd was enough to gain his total compliance. True, the boy enjoyed the acquisition of knowledge, and his tutors were impressed by the ease with which he acquired mastery, but one could not rightly call Mycroft demanding. His desires were in perfect concert with what his parents wanted for their son.

During these seven years, Violet enjoyed perfect freedom as a wife and mother. After producing the heir, having done her duty, she was essentially free to do as she pleased. Her figure had always been much admired, and after Mycroft, she quickly regained her former coveted silhouette. Her son reflected well on her, and she basked in the glow of his scholastic successes.

Her husband had reached a pinnacle in his career, a lofty position that afforded the family every comfort plus entrée to the loftiest echelons of society. A home in the city, a country house, servants, carriages, couture clothing, and so on and so on. Violet had everything a woman could desire.

And then she fell pregnant with Sherlock. It was, at the very least, a disappointment when Violet was forced to withdraw from the London social whirl. Sadly this pregnancy was not "easy" as the other one had been. Violet was older, and her body responded quite differently to her confinement. First came the terrible sickness that wracked her body so violently she burst blood vessels in her eyes. Next came the swelling that inflated her ankles, robbing them of their beauty. The glow she had enjoyed in her first pregnancy was replaced by the sallow, drawn look of her skin. As she spent more and more time in her own bed at home, Violet's emotional reserves were drained. The lack of joyful companionship left her morose and angry. The fact that Sherlock, who has never been punctual as an adult, came late as a baby, sent his mother into such a deep depression that she was watched by a nursemaid night and day as a precaution lest she hurt herself.

Sherlock was a breech birth. As a doctor, those simple words send a shudder through me. Oh, we do what we can, trying our best to turn the infant around. Encouraging the mother to adopt strange positions that may or may not entice the infant to change position. Yet at the last, we find ourselves helpless as the baby always does exactly what the baby wants. Knowing Sherlock Holmes as I do, I can affirm that his willpower is immense. I have been told he brought every ounce of this determination to his awkward pre-birth position. His mother's suffering was immense, and eventually the *accoucheur* had no choice but to resort to force. In the best of times, metal tongs are cumbersome. When a mother had already been in labor for seventy-two hours, as Violet had, they are both welcome and feared.

And so, Sherlock's arrival was more of a relief than a celebration. His mother looked on him and wondered how a mite so small could have wreaked such havoc on her life. Exhausted and in pain, Violet told her husband to take the child away. He did as asked, thinking she would soon be on her feet again when her spirits revived themselves. Alas, that is not how it happened. Violet turned her face from her newborn babe. She never looked on him with joy. Not once did she call the wet nurse and ask to hold him in her arms. Nor would she take subsistence. Instead, she closed her eyes and a week later, she died.

I share this with you because I believe it explains much of my friend's character. Without a mother's affection to yearn for, he grew to rely on his keen intellect to make his way in the world. It's not that Holmes has no passion, he does, but he reserves this passion for his work. This severance allows him to concentrate his energies on hunting down criminals.

There are times—albeit few and far between—when I envy Holmes his detachment. In those moments when the pain of missing Mary is so raw that I can scarcely draw my next breath, how I wish that Holmes and I could trade places!

11

The frozen streets of London had been churned like butter, as the snow and ice were pummeled by the hooves of horses and the wheels of carriages and the soles of countless weary boots. The slop was disgusting and dollops flew up and stuck to every surface. When the watery mess mixed with fresh horse droppings, this became nearly intolerable. I was glad the temperatures were rising, but I hated the mess that was inevitable when traveling in London proper.

Mrs. Morel's "maid" showed us to her parlour. Linton seemed as gruff as ever, and Mrs. Morel seemed preoccupied. Her manner of greeting us was subdued. Rather than her focused attention, as we had before, her mind was clearly distracted. Once Holmes and I took to our chairs, she muttered, "That will be all, Linton."

Turning to us, she said, "Mr. Holmes, Dr. Watson, thank you both for coming with such alacrity. May I introduce to you to Captain Hobbes-Nesmith, an old friend of my family?"

The newcomer was a patrician-looking man with a thin nose, a broad high forehead, and perfect posture. His eyes wore an air of sadness, and the pain they had seen caused a crease in the man's brow. His size and weight were not remarkable, but the naval uniform he wore made up for any ordinary aspect of his physique. Medals and ribbons decorated his chest and left no room for plain fabric to show.

Handshakes were exchanged all around. The roaring fire had dutifully heated the small room so that our outerwear immediately was too heavy. My hat and scarf came off first and then I unbuttoned my coat. Holmes was doing the same when Mrs. Morel's expression changed from expectant to horrified. "Linton!" she said. "Linton!"

I wondered why she did not ring the bell as it was within easy reach of her fingers. However, her repeated calls for the parlour maid seemed to do the job just as well. Linton raced into the parlour. Her small, narrow-set green eyes went from Holmes to me, from me to Holmes, and repeated the pattern. We were dripping the frozen water and wet horse droppings on the fine Oriental carpet that graced the sitting room.

Linton immediately saw the problem. "Oy, I suppose I ought to take your coats and things," she said at last. Clearly, such a courtesy was an afterthought. I could hear Mrs. Morel's pent-up explosion of frustration. "You will have to clean this carpet, Linton, as soon as the gentlemen are gone."

It struck me then that I had never heard a lady give housekeeping orders to a staff member when a guest was visiting. Never. The sign of a proper household was an effortless machine that hummed behind the scenes, offering a sanctuary away from the cares of the world. To speak of these cares was to note their existence. I wondered if Holmes had caught the slip, too.

"Once you've taken care of their outerwear, please bring us a nice pot of tea, won't you, Linton?"

The girl's eyes flew wide. "Tea?"

"Yes, of course."

"Actually," began Holmes, "I would much prefer a tot of rum."

"What? Rum?" The woman said, and then recovered herself. "Uh, sir, I shall try my best. The mister, um, he's awful careful about sharing his liquor, he is. It ain't like the cellar is open for me to grab whatever a guest is wanting, sir."

Holmes said nothing. The silence weighed on me and the detective, but Mrs. Morel did not seem to notice. Instead, she fussed with the ruffle on her sleeves.

"All right," Linton confirmed, but her voice betrayed her confusion. "If it's rum you're wanting, then I'll see to it straight away. After I get your outer garments sorted." Struggling under the weight of the coats, scarves, and gloves, she hurried out of the room.

"Captain Hobbes-Nesmith arrived a few minutes ago with news about my husband. I thought it prudent for him to share his thoughts directly rather than to hear them from me second-hand," said Mrs. Morel. In her lap was a linen handkerchief that had been twisted into a knot.

"Watson? Please take notes," said Holmes, as he slouched in his chair and closed his eyes. This meditative pose often disturbs others as they take it to mean the detective has dozed off. Nothing could be further from the truth. While his senses are turned inward, my friend marshals all his attention and directs it towards a problem.

I took out my notebook and pencil, balancing them on my knee. When I was ready, I said to the captain, "Please proceed."

Hobbes-Nesmith launched into a long dissertation. It seemed that he was in the port of Marseilles when he bumped into Mr. Morel. Morel told him that he expected to be home in less than a fortnight. Captain Hobbes-Nesmith duly expected to see Morel when he returned to London. But after making inquiries at the regular spots frequented by his friend, Hobbes-

Nesmith learned that Morel had not arrived. "My own ship, the Oriana, left Marseilles three days after Mr. Morel was due to depart. We docked in Wapping two days ago. By all calculations, he should have been home already. We took the same route as he did. We didn't see any signs of bad weather—and we would have sailed through storms too, if they'd been happening along the route we usually take. So I'm at a loss to say where Jonas Morel could be!"

Mrs. Morel dabbed her eyes delicately with her handkerchief. "Mr. Holmes, have you any news? I realise that it's only been one day, and I am pressing you on a matter that cannot be resolved easily. Forgive me, but the man I love is out there somewhere, and I fear for him." Her eyes moistened with unshed tears. She really was a magnificent creature.

Holmes confounded my expectations. I thought he would tell Mrs. Morel and her friend what we had learned about the ship's cargo. I imagined he would share, with some pride, that we knew the Celestial had a sister ship. Although I am long accustomed to Holmes surprising me, I had not expected for him to disappoint me by sharing none of the important information we had gathered. None! Sliding his eyes my way, I detected a message from him. Even though the gesture was coy, having known Holmes all these years, I trusted I had caught his drift. He was asking me to stay silent.

"Sadly, Mrs. Morel, we have learned nothing," Holmes said.

My mouth went slack in surprise. I thought he would at least offer a reassuring bromide. Instead, he'd totally neglected to share any portion of what we'd done to advance our cause. Again, my friend gave me a quick glance, mute testimony that I was to keep my counsel.

Holmes' eyes were alert and thoughtful as he said, "Captain Hobbes-Nesmith, would you be so kind as to trace for me the route your ships commonly take? Doctor Watson, I would appreciate if you act as my amanuensis so I can turn my full concentration to what the good captain tells us."

"Just so," I said. With pencil in hand, I waited until Hobbes-Nesmith recited a list of ports. "From Marseilles, we sailed to Algiers. From Algiers to the Suez Canal. Then on to the Indian Ocean."

His report was very much shorter than I had expected. Holmes queried him, "And the weather? What can you tell me of it?"

"Mild. Nothing out of the ordinary." Hobbes-Nesmith shifted in his chair. "I trust you are familiar with nautical life?"

"I have a modicum of experience." Holmes let the flicker of a smile cross his face. To Hobbes-Nesmith and Mrs. Morel, I am certain it seemed congenial. However, I knew that look. It was the same sort of sly expression that Holmes displayed right before he sprang a trap. Leaning forwards in my chair, I waited for him to shout, "Oh, ho!" But he did not. Instead, he jumped to his feet. "Well, now. We must be off. Come now, Watson."

The parlour maid scurried frantically to bring us our outerwear. Mrs. Morel's face closed down as if a veil had fallen over those fine features. Out of the corner of my eye, I thought I saw a message pass between her and Captain Hobbes-Nesmith. What that might have been, I cannot say, but my impression was that Mrs. Morel was pleading with the sea captain to do something. But what?

As Holmes wrapped a woolen scarf around his neck, he spoke in the most casual voice imaginable. "If the posters at the Argyll Rooms are to be believed, tonight is your last engagement. Is that so?"

"Why, yes," she said with a blush of modesty. "My obligation to the theatre will be fulfilled this evening at the conclusion of my performance."

"I see," said Holmes. "Tell me, how long did your contract run? I only stumbled upon your performance of late."

"Oh." She seemed to hesitate. "Ten days. No, two weeks."

"I see," Holmes said. "You expected your husband to be home before your engagement came to its conclusion? Is that correct?"

Her eyes narrowed. "That is correct. As I told you, I expected Jonas to be home by now. Captain Hobbes-Nesmith confirms that schedule. That is why I insisted that the captain stay long enough to speak to you. It was a matter of grave importance. I wanted you to know that my husband has been seen and that his plans were firm, despite the unfortunate result." Pausing, she rang the bell. The bewildered parlour maid appeared. "Linton? Fetch for me my reticule."

"After you left, Mr. Holmes, it occurred to me that I do have one picture of my husband." She reached inside her handbag and handed the detective a manila envelope.

Holmes nodded and bowed. "I am much obliged. Good day, ma'am."

I could scarcely choke out a good-bye, but I did it anyway.

As we walked to the street and waved to hail a cab, Holmes hissed at me. "Not a word, Watson. Not one word until I say you can speak. We are being carefully observed."

And so we climbed into the hansom, two silent men who said nothing to each other.

12

We were a half mile from Mrs. Morel's house when Holmes slapped his knee. The sound was muffled given the layers of wool, but the effect was still arresting. "What an actress! What an actor! I say, Watson, did they not play their parts to perfection? Even the parlour maid."

Such aspersions on our hostess did not sit well with me. "Really, Holmes. You have become paranoid. You are being ridiculous. The maid was overwhelmed, that is all. So Mrs. Morel is an actress. We knew that last night. It doesn't follow that her husband hasn't gone missing. One truth does not automatically negate the other."

"Jolly well said," Holmes agreed. "But even fine acting skills can't make up for a lack of preparation by the director. Did you not notice, Watson, that Linton forgot to take our coats? Or that the Captain, whose arrival was said to be a few minutes prior to ours, did not leave any trace of inclement weather on the carpet? No? Only you and I soiled that fine rug. How about my request for rum? What sailor would not naturally have laid in a good stock of fine spirits? Particularly since rum is especially aged during the trip that sailing ships make so often? And yet,

Linton was flummoxed when I asked her for some. In fact, she never did bring me the drink that I requested. How unusual! How completely and utterly wrong for the purposes of the little fake tableau presented to us."

"Aw, but Holmes, you are forgetting, we now have a photo. You can say all you want, you can say what you will, but once you open that envelope we will come face-to-face with a real man. Flesh and blood. What say you then about Mrs. Morel and her overly active imagination?"

"Anyone can take a photo, Watson. A casual passerby can step into a photographer's shop and purchase discards or duplicates easily enough. You put too much faith in human nature. Or in this case, you are too effortlessly distracted by a lovely face and a charming figure. Oh, do not look that way at me! I do not accuse you of adultery. No, I am simply pointing out that Mary left a gigantic hole in your heart, and no woman alive can fill it. Don't forget, I knew her, too. Although I did not know her as long as you did, I was able to train my powers of observation on her. You were not. You led with your heart, and I followed along behind with my head."

"What a load of rot. You think you knew Mary? Ha."

"Ha, indeed. I know enough of her to know she was everything to you. And with good reason. I hope you do not let this woman, this Mrs. Morel, inveigle her way into your heart just because you are in so much pain, my friend. She is not worthy."

"She is a client, Holmes," I said stiffly. Between the cold and the damp and Holmes, I was done in.

"You would do well to remember that," was his answer.

13

But we were not able to return to 221B and warm ourselves by the fire. Our hansom stopped to let us off and we were rudely grabbed by two burly thugs who pushed us into another hansom, holding us at gunpoint. How I wished I had brought my revolver with me! The whole ride I fumed and chastised myself for letting Holmes talk me out of being so provisioned. Holmes slumped down in the seat and closed his eyes, taking one of those naps that so infuriate me. The man can stay awake all night by catching sleep hither, thither, and yon during the day. While I eyed our assailants with distaste, my friend was deep in the arms of Morpheus.

While I did not dare look out the window, the sounds of traffic (muffled as they were by the slush) and the direction the cab was pointed, as well as the variety of turns we made, convinced me I knew exactly where we were headed. Once we pulled up to the kerb, I shouted, "Mycroft! This time he has gone too far."

Holmes woke to my loud protestation. "Did you not realise who sent these cretins and why?" His words would have made a less than congenial effect on our guardians had they the brains to understand what the term "cretin" meant.

The route the cabman took was well-known to me, as Sherlock Holmes and I have often visited his older brother Mycroft at the club he cofounded, the Diogenes Club. Unlike other gentlemen's clubs that extend membership to the most congenial of men, the Diogenes Club attracts the most unsociable and "unclubbable" men in town. Mycroft has gathered those who are witty and intelligent, typically with an obscure specialty. There are also those members who have made their mark in ways unappreciated by the world at large, particularly by society. Thus, this is a place for misfits of the highest order.

And yet...they serve the needs of both Mycroft and our government very well. Although Mycroft's office is below the club's first floor, it is easy enough for him to dispatch one of his many lackeys to the club proper and track down the sort of expertise the elder Holmes brother needs at any given time. In this manner, the club serves as a living, breathing repository of information. So congenial is this atmosphere that Mycroft keeps a flat on the top floor of the building. An elevator makes transit from office to residence easy for Mycroft, whose love of fine food is legendary and whose overindulgence in the same concerns me as a physician.

Sherlock bolted from the growler that served as our transport, leaving me to pay the cabman. Racing up the front steps of the Diogenes Club, and heaving himself through the front doors, he wasted no time. When the attendant on duty tried to gather Sherlock's details, my friend brushed past the man. "I am here to see my brother, Mycroft Holmes, and I don't have time to waste on your petty rules."

I was two steps behind Sherlock, so I saw the gaping mouth of the clerk and I watched as his saucer-sized eyes followed Holmes out of the side door into the front parlour, otherwise considered the club proper. Knowing that no conversation is allowed in that area—never!—I hastened to follow Holmes, realising that once we were in the club, the attendant would have no choice but to stand aside.

Whilst I did feel somewhat sorry for the clerk, as he seemed to be new to the post and our behavior was intolerable, I could not help but stifle a chuckle at the man's predicament. Either course of action was doomed. If he followed us and made a fuss, he was breaking the club's rules on silence. If he allowed us to carry on, he was breaking the club's rules on entry by nonmembers. Truly, we had presented the man with a quandary that would either stiffen his character or cause an absolute dissolution of all he held dear!

Even as I pondered this, I followed Sherlock through a door hidden under a stairway and down a flight of stairs. This entrance to Mycroft's office was well-hidden from the casual observer. We passed a series of guards. One lunged out to try to grab Holmes, only to be held back by a colleague who murmured, "Let him pass." As I was clearly an attaché to Sherlock, I was given safe conduit, too. Nevertheless, I stayed close to my friend as he hurried through corridors and bullpens filled with busy workers.

At the heart of this beehive of activity was a glass enclosure, Mycroft's office. The place had been designed with privacy as the amenity of highest value. Secondarily, Mycroft wanted the ability to oversee his fiefdom at all times, as he was a highly demanding supervisor. Sherlock yanked open the glass door to his brother's private space, a place we knew to be soundproof. With a flick of the wrist, Mycroft could lower shades that occluded prying eyes and this he did after a glance at his brother's troubled visage.

But then, after all, Mycroft had expected as much. We'd been waylaid and dragged here against our will.

Mycroft did not wait for Sherlock to speak. Instead, he looked up with a bored expression and said, "Brother, I have need of your special talents."

There was no apology, no suggestion that he might have interrupted Sherlock's life, nothing. Mycroft could be unspeakably rude, although an objective observer might chalk it up to being ruthless in the pursuit of his goals. And his goals were invariably the goals of the British government and the Crown.

Today Mycroft was firmly ensconced in a big office chair, a bespoke piece of furniture designed to cradle his large bulk. The formality of the chair and his desk was at odds with the mess surrounding him, as piles of reports to his left and his right teetered and threatened to fall. Behind him was a map of the world with various pins stuck in a variety of places. A second glance explained to me that he had marked shipping lanes. I found that curious, considering our most recent visit to the Registrar's office.

"But first, I think your friend needs to leave," Mycroft said.

"And I think he will do nothing of the sort," said Holmes. "I trust John Watson more than I trust any man on earth. Do I make myself clear?"

Mycroft huffed. "Very well, if you insist." Just as quickly, Mycroft changed his mind. "Actually, the doctor might be useful. Yes, in point of fact, I believe he will be essential to this effort."

The way Mycroft called me "the doctor" as if I was as common as dirt and not worthy of having a Christian name, rankled. "So glad you think so, Mycroft. Especially seeing as how you press-ganged both of us. You could have allowed me to return to the comfort of our rooms rather than divert my journey home."

"I have need of Sherlock's unusual talents," said Mycroft.

"And merely asking me to visit would have been far too

courteous? Too laborious?" Sherlock said, in a scoffing manner while pulling up a chair. I took one, too. Like his brother, when Mycroft fixated on a goal, he could be most discourteous.

"I haven't the time to waste on niceties," he said, proving my point. "Not when the whole of the British Empire is in jeopardy."

"Hyperbole," said Holmes, pulling his little black devil from his pocket.

Mycroft did not offer him a light. "Sherlock, when have you ever known me to exaggerate? Never! This particular situation is both delicate in a political sense and important in a way such as I have never seen before. In fact, given the circumstances, I shall not waste time asking you. I command you as a citizen of the realm to do exactly as I say."

This piqued Sherlock's interest. The casual observer might not have noticed the flaring of his nostrils, the subtle shift of his weight, or the way his fingers tightened on the bowl of his pipe, but I did. Accordingly, I too listened to Mycroft with full attention.

"A cab waits outside for you. It will take you to the morgue. There you will meet with Berthold, one of my men. He will instruct you further. Now begone." Mycroft struggled to his feet. "And know this, of all the tasks I've set for you, this might be the most challenging. If it were not for your specific abilities, I would not risk your involvement. But the Queen needs you and so do I."

14

Mycroft was as good as his word. Right outside the door of his office, we were accosted by a man built like a Toby jug, squat with a face compressed by time. He eyed us with suspicion before offering the quickest bow I've ever seen. "The name's Berthold. Follow me," he said in a brusque voice.

As we dutifully walked behind our guide, through the hallways and tunnels that ran beneath the Diogenes Club, I grew more and more cross with every step. My head ached from hunger. The cold had chilled my bones. Mycroft's overbearing manner, his lack of trust in me, and his high-handed way of ordering his brother around did nothing to soothe my jangled nerves.

"I say," I muttered, "before we embark on some sort of errand for your brother, Holmes, especially one that involves visiting a morgue, could we stop and get a bite to eat? I am famished, I am thirsty, and I am tired. I need such creature comforts if I am to perform whatever duties our new assignment might demand."

"There's a cab waiting for you outside on the street,"

Berthold said. "Makes me no difference but I darst say, you may want to wait for your food until after we've visited the, er, our destination."

This put me in a very gloomy mood indeed. "Then perhaps Holmes could go and I could wait whilst—" I began, but Berthold quickly disarmed my suggestion. "No, sir. That won't do at all. Mr. Mycroft Holmes was exceedingly clear on that one point: The doctor must go with my brother. I'll swear on a stack of Bibles, you'll be able to do your business and depart right quickly."

Swallowing my disappointment, because that was all I had to chew on, I followed my comrades out into the bright morning, even as the frigid wind slapped me across the face. As it did, I recognised the sun was warming the earth. Slowly the snow and ice were melting. Thankfully, the cab was waiting for us not ten steps away. We threw ourselves inside, and naturally I took the seat next to my friend.

Berthold seemed distracted so I put my questions to Holmes: "Whatever do you suppose Mycroft has in mind? And that bit about the Queen. Surely, if Her Majesty wanted your help, She would simply ask you directly. All of this sly maneuvering is really too much."

Holmes kept his gaze upon the changing scenery outside our window. "Watson, have you ever seen my brother so discombobulated? No? Neither have I. Whatever this is, rest assured, it is not trivial. Mycroft's curt manner increases in direct proportion to the seriousness of the task ahead. Search your memory and you will see that is true."

As usual, Holmes was right, so I abandoned that topic and sallied forth on another. "What are your plans regarding Mrs. Morel?"

"My plans?" He raised one eyebrow. "I have no plans regarding Mrs. Morel. Her cry for help is naught but a ruse. I must allow, however, that I need more facts if I am to draw a sound conclusion as to why she has gone to so much trouble. Let me guess: You see her as a damsel in distress? Am I right?"

My transparency made me uncomfortable. "She clearly needs help of one sort or another, Holmes. Why else would she bother with the world's most famous consulting detective? We know she asked for you specifically. No, I think you dismiss her quandary with too little concern. Is it not possible that she is at the mercy of another? That she is being forced to play a part?"

"Ha!" Sherlock Holmes guffawed. "A woman like that is never at the mercy of another. She has beauty, she has talent, and she has brains. Gold is pale when compared to what she can claim as her own. That makes me curious, I'll confess. But the story about her missing husband I find hard to countenance."

15

Our errand, for that is what I suspected it was, took us through various streets. The changing scenery warned me that we were drawing near to the Thames. Indeed, I soon saw proof of my assumption as the shops changed to reflect the nearness of the river, that artery that pumps water through the heart of London. Once again our conveyance lurched to a stop and we found ourselves deposited in a melting mound of snow. What had been a blanket of snowy white had turned into a coarse rendering in shades of gray. Despite the cold, a stench loomed over us and leaked in through the crevices of our vehicle. Dead fish, rotting seaweed, and that organic smell I always associate with the sea assaulted my senses.

Berthold had not uttered a word, yet at the jarring end of our transport, he snapped to attention and promptly hopped out of the cab. Holding the door open for us, he said, "Get out, gentlemen. This is our destination. We have arrived."

Sherlock Holmes' eyes fluttered to wakefulness. After a powerful yawn, he unfolded his lean frame and climbed out. I was right behind him, and upon clapping eyes on the building in front of us, I said, "The morgue? The Kew deadhouse?" It was not a question so much as an affirmation of reality. Of course, as a doctor, I was familiar with the Kew morgue. This small, plain building had been necessitated by the plethora of bodies washed up by the tidal changes of the Thames. The parish had long been responsible, but once the anatomists offered five shillings (a whole crown!) for bodies, no one could depend on proper examination of the dead before the corpses were carried off. Thus, many instances of foul play went undetected. In recognition of this failing, deadhouses such as these were hastily constructed. Even as Holmes and I waited while Berthold went to find the beadle, so that he might unlock the door, the stench from the place was nigh unto unbearable.

Holmes has trained himself to distinguish a great many odours and, typically, those emissions from a corpse arouse curiosity in him rather than disgust. Even so, he shook his head at the smell. "As the cold has retreated, so has every element that dampens the foul odour of death."

Berthold returned with a smallish man, costumed in a bright red jacket with cording at the shoulders. He held his ceremonial mace as proudly as any soldier ever carried the standard for the United Kingdom. Upon seeing Holmes and me, he seemed to put a snap in his step as he lifted his chin higher. With more than a hint of pomposity, he unlocked the door to the deadhouse. Moving briskly away, he spoke to us like a commander to his troops. "You'll not be wanting to linger, I'll wager. Yon poor soul rolled up in the tide, and if he's not claimed today, we'll commit him to a pauper's grave."

"We shall see," said Holmes enigmatically. He ducked to walk inside but I did not have to. Lighting a match and putting the flame to the wick of an overhanging lamp, Berthold did not say a word as he stepped as far away as the confined space would allow him.

The beadle had managed to bring his mace along. This officer of the church was spry and wiry, with a face like a map of London, all covered with lines and dots. Only his eyes were remarkable, as they gleamed with an uncommon intensity. I could see why the parish valued him, as I doubt he missed any tidbit of activity on his watch. This man might be elderly, but he was far from decrepit.

The beadle held his mace aloft with one hand as he tugged on the sheet covering the body with the other. Slowly the stained muslin came away to reveal a visage mauled by fish and crabs. Indeed, the flesh of this poor man had been chewed on by a variety of water-loving creatures. I reminded myself to look past these disfigurements. Instead, I concentrated on parsing what riddles the deceased might help us solve. His uniform was not completely intact, but large portions remained, owing to the density of the fabric. His beard needed trimming, as did his hair.

"The full beard suggests this man served in the Royal Navy, even if his costume is too beleaguered to wholly conform to regulations." Holmes tilted his head and stared at the subject before us.

"We must undress him," Holmes remarked. To wit, he unbuttoned the collar of the jacket and the dull brass buttons that ran the length of the placket. Then he unbuttoned the trousers. The shoes, thankfully, were missing, as were the socks. "Watson? Lift him from the head and shoulders, please."

I struggled to do as Holmes asked. One does not realise how rigidly we maintain our posture until one tries to coax floppy limbs into new positions and keep them there. Reluctantly, Berthold came to my assistance. Together we each took charge of an armpit and hoisted our portion above the slab. Holmes tugged and worked the fabric until the breeches came off.

Awkwardly, we rotated our positions, as Holmes worked the hands and arms out of the jacket.

When finally the corpse was naked, Holmes was the first to observe the letters "L.I.V." had been tattooed on the forearm.

"Do you see now, Holmes, that you were unkind to poor Mrs. Morel?" I said, feeling pleased that the body was marked as she had described.

"Watson, you have leapt to a conclusion. Yes, this is a dead man. Yes, he looks to be a sailor of some rank. True, his flesh is marked with three letters: L.I.V. But none of this proves that our poor friend is in any way related to Mrs. Morel."

I bit back an angry retort and settled for, "Have it your way, Holmes. I think we have seen quite enough."

"No, Watson," said Holmes in a kindly tone. "We have just begun. Observe, please, the chaffing at the wrists and ankles. What can we deduce from that?"

I peered closer. "That he was shackled for some time?"

"Yes. Quite so. Let me also introduce you to the many crusted irregular patches of skin on those parts of the anatomy that are extremely sensitive to pain." Holmes pointed out red dots near the groin, around the nipples, and under the arms. "What might that lead you to deduce?"

I unhooked the lantern to hold it closer to the flesh of our corpse. "Burns! My word! This man was burned. Probably a lit stick was held to his flesh!"

"Of that there is no doubt," Holmes agreed. "Turn your attention please to the deep indentation of flesh around the throat. See where the skin is sliced through in places? What can we learn from that?"

Moving to the top of the corpse, I trained the meager light of the lantern so I could explore the area under the beard more carefully. Holmes, of course, was right again: This man had been garroted. I said, "I suggest a wire was used in conjunction with a piece of wood. This wound is too deep, too specific, and too deadly to have been rendered by an amateur."

"I concur," said Holmes. "Now, Dr. Watson, please open the man up."

"Begging your pardon?" I asked as incredulity froze me to the spot. "You are asking...you want me to cut into this corpse? For what purpose, Holmes? It seems like a sacrilege to further defile this poor remnant of a human being. Has he not endured enough?"

"Ah," said Holmes, "I will wager you a shilling that he has endured much more than we presently know. In fact, I believe he has a secret, one that he would be eager to share with us if he could. Now, please, did you bring your medical tools with you?"

"No."

To the beadle, Holmes directed a question, "Sir, do you have a sturdy knife that the doctor could borrow? The sharper the better."

The man disappeared in the blink of an eye. Had the circumstances not been so bleak, I could have chuckled at his fervor, but in this depressing instance, I could only marvel at how agile the man proved himself to be. The smell of rotting flesh had become familiar to our noses. So much so that the corpse no longer seemed odiferous, although surely it was.

"Exactly how do you want me to open this body up, Holmes?" I asked. "Do you wish me to perform an autopsy? If so, we might want to move our friend. A knife won't work for cutting through bone."

"Fear not, Watson. I am not asking anything so onerous. No, I merely want you to fillet the corpse, exposing his digestive tract to us so that we can examine it. I am curious about what this man might have been fed in the last hours of his life. Did you notice that he is uncommonly heavy? Certainly, the dead seem heavy because their limbs are flaccid, but this man's weight seems excessive compared to his structure. I want to know why."

"Are you suggesting he ingested a large meal before he was garroted?" I was only halfway jesting.

"No, I am thinking along the lines of digestives that cannot be digested."

"Is this a riddle? If so, your sense of timing is abominable."

The beadle saved Holmes from more of my pointed irritation by offering me a leather case. "That's a Bowie knife in there," he said proudly. "My son's a cowboy out west in the United States of America. He sent that to me because I was worrying about him and Injuns. But he says that's just sensationalism, like them stories about Sherlock Holmes. Nothing but wild tales meant to sell books, he says."

Holmes raised a sardonic eyebrow. I said nothing beyond offering my gratitude for a tool worthy of my trade.

The knife was sharper than any knife I've ever used with the possible exception of a new scalpel. Following Holmes' directive, I plunged the blade into the xiphoid process, the third and largest segment of the sternum. Of course, since the man on the slab was nearly four decades old, that cartilage had ossified considerably. The Bowie knife did an admirable job of piercing the bony plate.

Across the room, Berthold responded by heaving. Racing out of the deadhouse, he must have only stumbled his way a few feet from the threshold because the sounds of his retching echoed through the small building.

"I may need help, if you want me to part the ribs," I said, looking up at Holmes.

"I doubt that will be necessary. The digestive tract is my goal."

"All right," I said. After extending the incision to a length of approximately eight inches, I cut free the spleen and the liver.

Using both hands, I lifted out the spleen, as it was closest to me. Then I reached over the incision and removed the liver. This exposed the stomach.

"Open that," said Holmes, pointing a long, thin finger at the stomach. He was leaning over the corpse with such interest that his head nearly collided with mine.

"Kindly move out of my way," I said. "On occasion, the stomach succumbs to bloating. Gases might turn this organ into a vigorous fountain of bile." After my pronouncement, I watched my friend. He took my advice to heart and stepped back, although he nearly collided with the beadle, a man whose keen interest seemed unfettered by any hint of nausea.

Delicately, I inserted the tip of the knife into the expanded organ. As I had prophesized, a *whoosh* of accumulated gases spewed from the inch-long incision I'd made. Once the noxious fumes exhausted themselves, I pressed the tip of the Bowie knife in deeper and slowly sliced a line perpendicular to the side of the marble slab.

Holmes hurried over. "Well?"

"Well, what?" I heartily regretted that I was wearing my good jacket. The bodily fluids splashed on the wool would never come out.

"Well, what do you see?"

After being sliced open, the stomach caved in on itself, rather like a hot air balloon does when deflated. If I'd been properly attired, I would have reached in and opened the pouch back up. Considering the damage to my outer garment, I used the tip of the knife as a tool, instead. I flipped back the side of the stomach closest to Holmes.

All three of us gasped in unison.

The dead man's stomach was filled to the limits of its extension. But instead of food, it was dense with nuggets of gold.

16

Berthold rejoined us, although he looked worse for wear. The cacophony of our gasps had lured him back inside the charnel house. His facial pallor indicated he was not up to the task of remaining at my side.

"Mr. Berthold, rather than faint and hit your head, I suggest you wait outside for us," I said curtly.

"No," Holmes countered my proposal. "Stay but one more minute. Berthold, we need to transport this body. My brother should see this."

"Pardon me, Mr. Holmes," said Berthold, "but your brother was quite clear. He asked only for a report. His schedule is such that viewing this with his own two eyes is a waste of his time and energy. That said, I suppose we better take the gold back with us, eh? I can't calculate how much is there, but it looks to me to be a king's ransom."

"At the very least, keep the body here for a day or so. I might want to bring the woman who claims to be the dead man's wife here for a viewing," said Holmes.

"Claims?" I cast Holmes an angry look.

"Claims," he repeated. I shuddered as I imagined Mrs. Morel in this horrid place.

Yet when I tried to turn my mind to other subjects, I was caught upon those words, that phrase Berthold had used: "a king's ransom." Berthold's comment was ill-timed and more to the point, wrong-footed. No king had sat on our throne for more than fifty years. Although I knew Berthold was simply repeating a tired phrase, the terminology roused a tangle of thoughts. All at once, I wished that Holmes and I were here alone, so I could discuss the matter with my friend. Talking to Holmes often gave me clarity. His manner of casting off the chaff and getting to the wheat kernel was integral to his deductions. Instead, such discourse would have to wait.

"We shall take the gold with us," decided Holmes. "After all, those pellets might be the only tangible proof we have."

"Proof of what?" I asked.

"I am not ready to say," Holmes demurred. "All in good time, Watson. All in good time."

Using the Bowie knife, I cut a piece of the shroud and folded the fabric into a pouch to hold the gold nuggets. The beadle's eyes lit up when he watched me transferring the pieces from the corpse to the linen. At the very end, I tossed a small pebble of gold to the beadle. "Sir? I believe you could do good for the parish with this token of our gratitude. Use it wisely is all that I ask."

Holmes fought a smile. I could almost hear him saying, "Watson, you are a sentimental old chap." Perhaps he would be right, but what harm could it do to give the beadle a bit of gold? No one seemed to be lining up to claim what we'd found. Surely the beadle could find a worthy cause enacted under the purview of the Church and thus the token would do some good in this sad, treacherous world. At least the token might fund the running of the deadhouse.

Certainly, someone had tortured this poor fellow. Admittedly, he must have been used as a carrier for gold. But why kill the transport after the fact? That didn't make sense to me. I could only hope that Holmes' piercing mind had a better grasp of these baffling points than I had.

We'd no more than taken our seats in the cab and rapped on the roof so the driver would know he should drive on, when Holmes sprang across the cab and locked Berthold's head in a choke hold such as I have never seen in my life. I flattened myself against the cab seat in shock. Holmes rarely uses force to make his point. This time he did.

"I ought to strangle you where you sit," Holmes hissed at Berthold. "You knew all along that man was carrying stolen gold. Yet you asked me and my good friend to play your foolish games. What is Mycroft up to? He had to have known the gold was there. Whose gold is it? Where was it going? How was it diverted?"

I blurted out, "How did it get inside that man? Holmes, I've never seen the like. Did he intend for nature to take its course? That defies all tenets of good sense."

Berthold made no attempt to get Holmes to leave off choking him. Instead, he endured the choking with a stoicism I could only count as admirable. His raspy voice said, "Go ahead, Holmes. Although I would have never guessed that the great Sherlock Holmes was a murderer as well as a thief. What do you suppose the Home Office will say when they learn the gold has gone missing from that poor dead sod? Can't you think they'll blame it on you, Holmes? Certainly no one will blame your brother. No, even if you care nothing for your own reputation, friendship demands you don't leave John Watson to be hanged for treason!"

"Good heavens, man!" I shouted. "Treason? I am a loyal servant of the Crown. I have given the Queen my years of service and I've naught but a splintered bone to show for it. In this adventure alone, I was following the directive of Mycroft Holmes, who is closer to the Queen as any other man in the realm. Yet you dare to threaten me?"

Holmes had not loosened his hold on Berthold's throat. "Explain yourself, man, and do it quickly if you hope to leave this cab on your own two feet."

"Back off and I shall!"

Slowly Holmes let his arms grow slack. Berthold rubbed his neck with open palms. "That gold belongs to the Queen. Regular shipments of gold from Australia fund the protection of the realm. Specifically, those nuggets will go to arm, dress, and feed our troops who will fight the Boers in our next conflict."

I stifled a gasp of shock. We'd heard rumblings but no clear trajectory towards armed conflict had been announced. This was news indeed, and the general populace would find it troublesome. I choked on the words, "The Boers? But I thought we had South Africa under our thumb."

Berthold brayed with laughter. "Just as I had *you two* under mine? Don't be ridiculous, Dr. Watson. As long as there are rulers in this world, there will also be the masses waiting for the opportunity to rise up. Defending the realm is an expensive proposition. The gold shipments from Australia are what keep our country solvent."

"Who was that dead man?" Holmes asked.

Berthold shrugged. "I could not say. I do not know. Nor do I think Mr. Mycroft Holmes knows about this man. Furthermore, I'm not sure that Mycroft cares. All we know is that gold from Her Majesty's mines in Australia is dug out of the ground and loaded monthly onto a ship departing from Sidney and bound for Liverpool. Once the ship docks, a military guard sees that the gold is taken directly to the Queen's Treasury in the Tower of London."

"So were you looking for Mr. Morel?" I asked. "Presumably he was on one of those ships and it sank. You hoped he could tell you what was happening?"

"Watson," Holmes admonished me, "there is no Mr. Morel."

I could tell Berthold agreed with my friend. I said, "Then whom did I just slice into? Whose body did I desecrate?"

Berthold's face twitched as he struggled not to smile. "We believe the dead man was Alton Baker, the second lieutenant on the Celestial. But we do not know for sure. As to whether he is married to a Maria Morel, that too, is questionable. These points of inquiry are what your brother hopes that you, Mr. Holmes, can find out. He wants to know who is behind the repeated sacking of our ships. Three of them have gone down, the Celestial being the most recent."

"But why would someone force a man to swallow gold?" I asked, voicing my thoughts. "And why would his body pitch up in the Thames? Surely, if the ships are sinking, there's no need for proving the gold is gone. Furthermore, why would a lost sailor be dumped into the Thames? Wouldn't he be lost at sea?" The deluge of questions kept on coming. In the midst of my recitation, my stomach gurgled. During my ghastly efforts in the dead house, I'd been so caught up in the deed at hand that I'd temporarily forgotten my need for sustenance. Now it came roaring back with a vengeance.

Holmes heard the noise and smiled at me. "I doubt that Mrs. Hudson will want to serve you, Watson, smelling as you do."

"Berthold, have the cabman take us to a public house. The Golden Ram is near enough. Don't worry, Watson. Your less than appealing apparel will not cause a great disturbance. I trust my brother laid on you a reasonable sum of money for expenses, Berthold? Good. The least that Mycroft owes us is a hearty meal and a fine glass of wine."

17

Frequent readers of my work will no doubt recall that Sherlock Holmes has at his disposal a vast network of helpers who function as a tributary does emptying into the vast ocean. This myriad of reporters hail from all walks of life and serve my friend with pleasure, as it thrills them to know they've done small services for the world's greatest consulting detective. Individually, they are unaware of how their bits and bobs of information fit into the whole, for they are those threads that only Holmes can weave into a complete tapestry. His unassailable logic, his keen intellect, his ability to use his imagination are the tools he alone can bring to this fresh new discipline that I call forensic detection.

Readers will also be aware that Holmes has established for himself a variety of bolt holes, spots known to him alone where he can retreat for any number of reasons, whether it is his desire to simply fuel his thought process with solitude or his need to prepare for another role that might assist him as he gathers necessary information, or his choice to absent himself when the criminal element is hot on his trail. One of these bolt holes, I was surprised to discover, was the Golden Ram, a public house not far from the Thames.

On the outside, the place looks like any other such establishment. From the pictogram of a stately ram with horns of shining gold to the mullioned windows, it was easy to identify as a place for food and drink. The floor was rough-hewn and uneven, worn by the abrasion of thousands of soles. A man taller than Holmes would need to watch his head, as the ceiling was low and the beams that crossed overhead were thick. A blaze in a large fireplace roared its approval, spreading light and heat throughout the dining room. As one walked straight inside from the front door, one could not help but come face-to-face with the publican, standing behind the counter at the bar and drawing pints with practiced ease. Holmes directed us to turn right and led us to a booth in the back corner, a darkened hiding place, or so it seemed, because we'd no more than taken our seats than a comely woman wearing a spotless white apron and a mob cap sashayed from swinging doors. She asked Holmes, "The usual, luv?"

That left Berthold and me to ponder the chalkboard menu hanging next to the barrels of port and Guinness. I chose the ploughman's lunch as I was too hungry to wait for food to cook. Berthold decided on the same. Holmes ordered a wine with a provenance so praiseworthy that it seemed wildly out of place for such a humble pub. Assured that such a marvelous vintage was indeed available, Berthold and I did the same. The barmaid was poised to walk away when Holmes crooked a finger at her. She bent her head close to his.

"Dolly, send Percy a message for me. Tell him I want to speak to the Duke." Holmes delivered this out of the side of his mouth, *sotto voce.*

"Yes, Mr. Holmes," said Dolly. "I shall do that first thing, before I get your wine. Be right back."

The woman disappeared and shortly reappeared carrying three glasses of one of the finest cabernets I've ever tasted. "Percy's on it, luv," said Dolly with a sly wink at Holmes. He reached into his pocket, pulled out a coin, and pushed it towards her so fast I barely noticed the exchange. Only after Dolly walked away again did I realise I'd watched a gold coin change hands. If I looked mildly astonished, it was only fair because such a sum was many times the expense of our meals combined. I was even more amazed when Holmes told Berthold, "That was to pay her for her time and expertise. You need to dig deep into your pockets and pay her handsomely for our food and drink."

Berthold might have grumbled some, but the wine was far too good and the cozy nook was far too pleasant for him to stay irritated for long. Indeed, I felt my eyes growing heavy as I leaned my head against the back wall of the booth. Holmes had nothing to say to Berthold, and Berthold had nothing to say to Holmes, so I don't believe I missed anything because I sat upright when the click of heels drew nigh unto our table.

There are those who suppose a kingdom such as ours is chock-a-block full of dukes. To read romantic novels, one might rightly conclude there are as many dukes as sheep on the hillsides, for only a duke will do when young ladies fall in love in books. However, I must set the record straight, for I do pride myself on well-informed readers. There are not that many dukes in Queen Victoria's realm. Not many at all. Fully half of those listed in *Burke's Book of Peerage* are related by blood to the Queen Herself. The others are likely related by marriage. To summon a duke to appear at a table, tucked away in the farthest corner of a pub, is a trick to be avoided by even the most celebrated magicians of the day. Nevertheless, Sherlock Holmes did just that, and he did it with such languorous ease that I was fair astonished when the Duke of Herrington strode his way to our table. I was even more flabbergasted when the Duke and Holmes embraced like long-lost schoolmates, which, as it happened, is exactly what they were.

The Duke looked to be the same age as Holmes. His gray eyes were soft, his brown hair was styled back from his forehead to emphasize the comely shape of his head. His lips twisted into an amused smile, not a grin, but nearly there. Not surprisingly, the Duke was by far the best dressed man in the tavern. Even so, he'd chosen clothing in subtle shades that blended into his surroundings. In short, he was the model of a man with a claim to royalty, yet his good breeding showed through and through because he carried himself without a scintilla of pomposity.

"Charlie," said Sherlock Holmes, getting to his feet, "meet Dr. John H. Watson, my dear friend. This is Berthold and he's one of Mycroft's lackeys."

This infuriated Berthold, which I believe was Holmes' desired effect. I stood up as the others had done and offered my hand, although I felt rather out of my depth. The stink of my coat had increased as we warmed ourselves by the fire, and my hands needed a good wash from handling the internal organs of a long-dead corpse. But Charlie did not turn a hair. He greeted me with the sort of aplomb that marks a true gentleman.

Rather than have him sit next to me in my disheveled state, I excused myself to find Dolly. Once I explained my plight, that kind woman clucked her tongue at my embarrassing problem. "Not to worry, Doctor. I remember how my late husband was always getting his overcoat soiled with this or that. Must have happened once or twice a week at least. I'll show you to a chamber where you can freshen up. If you'll trust me with your coat, I'll see to it and get it back to you, good as new. In the meantime, I'll see if I can't come up with a suitable garment you can wear so you don't catch your death of cold."

"Dear lady!" I exclaimed. "I should be forever in your debt. How much shall I owe you?"

"Not a farthing," said she. "Mr. Holmes pays me a goodly sum indeed. This is part of my service to him, and glad I am to do it!"

Once I had shucked off my coat, I was led to a private room upstairs, and there I availed myself of a delightful soap infused with chamomile flowers. After washing and drying with a clean flannel, I felt ever so much more sociable. My return to the table was heralded with smiles and invitations to make myself comfortable.

Holmes said, "Whilst you were gone, Watson, I bored my old friend with an accounting of our day's adventures."

"Bored? Sherlock, your vocabulary has deserted you when it was most important. I was decidedly not bored. My word," said Charlie, staring at me with wide eyes. "A man who swallowed gold? Surely, Doctor, that was not an easy task for him. I've been known to choke on a crumb of toast."

"True enough. Anyone can choke on almost anything. In this situation, we have evidence that suggests suffocation dealt the final blow. This poor creature was tortured within an inch of his life. As for swallowing small chunks of gold, under such duress, one can manage surprising feats and accomplish superhuman antics," I said. "Furthermore, we have cause to believe our dead man did not live long after his Midas-inspired feast. I hope he did not suffer long, but I am bound to say, his end was thoroughly unpleasant."

Coming out from the kitchen, Dolly carried a heavy wooden tray. She delivered to us our food. Charlie had agreed with my idea and asked the good woman for a ploughman's lunch. Since Berthold had done the same, we all watched with surprise as Dolly set a bowl of mulligatawny soup in front of Sherlock Holmes. The pungent curry was so enticing that all of us decided we must join Holmes, and Dolly was happy to facilitate our palates by bringing more bowls of the soup. "We keep a pot of it going all the time, just for Mr. Holmes, we do," she said with a charming smile.

The food went down a treat, a second serving of wine lubricated our goodwill, and thus we engaged in a lively conversation centered on the events of the day.

"There is a rumour," Charlie conceded, "one I am loath to credit. However, I needs must share it with you all in strictest confidence. I share it only because I know I can count on your sworn silence as gentlemen."

"I cannot vouch for Berthold," Holmes said.

When the other man took offense, Holmes pinned him with a candid gaze. "Would you have faith in a man foisted upon you? Would you entrust secrets of a highly important nature to someone you just met? No, you would not, so by what stretch of rational thought do you suppose I would trust you? There is none."

"I am your brother's man," said Berthold. "He trusted me enough that he sent me as his eyes and ears on this sensational mission. Is that not good enough for you?"

Holmes sat back and crossed his arms over his chest. "No, it is not enough. So hear me and heed my words. If anything that Charlie is about to tell us comes back to my ears, I shall call you out. Believe me, if you think my wit is sharp you will find it rusty compared to my skill with a sword. Are we clear?"

Berthold swallowed hard. His Adam's apple bobbed with barely disguised fear. "Y-Y-Yes."

Charlie raised his eyebrows and gave a slight shake of his head as emphasis. "Berthold, I do not know you, so in the spirit of Christian charity I give you this free advice: Do not cross Sherlock Holmes in a fencing match. I have never seen a man handle a sword with such finesse. Never. And believe me, I have seen the best the world has to offer."

"So I ask you again," said Holmes in a voice so cold I thought ice might form on his wineglass, "are you able to hold your tongue?"

Berthold nodded. When he realised a bob of the head was not enough, he said, "Yes. I give you my word on my life."

"Then, Charlie, loosen your tongue, my friend. I suspected you might harbour information vital to our cause. Do not fail me now," said Holmes.

18

"For the sake of delicacy and due to my immense respect for the Queen," said Charlie, "this is a story I am loathe to tell. I share it only because of my long friendship with Sherlock, and because I worry that this information might soon be used against Our Queen, even as She continues to rule over the world's greatest empire.

"You are all aware of the Queen's grief, both as a woman and as a ruler, when Her beloved Prince Albert died. Suffice it to say, no one gave our Queen more joy, more love, and more support than the man she married. Albert was a rare man. Despite the fact he was ostracized by many in the palace—his German accent was mocked at every turn, as was his brusque manner—he worked tirelessly to promote the interests of his adopted people. Losing him was such a blow that the Queen has never fully recovered. Thus, Her friendship with John Brown provided hours of amusement for Her family. They could not see what She saw in a man of low breeding. As you might guess, when one is born into Royalty, one is set above the common man on so very many levels that seeing others clearly is nearly impossible. Then, of course, John Brown died. Again Our Queen grieved.

"She was forlorn and lonely during Her Jubilee. It had been hoped that a token of esteem from India would lift her spirits. Two men were sent with a gift for HRH. The taller of the two men immediately caught Her eye. His name is Karim Abdul, and he has since become her beloved *munshi,* a sort of teacher and advisor."

"How could this happen?" I asked. I had understood the appeal of John Brown, at least somewhat. Brown had known Prince Albert and served him as his ghillie. Brown was a Scot who loved the out-of-doors as much as the Queen did. Brown's penchant for fresh air and exercise was exactly what the Queen's doctors had prescribed for Her. But a man from India? From another country and another culture? This was a sticking point for me.

Charlie nodded. "I am embarrassed to say that the absence of a masculine figure in Queen Victoria's life has left Her incredibly vulnerable to *any* male who can fill this vast emptiness in Her life. Surely, you've wondered how Mycroft has managed to keep the Queen on the end of a leash? See? There are those who talk of yin and yang, the two portions of the soul that crave balance. I cannot help but believe that Our Queen fully desires an opposing force to even out Her strong personality. Therefore, it is not surprising that She falls under the spell of strong men who stand up to Her or who offer Her the sort of male attention she craves."

"But an Indian man?" asked Berthold. I had forgotten he was there with us at the table. "A brown-skinned creature with no status or breeding?"

This infuriated me. Berthold was fast becoming the object of my most extreme dislike. I could not contain myself. "Sir, I served in Afghanistan and I can tell you there are many an

Afghan whose moral code is higher than some of the Brits I know. As for the color of their skin, as a doctor I can tell you that is only the wrapping on the gift. Once I peel back the outer layer, what is left looks that same no matter whether the epidermis was white or brown or even yellow or red."

"Pray go on, Charlie," said Holmes after sending a glance of irritation towards Berthold.

"This man Abdul, or *Munshi* if you will, charmed her endlessly, and while there are those who suggest an unwholesome relationship, I prefer to believe this was a particular conflagration of masculine thinking, foreign intrigue, and wholehearted allegiance to Our Queen that has won Her over so completely. In all fairness, I must also tell you that his loyalty to Our Queen is unparalleled. Indeed, the man has left behind his entire family in India in order to wait on the Queen, hand and foot. At the best of times, Victoria has always been querulous, and at the worst, She can be hardheaded, sarcastic, and shortsighted. Even so, Munshi seems to have tamed Her less desirable aspects, although I know that word 'tamed' will sound repugnant to many, it is undoubtedly the correct one in this situation."

Holmes often lets people meander in their thinking as he claims unguarded commentary is incredibly revealing. Today was not the time for a lengthy exploration of Charlie's thoughts. So Holmes broke in and said, "Charlie, why does all of this matter? What does Our Queen's favoritism have to do with a dead sailor who has a belly full of gold? Isn't the concern here that the gold isn't making it to the coffers of the Realm? Is it not true that the gold will pay the troops who will be fighting the Boers?"

"Yes, of course, it's true," Charlie agreed. "But isn't it clear to you that someone desperately *wants* the public to know the gold is being diverted? For goodness sake, Sherlock. Someone deliberately told Mycroft about a dead sailor's body washing up in the Thames. Honestly, is that such an unusual occurrence? No, it is not. Yet someone went to great lengths to make sure that Mycroft Holmes, in his lofty perch at the top of the British government, caught wind of this particular floating corpse. Furthermore, someone not only brought the corpse to Mycroft's attention, they did so with an aim to entice Mycroft to get his brother involved. Knowing full well that once Sherlock Holmes is on the case, he is like a terrier with an old shoe. He will not let go!"

Holmes nodded and I leaned closer so that I would not miss a word. At first, I'd considered Charlie as a man whose station in life had encouraged lazy mental habits. Now I was forced to consider him in a new light. Charlie had made an excellent point: if you wanted a problem to go away, you certainly did not bring it to the attention of Sherlock Holmes. But someone had done exactly that.

"So tell me, old friend," began Holmes, "is there any scuttlebutt in Court or in society that might shed light on this conundrum? What have you heard or seen that might explain this phenomena? Who would want the world to know that gold bound for our troops is being diverted? And why?"

"There are indeed, certain unsavoury rumours flying around in society," Charlie said, in a voice barely above a whisper. "One is accustomed to this, as the Palace is chock-a-block with sycophants jockeying for prime positions. Their rise and fall is as cyclic as the seasons. Yes, Buckingham always has been and always will be a place filled with intrigue, as that is what the idle rich do for entertainment. But this new thread, this new commentary, is different, my friends. Very, very different."

"In what way?" Holmes leaned into the conversation and lowered his voice.

"I fear these particular rumors are the underpinnings of a

plot to overthrow the Throne." Charlie said this so flatly that I almost missed the import. He was not talking in an hysterical tone, nor did he seem to relish this world-shaking theory. No, he was speaking in a matter-of-fact way, brimming with concern. "I think someone wants to make it look as if the Queen is filling the coffers for Her own use – or worse."

"Why should that matter?" asked Holmes. "As a point of fact, one might argue that all the money in the coffers is Hers. She is the ruler of Our Country and this Empire."

"True, but to divert money needed to supply soldiers with necessities will cause the people to rise up against Victoria, will it not? The towns and villages supply the young men who go to war. They are our Country's finest crop, and it is the Queen's responsibility to see that they are armed and clothed and fed. But if there is no money for Her to fulfill Her end of the bargain, if families watch their young men fight against an army in a faraway land, they'll react with fury if they learn She did not provide those soldiers with the barest of necessities."

Holmes frowned ever so slightly. "So you are saying that you think all of this is a complex plot to overthrow the Monarchy? But the people of this country love their Queen. Why would they choose to rid themselves of a woman so universally admired?"

"Ah," said Charlie, "that she is. For a moment, conjure up a battleground scene with thousands of young men slaughtered for lack of proper ammunition or sick from dysentery or bleeding to death without proper nursing care. Certainly, citizens of the Realm would turn on the Queen, especially if they learned that the money to supply those lifesaving necessities had gone instead to a lowborn man, a brown-skinned man, from one of our Colonies."

Pitching his voice even lower, Charlie added, "And ponder this. Queen Victoria calls Munshi Her son. Imagine how this angers Bertie. Imagine how irrational he can be at the best of times, and then multiply that a hundred times over. Bertie could whip up the crowd and encourage them to turn on his mother. Yes, he well might! His peccadilloes, his profligate manner of spending, his romances with unsuitable women, his whining...need I go on? In one generation, he has managed to squander the goodwill his father built. Imagine if he were to ascend to the throne! The fury of the populace would be immense."

"Would he do that?" This came from Berthold and yet, he voiced the question all of us were asking.

Charlie raised his eyebrows and nodded very slowly. "Indeed, I would personally tick this box as being the one scheme most likely to happen. Bertie seethes with anger whenever his path crosses that of Munshi. He hates the man with an undimmed passion. For John Brown, Bertie felt distaste. For Munshi, Bertie feels disgust. Towards His mother, the Queen, Bertie seethes with anger. Truly, my friends, I would put nothing past Bertie. Nothing. Would he rig a scheme to steal gold meant for our soldiers? I think he would, if it might convince his mother that She was wrong to speak so affectionately about Munshi. Would he let his future subjects die in distant wars? I believe he would, if his actions would cause people to rise up against his Mother. He is not a deep-thinking man, but he is a man whose passions run hot. If he could strike back at his Mother, if he could convince Her subjects that She cares more about a man from India than about our English native sons, the result could be anarchy."

19

Given the shocking nature of Charlie's information, it was only a matter of time until we would see a bloodbath such as happened in neighboring France. Of that I had no doubt.

Charlie's commentary ended, and the four of us sat silently around a battered table. If what he'd observed was true, we were poised on a precipice. One false move either way could plunge our country into civil unrest. Of course I'd heard rumblings about Bertie. They were impossible to avoid. The man embodied all the worst problems with hereditary rule. Although Victoria and Albert, his mother and late father, were loving parents, they failed to curtail Bertie's bad habits, his weak points, and his overwhelming sense of entitlement. Worst of all, these negative aspects of the man could not be brushed aside or hidden away. He was flagrant in his sense of style, and he craved attention from the masses. He was morally weak and impulsive in his judgements. He was and had always been a disappointment to his mother on many, many levels.

Of course, I was getting ahead of myself. It might not be Bertie behind the rumors. It was possible that the Queen

Herself was diverting the gold. Or that some other entity was hijacking the gold either to embarrass the Queen or to use for other nefarious purposes. All in all, there were too many possibilities to count. Nor could I see a clear path forwards for narrowing down the number of options.

So I turned my mind to the matter of the dead seafarer. Was he the husband of Mrs. Morel? I hadn't bothered to ask Holmes if I could see the photograph. The tattoo was exactly where Mrs. Morel had told us to look. The letters—L.I.V.—were plain to see. Who else could the man be? How many dead men would wash up with similar tattoos? Then, of course there was his uniform. This had not been an ordinary seafarer. Taken as a whole the man in the deadhouse fulfilled all the requirements to fit the part of Mrs. Morel's missing husband.

So had he docked and been waylaid on his way home? Had he never made it to port? Had he been kidnapped or press-ganged and tortured and killed and then dumped into the Thames? Mrs. Morel had expected to hear from him at his last port of call. Was he taken before the ship docked there? Or after? If so, how long before or after? And what did that tell us about the manner of his demise? There was much to learn before we could confidently go forwards. Yet it seemed to me that we had to start with the Celestial. We simply had to find out when the paths of Mr. Morel and the Celestial diverged. That was paramount.

Tomorrow Holmes and I would go to the shipyard and ask around. Perhaps the Celestial had docked and then shipped out again. If we were lucky, and the ship was still there, we might be able to interview sailors and find out whether Jonas Morel had been with them when they arrived in port. If not, what had happened to him? What did they know?

That night back at our flat, I could not help but break Holmes' reverie. "Is it possible? Could it be? And how does one go about verifying a tale so wild? So improbable?" I asked. "How credible is your friend, Charlie?"

Holmes smiled faintly. He had been reading a book on philosophy and now he rested it open on his knee. A pleasant fire warmed our sitting room. Bryony had left me a note that she was nearly done knitting the pair of mittens. This tiny portion of good news cheered me immensely. Imaging Evans with warm hands lifted my spirits and I could not help but reflect how when we do a good deed for others, we are our own beneficiaries.

But that joy quickly faded. What we'd learned from Charlie had thrown a pall over all of us and the ride back to 221B had seemed endless. Holmes frowned as he responded to me. "Do I trust Charlie? Next to you, I trust him more than anyone on earth. He has no reason to lie and every reason to keep tawdry details to himself. Imagine what would happen to his standing in society if word circulated regarding what he told us today."

"About Bertie," I said. I picked up a poker and aimlessly jabbed a coal. "Could it possibly be true? He is the son of Our Queen and of Prince Albert. Surely he cannot be so selfish as to willingly destroy their legacies? He has to know that he is lighting a match and setting it to a tinderbox. No matter how angry or resentful he feels towards his late father and his Mother, he must have an ingrained sense of loyalty to the Throne and to the Realm!"

Holmes chuckled quietly. "Watson, you are an incurable romantic. You truly strive to see the best in other people, don't you? I could watch your face and sense how you were struggling with Charlie's report on Bertie. You could not believe it! To you, a man who betrays his sovereign is a traitor, pure and simple. The fact that in this case the traitor might be next in line to the Throne is a conundrum, isn't it? And yet, have we not spoken of 'cutting off one's nose to spite one's face' countless times? I'm sure we have, and this would be a perfect example of such ill-advised behavior, would it not? I daresay that Bertie's emotions have often overruled his good sense, so this would be yet one more incident of the same."

"This is like an octopus with tentacles sprawling out in every direction," I said. "Where can we start to make sense of this puzzle?"

"There is but one way to find out. One way and one way only."

"You will ask Mycroft. He will know."

"No," replied Holmes with an enigmatic smile. "I am sure that Berthold has already reported back to him. If I go to my brother, he will have had ample time to come up with a reasonable explanation or a way to send us racing in the wrong direction. If this is a palace intrigue, Mycroft will do everything in his power to cover it up. That may or may not include getting to the heart of the matter, as my brother's motivation is different from mine."

I had to agree with that.

"No," Holmes repeated. "This case reminds me of a tangled ball of yarn. We do not yet know exactly what we are dealing with or who is behind all this. Someone certainly is going to a lot of trouble. But why? And how did this start?"

I nodded. He was right about that. We knew ships had disappeared, but we knew nothing of the circumstances. If there was a pattern, we needed to discern it, and we could not discern it without all of the pieces.

"I shall requisition paperwork from Mycroft's office," said Sherlock, as he lit his pipe again and blew a wobbling smoke ring my way. "As you know, my brother never destroys a scrap of paper. Of late, he's tasked a group of eager young men with the job of sorting and organising Mycroft's collection of treasure: his extensive documents. I've become acquainted with

Lewis, the student who oversees the effort. Rather than go through Mycroft and suffer the indignities of convincing him we really do need his help, I shall circumvent my brother. I shall tell Lewis I am conducting a sort of test, in an attempt to ascertain whether the method of cataloging this information is useful."

His scheme was elegant in its simplicity. I could not help but be impressed and said as much.

"Yes," said Holmes as he chewed on his pipe. "Before you wax enthusiastic, let us avail ourselves of the papers. There might be nothing for us to see or there might be so much dreck that we cannot accurately search for gold."

20

The next morning, Holmes rapped on my door at an early hour. "If you would kindly get dressed, it would be much appreciated. Now, there's a good fellow. I'll have Mrs. Hudson send up some food. Hurry, Watson! Oh, and by the way, we're going to be receiving some cartons. We must read and absorb the materials in them as quickly as possible. Now, off with you."

He shut the door and left me alone. Whilst attending to my toilette, I heard Mrs. Hudson's arrival and departure, as well as the muffled voice of an unknown visitor.

When I stepped out into the parlour, I discovered Holmes deeply immersed in some new reading material. He sat cross-legged on the floor with an open carton at his side. More cartons were stacked neatly on the floor. A slate board was propped up next to the unused fireplace. The table had been set for breakfast. A steaming cup of coffee sat waiting for me.

"Ah, Watson, you're just in time," Holmes said, looking up from the papers in his hand.

"Four hours for what?" I asked, "What's this all about, Holmes?"

"Intrigue! Intrigue of the highest—and the most dangerous—sort." Holmes leaned forwards, resting his elbows on his knees. "Have you ever heard the name Erich Jaeger?"

"Yes. Isn't he that bumbling anarchist? The one who attempted the abduction of the Queen? If my memory serves, he was found wandering the halls of the palace with a ransom note in his pocket, yet!"

"One and the same. Well, he is on the loose again. Somehow, he managed to walk straight out of Bethlehem Hospital."

My blood chilled at the mention of Bethlehem, a place so horrific that its nickname "bedlam" had spawned a pejorative for chaos. I was equally surprised to learn that Jaeger was a patient there.

"Yes, Watson, seeing your expression, I must concur. I thought the same thing. The last I heard of Jaeger was that he was at Pentonville Prison. But for reasons yet to be made clear, he was transferred to Bedlam. I have my suspicions as to the culprit responsible, but we shall bide our time regarding that. For now, at least."

"But, Holmes, the man's an incompetent! Do you remember how they captured him? He simply walked up to one of the Palace guards and asked for directions to Victoria's quarters! The man is not only incompetent; he's a dolt as well!" My voice rose a notch as I contemplated how unsettling this news was.

Holmes eyed me, curiously. "Perhaps. Then again, would you explain how this incompetent dolt was able to penetrate the palace's defenses? How he appeared out of nowhere and tapped one of the guards on the shoulder? On the third floor, no less! And how this incompetent dolt was allowed to walk out of Bedlam? No, Watson, there's more to this man than we are led to believe. He's cunning and well-schooled. Mycroft told me that Jaeger is brilliant, although unhinged. He can, it would seem, appear or disappear at will."

"Even if what you say is true, Holmes, what has all of this to do with Morel? I haven't the foggiest idea as to what is going on."

"Sadly, at present neither do I. But I'm sure that we haven't heard the last of Erich Jaeger."

Holmes gave me my orders: "Separate everything that is relevant to this case, Watson. I shall join you once I've finished reading this. We have a scant four hours before I have to return these boxes."

"What am I looking for?" I asked, grabbing my coffee and sidling up to the boxes.

Holmes sprang to his feet and walked to the slate board. "I've taken the liberty of jotting down the names of the individuals involved. If you come upon any document with any of these names, place it to the side. We'll come back to it, after we've sifted through everything. Take note of anything at all, no matter how innocent in appearance."

Holmes rapped a piece of chalk against the board for emphasis. There he had listed twelve names: Johann Voort, Linton, Maria DeMare Morel, Erich Jaeger, Mikhail Barukin, the Celestial, the Clarity, the Bard, Jonas Morel, Barlow-Smythe, Thomas Connelly, and Captain Hobbes-Nesmith.

"Who are Johann Voort and Mikhail Barukin?" I asked.

"They were listed as the ship owners for the Clarity and the Celestial respectively. Mr. Connelly is a shareholder in the venture. I believe he is the man who obtained the financing for the ships. Erich Jaeger dreamed up the system for refrigeration and many other inventions. As Mycroft suspected, the man is a genius. The Bard was a name mentioned by Maria Morel, if you recall. Obviously it's a pseudonym or nickname, but I figured there might be a clue as to the Bard's real identity in these papers."

Confused and flustered, I kept my wits about me. I refused

to give Holmes the satisfaction of knowing that I had been duped, once again, by one of his charades. Instead, I spoke calmly, "You may as well tell me everything, Holmes, and stop grinning like the cat that ate the canary. I am entitled to at least that much consideration."

But he didn't satisfy my curiosity. I took a seat across from Holmes. Although I struggled to seem unperturbed, my demeanor was more of a parody than the circumstances warranted. Indeed, I groused under my breath before stealing a doleful glance in Holmes' direction.

His response was contrary to what I had hoped. He burst out laughing! "Good old Watson! It's a fortunate thing that your chosen field is medicine, for I surely think that you would have failed as a cardsharp! Your expressions are too telling!"

Mimicking my pouting face, he walked over and clapped me on the back. I should have been cross with him, but sadly, all I managed was an embarrassed shaking of my head.

We pored over the contents for nearly a full hour with nary a word between us. Once the initial inspection was completed, we had a separate pile of documents, neatly divided according to each name listed on the slate. Surveying the expanse of our accomplishment, I was thankful that the stacks were not overly cumbersome. After eliminating the irrelevant documents, the remainder seemed manageable.

"Aha!" Holmes waved a scrap of newspaper in the air. "An illustration of Jaeger. A most singular visage, would you not agree?"

I took it from him and studied it. Jaeger's close-set eyes were interrupted by a much-maligned nose, evidence of involvement in a great many pugilistic endeavours. One ear was badly damaged as well, resulting in that sort of deformity first catalogued in ancient Greece amongst wrestlers. The trauma the appendage had endured resulted in thickening, loss of circulation, and a general deformity. Added to these battle scars was a nevus, an unattractive mole, blossoming over one eye. Taken as a whole, the man was incredibly ugly. Sadly, that was the long and short of it.

I was delighted to have a vivid rendering of the fiendish persona behind these many woes. Holmes, on the other hand, believing that one could never have enough information, bemoaned the meagerness of our spoils. "Confound my brother!" he cried aloud, to no one in particular. "Ever since childhood, Mycroft had a most admirable trait—he could never discard anything. He would often say to me, 'Leave nothing to chance; always possess the tangible. Everything will be of some use in your life.' These blasted inserts!" Sherlock Holmes railed, holding one of the cards in the air. "'Material removed and destroyed. Dated/Duplicate/No longer critical—M.H.' Of all the times for my brother to become a conscientious bureaucrat!"

With an air of disgust, he tossed away the card. He got to his feet and paced the parlour. From the pocket of his waistcoat, he withdrew the gold sovereign given to him by Irene Adler, now suspended from his watch chain as a memento. When contemplating a particularly thorny problem, Holmes would rub his thumb and forefinger against the coin repeatedly, a habit that quelled his overactive nerves while helping him think.

"Holmes," I said, tentatively, "you yourself have said numerous times that if Mycroft finds something to be of little or no importance, then you can wager a crown that that is precisely what it is—not important!" I watched my friend, waiting for an impatient rebuke of my observation.

Much to my surprise, Holmes stopped, tucked the coin away, and said, "Perhaps you're right. Perhaps the information gleaned from these cartons is the cream rising to the top. It's possible that the destroyed files would have sent us off on a fool's errand. Yes, Watson, you're quite correct. Our meager reward for our efforts must be *tant mieux*. Of course, one must assume that the actions of an individual working for the government will, at all times, be virtuous and altruistic—never contemplating a separate or ulterior agenda!" Holmes' words dripped with sarcasm.

"You've made your point, Holmes," I agreed in an exasperated tone. "But if this is all that we are given, then let's make the most of it. I'm growing tired of being manipulated and held in the dark."

"Quite right, Watson. Bravo! It's time for us to take matters in our own hands—and let them rue the day that they've decided to cross swords with us!"

21

He clapped me on the back and took one of the piles of documents over to the sofa. “Come,” he said, tapping the sofa’s cushion. “Sit next to me. We’ll sort this out together.”

We scoured each document, checking for any correlation of previous pages against the others. After placing the documents back in the cartons three hours later, we had a fairly accurate picture of the fiendish plan.

Sensing my excitement to discuss the matter in greater detail, Holmes gestured for me to remain silent. I opened my mouth to protest, but a flicker of a muscle in his jaw warned me to stay mum. Holmes pressed himself deeper into the sofa and stared at the door in an expectant manner. I sat by docilely, not sure of what was to happen next. Holmes lit his pipe and peered through the smoke.

Never taking his eyes off the door, he fished his watch from his pocket and raised it to eye level. A crooked smile played along his lips, as he silently bobbed his head up and down in rhythmic time. I craned my neck to better see his watch and noticed that it was about to come up on one o'clock, four hours from whence Holmes had started his quest.

"Enter!" shouted Holmes. The door opened a crack, then wider still. Five men entered without uttering a word or acknowledging our presence. They removed the cartons from our apartment and, silently but swiftly, closed the door when they left.

Holmes laughed, startling me with his boisterous manner. "Ah," he said, shaking his head. "It must be comforting to be in the employ of the government—following instructions and never having to make decisions. This government of ours, filled with uninspired people placed in positions requiring little or no thought—laden with intellectual theorists, who've never toiled —practicing their theories and grand schemes on those who work. People in exalted positions of trust, who cannot be trusted. Yes, Watson, our government is truly a marvel. It's a wonder that anything good is ever accomplished."

Sadly, I nodded in agreement. Mrs. Hudson came up immediately after the men left with the cartons. She had fixed us a fine assortment of cold meats, cheeses, and bread. I was happy to eat it, as working our way through so many papers had proved more taxing than I had imagined it would.

"Now, to business," said Holmes, facing me. His face heralded a look of anticipation. "With your help and inspired intellect, we'll sort through the most obtuse and obfuscating facts that mark this case and bring these fiends before the mast."

My chest swelled with pride at Holmes' high regard of my opinion, but silently I prayed that I was up to the task.

"I would like to put this entire, sanguinary plot into chronological order, so that we will know where we stand," Holmes said as he dragged the chair over to the sofa. He set it in front of me and plopped himself down. Then he leaned forwards, placing his elbows on his knees and cupping his chin in the palms of his hands. "Take notes, if you feel it's warranted."

It has long been his custom that whenever he would put his thoughts into words, he would do so in a monotone. But in this instance, his demeanor was energized. His eyes were alert and keen, and most of all, his words were vibrant, filled with excitement and awe. In his mind's eye, he was one of the villains: he thought like them, he spoke like them, he breathed their air, he ate their food, and he understood them. Such were the powers of his imagination.

I would often take copious notes when Holmes interviewed a client, witness, or suspect. However, when we were discussing the merits of a particular case in private, I usually abandoned this laborious practice in order to actively participate in the conversation. It was precisely because of the complex nature of this case that I felt it a moral imperative, as well as a sincere desire, to place the events into their proper historical perspective and context. I decided to take Holmes up on his suggestion and selected a new journal from a ready stack. I also grabbed a pen and a lap desk. With those implements at hand, I sat down in one of the armchairs.

There were other advantages of committing Holmes' words to paper. Besides providing a concise accounting of the events that had already transpired, it would allow my readers a glimpse of the inner workings of Sherlock Holmes and the ofttimes circuitous nature of his logical mind. Holmes waited patiently, as I titled the ledger and prepared to chronicle the affair to date.

Holmes nodded at my readiness. As is often the case, he paced the floor, walking in circles as he chewed on the stem of the little black devil. "First, let us presume that we have all of the information there is to possess. Or, at least, we can presume that all that we possess is all that we will receive. With that in mind, would it be possible to solve this case and bring the guilty to the dock?"

I glanced up at Holmes, not sure whether or not I was to answer him. His faraway look indicated that his question was of a rhetorical nature, so I sat by silently, waiting for him to continue.

"Sadly, the answer is no," remarked Holmes. "At this juncture, we know we have a dead man who was tortured and killed, and a quantity of gold. We might have, and cannot be sure of, a missing husband. We might or might not have a missing ship. So far, we don't even have enough to link the two parts—those of which we are sure and those that are possibilities—together. I believe that we have not entered this case at the beginning. Then we must go back and figure out how long has this been going on? Has the gold from Australia been diverted for long?"

I waited. His question seemed unanswerable and yet he seemed to have a response to the riddle he had posed. Holmes continued, "To answer *that*, we must go all the way back to a ship called the Elvira Stockton. If you recall, her circumstances are shrouded in mystery. Alas, her inglorious demise shall forever be the fodder of those whose pitiable existence thrives on vague rumours and innuendo. They have fallen prey to the belief that sea monsters or other such rot caused the horrors that befell the Elvira Stockton."

"Of course," I said, "now I recall. The Elvira Stockton was found roaming the seas under full sail. The initial reports stated that her entire crew had gone missing. However, at the trial, there was testimony that half her crew was missing and the other half had been killed. I recall speaking with a sailor, who said that his ship was nearly swallowed whole by the very same sea serpent! Holmes, you're not suggesting a connection? Why, that was nearly a year ago!"

Holmes stared at me slack-jawed, his eyes bulging with incredulous disbelief at my firsthand accounting of the existence of the monster. "Watson, do not let the facts stand in your way. By all means, enlighten me with your tale of Poseidon's minions."

Acutely aware of how my näiveté had placed me in such an indefensible position, I replied huffily, "There's just no talking to you when you're in such a carping mood. I knew the sailor's tale was a lot of poppycock. I just wanted to share what I had heard." My cause was hopeless, and I knew that had I uttered another word, my pompous indignation would become almost comical. I sat with my head bowed, stoically resigned to accept his mocking smile with a modicum of dignity—sea serpents, indeed!

"Ah, Watson, it's not your fault. If you cannot trust the government, then..." His eyes narrowed slightly, prodding my reaction. Slowly, I lifted my head and peered at Holmes, questioningly.

"That's right, Watson. Our government planted the seeds of this mythical sea monster. The case of the Elvira Stockton was of such disastrous proportions, the government, in order to hide the true facts of the matter, fabricated this sea monster nonsense."

I shook my head, stunned by his revelation.

Holmes continued, "There were several sightings of the Elvira Stockton when she was first reported missing. She was seen with her tattered sails billowing in the wind and showing no signs of life. She drifted in and out of fog banks, almost purposefully staying clear of any attempts to board her—much like the fabled ghost ship, the Flying Dutchman. As the weeks wore on, rumours swirled in the docks. There circulated tales of this phantom ship and her ghostly crew. Of course, these flames were fanned ever brighter still by agents within our government, who under orders, spoke of demons and monsters until it became impossible to separate truth from fiction!"

"I remember, Holmes," I remarked. "There was even a report of finding settings for tea left untouched in her saloon. Tea that was still piping hot! I'll tell you, Holmes, the further we go into this mess, the more bizarre it becomes."

My friend groaned in agreement. He walked to the side table and lifted one of his large reference books. Leafing through the pages as he scanned the text, he slammed it closed with a thud.

"Of what useful purpose is it to have these books, if the information that I need is not within their covers? Ah well, I shall have to make do with my memory. If you recall, Watson, one of the stories concerning the Elvira Stockton was that on her manifest, she was listed as carrying alcohol?"

"Yes, and the alcohol was left untouched. Everything was as it should have been, excepting that the crew was missing."

"Right you are, but like the Celestial, there were two other items that were not listed, though she was heavily laden with both! First, she was carrying a queen's ransom in gold, and, second, every inch of space below deck was crammed from stem to stern with munitions."

"Are you telling me that our government was in league with these scoundrels?"

"No, Watson, not in the sense that you mean. You see, an ambitious young man, Erich Jaeger to be precise, had a plan. A few months before the Elvira Stockton affair, there was a brazen robbery. Scoundrels attacked a munitions shipment bound for Aldershot. There was also a very highly-placed foreign dignitary on that train. He was taken hostage, and twenty-three soldiers killed whilst defending the shipment."

"Twenty-three men killed!" I shouted, leaping from my chair. The writing desk clattered to the floor. "Why am I now hearing the first of this? What's this world coming to, Holmes? Twenty-three men killed, and no one knows anything about it!"

"Don't feel put upon, Watson," Holmes replied. He picked up my writing desk and handed it to me. I sat on the sofa, and he then took the chair opposite it, leaning back in it and crossing his arms over his chest. "It is my business to know of these things."

"Actually," he continued, through clenched teeth. "I would not have learned of this at all had it not been for an apparently errant remark by my brother at a Buckingham Palace garden party. Before we sat down, he and Queen Victoria were off to one side, whispering and thinking that I couldn't hear their conversation. But I overheard them as they spoke of resurrecting the Elvira Stockton and the sea monster."

"Sea monster?" I cried. "Do you mean...?"

"The very same," replied Holmes. "Having heard this, I decided to press them both, regarding the Elvira Stockton. I thought it better to bring the entire episode to light. It was then that Mycroft told me of the robbery and the ambush."

"And what of the sea monster?"

22

Darkness descended upon Holmes' pale features, "Hmm, that question elicited a most peculiar reaction, when I myself posed it. It was clear my query placed both my brother and Our Queen in an uncomfortable predicament, and they chose not to answer it at all. In fact, their response was so evasive and convoluted, that I'm surprised they didn't hurt themselves with their verbal acrobatics. All that I could obtain from them was the promise of complete disclosure should I, on my own, uncover the truth."

"Ridiculous!"

"We shall see. As to the facts surrounding the Elvira Stockton, though I'm loath to admit it, most of what I had believed was a complete sham and erroneous. It was the First Mate, Ponsonby, as you may recall, who was charged with the murders of the crew and subsequently hanged for his crimes."

"Yes, we've covered all that. We've determined that the wrong man was hanged."

"Ah, but suppose he wasn't?"

"You mean he was the right man, after all?"

"No. What I mean—suppose he wasn't hanged?"

"Wasn't hanged? What the devil are you saying? There was a trial! Posonby was found guilty and hanged. It was in all the papers."

"But that's just it—it wasn't in all the papers! A case of this magnitude should have generated an avalanche of horrific articles in *The Daily Gazette, The Telegraph, The Globe* and the other rags. Curiously, all of the articles regarding the hanging appeared in only one newspaper, *The Times.* Furthermore the hanging did not take place at the Tower or Tyburn or any of the usual spots. Instead, it was supposedly held at St. Thomas-a-Watering on the way to Canterbury."

"But that hasn't been used for more than a hundred years!" I said.

"I know," Holmes agreed. "Exactly so."

"I don't understand what you are saying, Holmes. Obviously, you're in possession of facts that I do not have. Speak plainly, if I'm to understand this at all."

His exasperation was evident, as he tried to coax a glimmer of understanding from my dull brain. "Oh, very well," he said, obviously disappointed that I was not up to the challenge. "The press at times seems to exist for one purpose only, and that is to annoy the government at every opportunity. But suppose the press becomes a willing partner with agencies within the government, if not the very government itself?"

Noting my skeptical expression, he pressed on patiently. "Explaining this conspiratorial relationship between the press and the government will be put off for another day. Suffice it to say that I was informed that such a relationship did exist, regarding the Elvira Stockton. Some of what's been printed in the press, as far as it went, was factual. But all of the information originated from the back rooms of some unknown, obscure department of the government. When the first facts filtered through this office, they realised that they had a traitor on board the ship. Their first reaction was to deny that any such event had occurred at all, but it was too late. Some of the facts began to leak out. It was my brother's idea to sacrifice Ponsonby."

"Do you mean that Ponsonby wasn't the actual traitor?" Aghast at the implications, I was reluctant to pose the obvious question. "Ponsonby was, what? He was made a scapegoat? Holmes, that's barbaric! That means your brother is a murderer!"

"Wrong again, Watson. Ponsonby was an agent for our government. He was investigating the stolen arms shipment. That's how he came to be aboard the Elvira Stockton. He had followed the goods there. Unfortunately, he was found out and tortured for information."

"The keelhauling?"

"Yes, but he revealed nothing. Ponsonby didn't know that a large contingent of the crew were active and willing participants and in league with the traitors. That's how the rest of the crew was murdered so easily. They were outnumbered! The truth is that the crew had been killed prior to Ponsonby's torture."

"They didn't stand a chance."

"No, they didn't." His gaunt features went cold.

"But the hanging? The trial? If the government knew all of this, why did Ponsonby have to die?"

"He didn't."

"I am aware that he didn't!" I snapped. "But he died, nonetheless!"

"I'm sorry, Watson, you misunderstand. I mean that Ponsonby is not dead. Don't you see? The stories in the press, the trial, the verdict and the hanging, were all a sham! The reports were bogus."

"Allowing that what you're saying is true, why would the

press permit itself to be used in such a way? Why, it's unheard of!"

"Not at all, Watson. There've been many cases in which the press allowed itself to be used. Have you forgotten the matter of the suicide of Lord Hume?"

"Yes, of course," I answered, snapping my fingers. "That was an inspired bit of sleuthing on your part, I must say. How you deduced that it was the coffin maker who was the murderer and the spy, I still don't understand. But, yes, I remember it was at your suggestion that the government agreed to plant the news article that Lord Hume's body was to be exhumed the following day. It was that very evening that the coffin maker dug up the body and was caught red-handed with the schematics of a mysterious ship that was being designed. The plans were in a hidden compartment in the coffin. What was the name of that ship? It had something to do with an exotic sea shell or something. I can't recall."

Holmes smiled, appreciative of my memory. "Very good, Watson. The coffin maker's plan was simple. After a proper amount of time, a long-lost relative would come to claim the body and request that Lord Hume be buried at the family's estate. During the disinterment, the papers would be removed and sold to the highest bidder. It was the fault of the coffin maker that he panicked so badly."

"Still," I interrupted, "if it hadn't been for you, the plans would have never been found."

"Very well," Holmes accepted graciously. "But getting back to the Elvira Stockton, the Ponsonby trial was a sham. Upon finding Ponsonby still alive on the ship, this was a golden opportunity for our government to capitalize on an obviously serious mistake by the pirates. Ponsonby should have been killed, but that task was overlooked by something that had panicked the crew."

"And what was that? What panicked them?"

"I don't know," replied Holmes glumly. "But I will say this, when I attempted to address the matter with Mycroft and Her Majesty, they were clearly very worried that I would find out. I'll tell you one more thing: I will!"

I shook my head. "It's impossible to investigate under these circumstances, Holmes. Just drop the matter and be done with it. I can see no winners regarding this cursed case."

Holmes growled. "If this was simply a case to extricate the government from an embarrassment, then it might be worthy of that particular consideration. However, since that is not the situation before us, we shall pursue the matter with all intensity."

"Very well, Holmes," I responded, "but it would serve them right if we just washed our hands of the matter."

"Perhaps. Then I would be under your feet all day, until another case could be found. No, it's better for you that I continue with this case. I don't think your fragile nerves could suffer me for long." Sherlock Holmes chuckled softly.

"Hmm," I replied, falling in with the spirit of the moment. "I hadn't thought of that. Of course, you're right. This is a case that begs for your expertise. You must pursue this, no matter how long it takes. I'll muddle through, somehow."

The playful jousting acted as a medicinal elixir, and we reluctantly turned our attentions back to the Elvira Stockton.

Holmes groaned wearily. "Ohhh...I feel as if this case has been my life's work, yet it's barely a few days old. Watson, you're my anchor. It is your lot in life to keep my feet firmly on the ground. Now, where was I? Oh. Yes. Ponsonby was rescued from the ship, and he informed the authorities what had happened. After an untold amount of conferences and debates, an idea was formulated. They decided that Ponsonby might be of some further use to the government, and the sham trial was set in motion. The editor of *The Times* was approached and, under the threat of releasing information about a past indiscretion, acquiesced to Queen Victoria's entreaties. The editor, feeling that he had no choice, agreed to accept and publish articles written by the government about the Elvira Stockton and the trial."

"You mean the editor was being blackmailed by our government?" I asked. "But why? You yourself said earlier that cooperation between the press and our government is an everyday occurrence."

"Ah, yes, but what if *The Times* was already working on the true story regarding the Elvira Stockton? Remember that some time had elapsed, and some of the facts had filtered through channels. Somehow, the other papers had not yet caught wind of the story. It was only through chance that *The Times* had stumbled upon it. Queen Victoria, in Her wisdom, seized the opportunity and quashed the real story, whilst at the same time, She granted the editor an exclusive story should the truth ever be told."

"This is insane!" I was indignant.

"Not really. But suppose you tell me what's going through your mind?"

"Well, now that you've asked, why was it necessary to perpetrate this hoax? I mean, why the trial and the mock hanging? Why didn't they just report one survivor and be done with it? Was it necessary to fabricate this preposterous story about sea monsters? Or, for that matter, why didn't they just say there were no survivors and let the lad live in peace?"

"Why? Why, indeed? Because, my dear fellow, if they reported him alive and did nothing, he would have been killed by the pirates. If they reported no survivors, they couldn't be sure if the truth wouldn't surface—again, placing his life in further jeopardy. Queen Victoria did what She felt she had to.

No one would search for a man who had supped at the gallows. He is now living a quiet and comfortable life abroad."

"But the sea monster—what of that?" I demanded.

"That, Watson, is a part of the story that will not surrender its secrets willingly. To this very day, as far-fetched as it may seem, there are still reported sightings of this mysterious leviathan from the deep."

"But surely, Holmes, you can't put much stock into these ridiculous fables! Why, in this very room, just a short while ago, you made me the fool for even mentioning it. It's twaddle—that's what it is!"

"It would be folly to dismiss these sightings out of hand. There are too many similarities. Each witness describes, almost in the very same language, what he or she had seen. The descriptions are identical."

"Exactly," I exclaimed, triumphantly. "That proves my case. These supposed witnesses are merely repeating what they had already heard or read. I need not remind you of some of the incredible stories we have dealt with over the years, much less the more sensational cases we have worked on. By all that's holy, there were times when we had more confessions than we had crimes. These stories are nothing more than people seeking recognition and ill-gotten fame. If one person starts a rumour, you can bet a crown that another will swear to it."

"Normally, I would agree," Holmes said, "but you've failed to take note of one very important fact."

"Oh, and what is that?"

"The witnesses had one other thing in common, besides their testimony."

"Precisely!" I cried, pouncing on his observation. "Holmes, my head is dizzy. On whose side are you arguing? How can you be contrary to my point, when you've just stated that these so-called witnesses share commonalities?"

"Be quiet for a moment, and I will continue, because I still think we are talking past each other. The strand, the single ribbon of commonality these witnesses all share, is that they have *nothing* in common, save the sightings. In other words, they do not know one another, have never met one another, nor in any way whatsoever have they come in contact with one another. They were on different ships and sailed from different ports at different times, months, and even years apart. No, Watson, the singular aspect of these sightings is not the familiarity of the witnesses with one another, but rather the incalculable odds of having this many people, unknown to one another, describing the exact same thing."

"Suppose that I accept what you've just said. Then are you telling me there really is a sea monster?"

"No," replied Holmes, as he stared vacantly. "But there is *something* out there."

"Poppycock! I've read the reports. A giant serpent with glowing eyes, indeed! Holmes, if I didn't know any better, I would swear that you're toying with me."

"We shall see, old chum. We shall see. As I have often said, 'Once you eliminate the impossible, whatever remains, no matter how improbable, must be the truth.' In this particular case, there is a truth out there. We have yet to discover it. To be plain, I need only to quote Cicero: *Not to know what has been transacted in former times is to be always a child. If no use is made of the labours of past ages, the world must remain always in the infancy of knowledge.*"

"What does that mean?"

"It means that the Celestial is merely a reenactment of a specific history—the travails that plagued the Elvira Stockton and perhaps also the John Sebastian! Since it would seem that our government has learned nothing from the Elvira Stockton affair, perhaps the Celestial was a cunning and deadly variation of a tried-and-true scheme to steal arms," Holmes said as he got to his feet and paced the room. "Again, why would Mrs. Morel set us out on a course of action and then disappear? What we have here is an ouroboros, the mythical snake eating its own tail."

I could not hide my confusion and so I felt relief when Holmes added, "The ouroboros is a symbol for infinity. There is no beginning and no end, so one is condemned to going 'round and 'round. This is a senseless circle designed to be trod in perpetuity."

After a pause he spoke again. "They underestimated me. I shall prevail."

23

At that moment, there came a knock at our door. I opened it to find Mrs. Hudson, holding a message. "For Mr. Holmes," she said. "I'm almost ready to bring up a tray with your supper, but the courier insisted you have this immediately." After passing him the note, she went back down the stairs.

The text reads:

To Sherlock Holmes,
See the Bard, he knows!
Mrs. Morel

A loud banging on our door startled us to action. The sound came from the lower door panel, and therefore, it was easy to distinguish it from Mrs. Hudson's higher placed and ladylike knock. This was a full-throated slam of a fist. Holmes crept towards the entrance and gestured me to follow him with my revolver drawn. I stood to the left, behind the wall, as Holmes placed his hand on the knob, and yanked it open. My pistol was aimed at a very startled young boy, whose eyes bulged in fear.

Slowly, he raised a dirty little hand in which was held a rolled-up piece of paper. Without uttering a word, the boy dropped the message on the floor and fled down the stairs, never looking back.

"Not one of your Irregulars," I noted.

"No," Holmes answered, as he stooped and retrieved the item before slamming the door shut. Before opening the missive, Holmes eyed the rolled-up paper and felt its texture. Inspecting the ribbon that held the parchment closed, he slipped it off and placed it in his pocket. He unfurled the note and read its contents aloud.

"*Never was there Queen so mightily betrayed! Yet, at the first I saw the treasons planted.*"

Holmes smiled, shaking his head from side to side. "I think, Watson, we have just heard from the Bard. A quotation from *Cleopatra,* I would think." He tossed the paper at me.

As I perused the note, Holmes asked me. "Well? What do you make of this?"

"You must take this to your brother," I said, handing him back the note. "Mycroft may well know who this Bard character is. In any event, you need Mycroft's benediction and his assistance. This is a plot as twisted and convoluted as any we've ever come up against. I shall say this once, and only to you: It is possible Our Queen has acted in ways that are nothing short of treasonous. I fear that after the death of Her dear husband, Albert, She lost Her will to govern and with it Her will to oversee the day-to-day workings of Parliament and those entrusted with power. In short, I find it possible that these deeds are not done despite Her but for Her! What if She has decided to divert the gold and use it for a purpose totally unbecoming of Her rank? Remember, She has been spending more and more time with that Indian man who seems to have a strange hold over Her."

Satisfied that I had spoken with enthusiasm and elegance in my reasoning, I waited for Holmes to put on his coat and leave the flat.

He, however, had other ideas. "I shall do no such thing. I refuse to take this up with my brother. I cannot count on his probity. He has long since decided that those with brown skin are a race of inferiors."

"You are joking!" I said. This was an aspect of Mycroft's personality that I had never had any reason to examine. As I'd said to Berthold, war had taught me to value each and every man for his character and not for the color of his skin or the place of his birth. On the battlefield and in the heat of the moment, I had found highborn men who were lacking in courage and lowborn men who were more virtuous than any of the saints in the Bible. You could not tell me that because a man was brown that he didn't deserve the same protections and comforts as any of the rest of us.

Holmes went on to say, "Rather than assist me in the search for the truth, Mycroft would use a rumour such as this as a way to run Munshi out of the palace. Mark my words, my brother would turn this slander into a weapon."

"Holmes, are you delirious?"

"Not at all. I must say, Mary has left very little mark on you."

I was wounded to the quick. "How dare you speak like that of Mary!"

"How dare I? Think back to how your heart grieved when first you lost your wife. Multiply that by a hundredfold and that is the grief Our Queen has endured. Unlike you, Watson, She is never known any other real companionship or camaraderie. She can never find comfort in the arms of another human being. This woman was raised in isolation, treated as a pawn by Her mother and Sir John Conroy, and purposely isolated from free society. She grew up in the shadow of the Tower, knowing that

Her uncles wanted Her to die. She was all that stood between them and the greatest empire ever known to mankind! And then She fell in love with Albert. Not a paragon, but a man, and She gave him all the affection She had been missing in her life. He returned it in kind, over and over again. He was Her husband, Her lover, Her father, and all that She ever hoped for. Then he died, in part due to the carelessness of Her callow oldest son, an odious throwback to Her feckless grandfather." Holmes spoke with barely controlled fury.

"Since Albert's death, the world has turned on his Vicki the way a cur turns on its master. No one has allowed that woman the sort of grief She is entitled to. No one. The demands of state have nipped at Her heels. She is lost without Her Albert. Or rather, I should say, She was lost until John Brown prised Her from Her miserable existence, showing Her that true devotion still exists in this heartless world, and that She, of all people, was worthy of undemanding love."

"That has nothing to do with this man from India!" I shouted back at Holmes. "Surely this Munshi has not stepped into Albert's shoes!"

"Really? And who are you to judge, John Watson? You who can find another wife? You who can lose yourself in work of your own choosing? What do people say of you behind your back? Do they not suggest you've made yourself wealthy by gripping tightly to my coattails? You know they do! People talk; that is what people do. They talk because they cannot think. They talk because they cannot imagine. You might concern yourself with my cloistered lifestyle, as you have aptly called it, but I tell you this, John Watson. When I imagine what it is to have a great love and to lose it, I find the pain so daunting that I have promised myself I shall not ever accede to such a folly. Pity those who love with empty arms. Thank you, but I shall tend to my chemicals. And if the memory of Mary meant as much to you as you profess it does, then have a care for that poor widow all alone in a cold and loveless castle. If a man from India gives Her an iota of relief from the cares that She was born to shoulder, then I bless that fellow. Certainly, I shall not stand in the way of their friendship because I know exactly how much a true friend means to me!"

Fortunately, at that moment Mrs. Hudson arrived with our evening meal. We ate in silence. I don't remember a time when I've been so angry with Holmes as I was that particular evening.

24

What happened next I know only because Holmes was kind enough to report back to me. "If I do not tell you and one day you hope to turn this entire enterprise into one of your popular novels, you will miss such a portion of important investigation that my actions afterward will seem in turn treasonous, ill-considered, and foolhardy. What I propose to do next is none of those. All my actions are grounded in sound logic, as I shall prove by the time this adventure comes to its conclusion," he said later.

After I had stormed off to my room, and after I had imbibed from a flask I keep in my top drawer, Holmes slipped out of the flat on a mission of some daring and weighty importance. Hailing the first cab that he encountered, Holmes took the transport, directing the driver to drop him off in the mews behind Buckingham Palace. Gliding from one shadow to the next, he approached the tall fence surrounding the palace. Since it was gone two in the morning, the Queen's beloved Turi, her white Pomeranian, was secured in the chamber of her First Lady of the Bedchamber. Holmes knew this and did not worry that Turi would detect his presence, since even at two in the morning there are those who roam around the palace, doing their jobs in the dead of the night so as to disappear when the sun comes up. They are rather like the fairytale brownies who aid the cobbler in that way, as their efforts are best expended in the night so the results can be admired during the day.

Not the least of these are those who labor in the kitchens, and Holmes was well aware of that, being an astute observer of humanity, no matter what role those people play. Before Big Ben struck three, Holmes spotted a cart pulled by a solitary mule. The letters on the side proclaimed the lowly wagon to belong to a butcher's boy who reliably delivered haunches of venison to the palace. On this particular morning, Holmes was dressed as a kitchen worker in black trousers, black waistcoat, and starched white shirt. This he had done in preparation for his nighttime excursion. When the driver pulled the handbrake on the cart, Holmes sidled around the palace, taking care not to dirty his clothing, and managed to converge on the space between the butcher's boy and the entrance to the kitchen. "Stepped out for a bit of fresh air," Holmes explained in perfect congeniality. "Need any help?"

The tired young man had been driving all night through the bitter cold. Holmes' offer was received with pleasure. Thus, Holmes easily slipped into the palace without raising any semblance of alarm. Knowing the floor plan of Buckingham, Holmes crept up the grand staircase and found a linen cabinet where he could hide. There he stayed until Big Ben tolled six, the hour when the Queen was awakened each morning and Her breakfast was delivered. Having positioned himself down the hall from Her room, he waited until the final stroke of that old clock that keeps all of London unified. Stepping out of his hiding place, he smoothed his jacket, shirt, and pants. When the footman turned the corner with the breakfast tray on his shoulder, Holmes smoothly intercepted the servant.

"Do you not recognise me?" asked Holmes. "I am Sherlock Holmes, as you can plainly see from this newspaper article here." At this juncture, Holmes withdrew a copy of *The Times* with his photo on the front page.

Before the astonished footman could cry out, Holmes hastened to add, "I am here on official business, doing a survey of the palace security. Now if you'll kindly give me that tray, I'll see that Her Majesty gets Her breakfast. Oh, and for your trouble, here's a signed copy of John Watson's latest book."

At this point, I could not help myself. "This is preposterous, Holmes. Whatever made you think that footman would care about my scribblings?"

"Ah, Watson, you underestimate me and you underestimate your popularity. As always, I had done my research. I knew that the Queen's footman was a mad keen fan of your work. Once I had that small detail tacked down, I was able to use my celebrity to my advantage. Why not? We suffer from it. On occasion, we are plagued by it. Do we not find ourselves at the mercy of readers who question my actions and your work after the fact? Indeed we do, so why should I not also profit from our mutual exploits?"

As the happy footman walked away, Holmes carried the tray on his right shoulder, rather than his left. This effectively blocked the view of his face. At the time, it was naught but an insurance policy, as Holmes fully expected to knock on the door to the Queen's Bedchamber without encountering any resistance. However, to his surprise, outside the door was a man dressed in robes and snoring loudly.

Yes, Holmes had come upon Munshi, the Queen's own "adopted son."

"I must tell you, Watson, he sprang up with a dagger drawn and he would have cheerfully disemboweled me if the door did not open to the shocked face of the First Lady of the Bedchamber. She, too, is a fan of your work. One look at me and she shrieked with joy."

"You are joking, Holmes. Again, I say to you, this is preposterous."

"Not at all, Watson. You are not familiar with life at court. I am. Mycroft has told me more than I ever hoped to know. As exciting as it might look from the outside, those drawn into the royal orb find it tedious beyond anything they have ever known. Think on it. Their lives revolve around the Queen. They get up before She rises. They cannot go to bed until after She retires. When She is working, they must be at the ready, which is where we get the very descriptive nomenclature 'ladies in waiting' and 'men in waiting.' That is what they do. They wait. They cannot entertain themselves. They cannot ask guests to come and visit. They cannot leave unless they are given permission. Their lives are circumscribed in a manner much like those who enter a convent or a monastery. So my unexpected appearance was a delightful surprise to a woman bored silly with tedium. I tell you she was never so happy to see a stranger at the door. Better yet, the fact she recognised me saved my life, as Munshi was poised and ready to vanquish me on the spot.

25

"Sherlock Holmes?" called the quivering voice from the depths of the bedchamber. "Is that he? Don't just stand there! Fetch my dressing gown and show him in, immediately!"

The Queen's First Lady of the Bedchamber raced back from whence she had come. For propriety's sake, Holmes did linger in the hallway, immune to the scowling face of Munshi. The tray he was holding grew heavier by the second, but Holmes decided against asking Munshi for help. "Not when the man kept his dagger pointed at me as he did. I tell you, Watson, he was most unimpressed by my arrival, and if ever there was a more devoted guardian, I am unaware that one exists."

Holmes' arms ached with fatigue by the time he was bade entrance into the darkened room. A tiny figure was propped up against a phalanx of lacy pillows. On Her head was a white mob cap that Holmes admits was almost comically askew.

"She had so much lace and so many ruffles around Her throat, that Her face was nearly lost in the froth," Holmes explained. "A small wicker bed tray was positioned across Her lap, and Her tiny plump hands gripped the sides of it in eager anticipation of Her morning repast. I found centering the silver serving tray on the small wicker one to be rather an interesting challenge, as it occurred to me midst delivery that if I erred in judging the correct placement, all the comestibles would land in that most regal of laps. Once I let loose of the tray handles, She turned Her face up and pouted at me. 'Pray remove the lids, Mr. Holmes. I cannot enjoy my breakfast if I am not allowed to eat it!'

"Begging your pardon, Your Majesty," I said.

To that She laughed! "Next time you choose to disguise yourself as a servant, Mr. Holmes, you had better know the duties incumbent on your employment. Otherwise, you might find yourself getting the boot before you achieve your desired results."

With that, She stuck Her knife into a pot of marmalade and added a generous slather to Her toast. After taking a huge bite, She used the knife as a pointer. Indicating the teapot, She asked Holmes, "Will you be Mother?"

As She gestured towards the teapot, She exposed the ring She'd had crafted as a memento mori of Her beloved Alfred. A miniscule photograph of the man rested under a small crystal. Black onyx pieces were inlaid in the band. The piece looked shockingly heavy, and the bulk promised it would be cumbersome, but Holmes had read that the Queen never took it off.

This telling detail he related as his voice took on a mystical quality. "I poured tea for the Queen," he said in a manner that betrayed his abiding shock. "A fine Darjeeling by the smell of it. I had no idea what else to do! She, being raised to Her position at such an early age, acted as if this was the most natural event ever. Once I'd filled Her cup with tea, She called out, 'Munshi? Bring Mr. Holmes a chair so that he might sit beside My bed while I have My breakfast.'"

The chair arrived promptly. Munshi positioned it as the Queen instructed, and Holmes sank down upon it gratefully.

Sipping Her tea, the Queen studied Holmes. Setting down the teacup, She asked, "I suppose there is a reason for this visit? Is My life in some sort of danger? Has Mycroft sent you? I am eager to hear what brings you here like a thief in the night. But before you say a word, may I suggest that next time you send a message first? If you truly do have a great need of meeting with Me, I shall agree to see you. There's really no need for skulking around the palace like a stray cat that's found its way into a warm barn."

Only at that point did Holmes relax his guard somewhat. The near miss with Munshi had been worrisome, and of course, his method of gaining an audience had been entirely unorthodox. However, his cause was just, and Holmes knew he needed to glean that information absolutely necessary while Her Majesty seemed tolerant of his presence.

"Your Majesty, my sources have reported a rumour circulating through the royal household. Normally, such tales would quickly be rebuffed or happily be ignored, but this particular rumour must be put to rest for a variety of reasons, not the least of which is the safeguarding of the monarchy."

The Queen frowned at Holmes. She picked up Her second piece of toast and this time She jabbed Her knife into the pot of marmalade with such force that it almost flew off the breakfast tray. "Do you think this is the first time a rumour has threatened Me and My Crown? Do I seem so feeble-minded that a rumour will bring Me to My knees? Really, I thought better of you, Mr. Holmes. You dare to disturb My equanimity first thing in the morning by bothering Me with tittle-tattle? I had assumed you were here on a matter of some importance, but no, you are a common gossip like all the rest of those nattering fools."

Holmes did not let Her finish. "Rest assured this is no ordinary scurrilous story, Your Majesty. Gold is being diverted from your ships sailing out of Australia. Surely you have noticed that in the past month alone, three ships have gone missing!"

"That is not a rumour," she said, her voice raised to a forceful level. "Nor is that news to Me! I am well aware that pirates are targeting My sailing vessels. I have taken steps to increase security on My ships. I have even gone so far as to authorize subterfuge of the most dangerous kind, requesting that loyal men join the crews and report back to Me. So, explain to Me why you think this has escaped My notice."

"Yes, yes, you've done all you can, except you have not chopped off the poisonous vine at the root. The rumours suggest you yourself are diverting these funds! And even more distressing, they say you do this for the sake of setting up a new kingdom, one where Munshi will be your chosen king!"

Until then, Munshi had stood in the threshold, glaring at Holmes with malicious interest. Now the tall Indian man sprang forwards and knocked Holmes to the ground. His hands grasped the detective by the throat as he choked my friend nearly senseless.

"I vaguely heard the Queen shouting for him to stop," Holmes told me. "I knew that returning his aggression would only make me seem less trustworthy. It seemed to me at that bleak moment that I was destined to give my life for the Crown, but in a manner so ignominious that I should be a laughing-stock even after I was buried."

Gradually, Holmes was revived by dint of salts waved under his nose, and helped to regain his seat. The First Lady of the Bedchamber offered him a glass of cool water. His throat ached as he swallowed.

"Tell him you are sorry, Munshi," the Queen instructed Her

servant. Her tone and manner was much like a mother chastising a child.

"I beg your pardon, sir," said the Indian, as he bowed at the waist.

Pausing in his recitation, Holmes explained to me, "I decided not to engage with the fellow, as his actions were so totally unwarranted. Instead I turned my attention back to the Queen.

"I told Her, 'Your Majesty, I came to you and no one else because as a loyal subject of the Crown, I believe You have every right to do with the Australian gold as you see fit. If You wish to fill the royal coffers, do so. If you want to decorate Brighton Palace, go ahead. If You want to set aside a fund for a servant who has made Your life more pleasant, then I believe You should do exactly that.'"

She leaned forwards as best She could with the tray blocking Her change of position. "You would support Me in this?"

Holmes paused at this point to make an aside to me. "Although I am not myself sentimental or given to emotional responses, Watson, I have trained myself to observe them in others. I can honestly tell you that the woman before me sounded more like a small child than like the Empress of the largest Empire that history has ever seen. I have heard there are psychologists who theorize that each of us has inside the residual emotions of our younger selves. My recent experience would seem to bear that out. Queen Victoria sounded surprised, relieved, and thankful when I indicated I would not question Her desires. Until I made those utterances, She was ready to do battle. Boudicca was never so fierce as the tiny woman in that huge and lonely bed. She had feared I was yet another voice in the chorus demanding that She give up another one of the very few who loved Her without reserve. How proud I was to prove Her wrong."

Holmes resumed his story, explaining how he answered the Queen. "I would support You in each and every one of Your desires," he said in an earnest voice. "That is the point of being our anointed Queen, is it not? I have pledged my skills and my life to Your service. How You use me in that service is of little consequence."

She seemed to mull this over. Her finger played with the lace trim on the napkin in Her lap. Taking a shuddering breath, She wiped her mouth. "Truly?"

"Truly. You have my word as an Englishman."

Her eyes filled with unshed tears. "Most of my subjects would disagree with you, Mr. Holmes."

"It has been said repeatedly that I can be a very disagreeable fellow," Holmes admitted.

The Queen looked down Her nose at Holmes. "I am not diverting the gold on My ships. My Navy exists to keep Our Nation safe from all who would do her harm. Never would I give an order that would lead to the death of my fine sailors for a cause so at odds with the common good of Our Nation and Our Empire."

Holmes nodded to let her know he'd heard and absorbed her response, but she seemed too overcome with emotion—or perhaps anger—to continue. When he engaged her attention again, he said, "Then I have the answer I was seeking. That is what I needed to know, and I was loath to believe what was told to me secondhand in a matter of such grave importance. You see, I've been asked to find a missing husband, but that, Ma'am, I feel certain is a smoke screen. My quest pointed me to a dead-house where there lay the body of a sailor in your Royal Navy. A lieutenant, actually. The man had been tortured and forced to swallow an impressive amount of gold. I believe this is why I was asked to find this missing husband. The truth is far more sinister. Someone wanted me to find evidence that supports these terrible claims against You. Now I have my mandate: I shall uncover what is behind all this. We shall see what scoundrels there are out there, plotting to blacken Your name."

The Queen was eager to hear more. "And can you? Can you discover the person or persons behind all of this? Those rumours are egregious. To say that I would kill members of My own Navy! What sort of leader would I be? Perhaps it is simply a happenstance, an unhappy coincidence that this man was found with gold inside his body and so someone spun a tangled web from the weakest of silk thread. Perhaps knowing about the pirates, those who do not approve of my friendship with Munshi are using this opportunity to force Me to give up My reliance on someone I can trust." At this, she fiddled with the lace of her bedclothes. "In My life, there have been such a small number who truly care for Me as a person, not as the figurehead for a Country. Why it is incumbent on others to seek to destroy those few friendships that hearten Me, I cannot say. It grieves Me to My very marrow."

Holmes rose from the chair and bowed at the waist. "I shall do my best to give you relief from such churlish behavior, Ma'am. At the very least, if I cannot quiet their wagging tongues, I shall uncover the proof that exposes them for the liars that they are."

26

"My word, Holmes," I said, as I wiped my brow. With a trembling hand, I helped myself to a second cup of hot coffee. "You could have been killed. Or worse. Thrown into the Tower of London and never heard of again. To trespass into the Queen's bedchamber takes a man with an unlimited portion of bravado—and a miniscule scoop of good sense! If you had written me a note, at the very least, I could have gone to Mycroft and secured your freedom. But as you left it, I should have awakened and not had a clue where you were, what had happened, or how to offer you assistance. Dash it all, that was blasted unkind of you."

Any anger from the night before had dissipated in the realisation I'd nearly lost my dear friend. Truly, how could I stay angry? Furthermore, the Queen's actions underscored what he had suggested earlier, that She was a very, very lonely woman who had found a loyal protector.

Sprawling on the sofa, Holmes lit his pipe. He puffed a large smoke ring into the air where it floated like a wrongly coloured halo over his head. He'd gulped down his coffee and passed up breakfast, explaining that he had been escorted back through the royal household by one of Her Majesty's equerries. That particular servant had been admonished to make sure Holmes was properly fed before being turned out onto the street.

"I chose not to leave a note to protect you, Watson, in case this adventure went pear-shaped. You could honestly claim to know nothing of my plan to gain entry to the Queen's bedchamber. No matter what they did or how they asked, you would be at a loss to respond."

That was true enough.

I lay the cause for this squarely where it belongs...at the feet of Bertie, the Prince of Wales. Never was there a more contemptible excuse for a man than our heir apparent. Bertie is self-indulgent, surly, self-aggrandizing, and worst of all, a man whose habit of excess triumphs over any shred of decency when it comes to the fairer sex. Before he married the gentle and long-suffering Alix, I (like many other citizens of the Realm) held out hope that the love of a good woman would persuade Bertie to stay at home and quit prowling the streets of London like a tomcat. Sadly, I was wrong. As each year passes, and his mother moves closer to the grave, Bertie's bad habits pick up steam. Truly, I fear for our country when I allow myself to speculate on what sort of ruler he will one day be.

"You could have awakened me," I said, returning to my complaint. "Holmes, even if you did not want me to accompany you, surely alerting me to the possibility you might be hauled away to prison would have been a small but thoughtful gesture."

"Perhaps," he said. "Wake me in an hour, please."

"Why?" I wondered. "Are you planning another gadabout?"

"No," and he rested the heels of his shoes on the sofa so that the soles did not come in contact with the fabric. "I am planning to go back to the home of Mrs. Morel. I assume that you would like to come, too?"

"Whatever for? She's gone. We both heard as much."

Holmes nodded. "So we've been told. However, she might have left something behind, a clue to where she has gone. Getting into that house should not be difficult. I have my lock picks in my pocket."

I did not get the chance to answer before he commenced snoring lightly.

27

True to his word, when I awakened him a half an hour later, Holmes was alert and ready to go. "Hurry, Watson," he admonished me whilst I was wrapping a scarf around my throat. Glumly, I realised that I should have to do without my warm overcoat and make do with the thin coat Dolly had loaned me. Given the chill in the air, that would make our trip in a cab miserable, indeed.

But I was saved from such discomfort when Mrs. Hudson met us at the bottom of the stairs. "A lad brought this by not more than an hour ago, Doctor. He said to tell you that the lady sends her regards."

A blush of embarrassment crept up my throat and warmed my face. As she held the coat open for me, I could imagine the landlady's curious eyes upon my person. I had resolved not to offer her satisfaction when Holmes said, "Dolly did a fine job of cleaning your garment, didn't she?"

With that, Holmes opened the door wide enough to whistle for a cab. Since we needed to keep watch for our ride, Holmes left the front door unlocked. That way he could espy a hansom as it approached and wave it over to the kerb.

"Dolly?" Mrs. Hudson repeated in a querying tone. "My, my. And you are on a Christian name basis with this woman, Mr. Holmes?"

"Everyone is on a first name basis with Dolly," Holmes explained. "That's the sort of woman she is. Even before her husband died, she was a friend to all who came into the pub. Now even more so, as the pub is all that's left of her married life."

"I see," said Mrs. Hudson with a hint of reproach in her voice.

The subject was exhausted, but it might have been dragged out longer by the ever curious Mrs. Hudson, except that a young lad bounded through the unlocked door. Hopping from one foot to the other, the child said, "You've got to come. You have to! It's a matter of life and death, don't you see? Please, say you will!"

Holmes put a hand on each of the boys' shoulders to steady the young man. "Stuckey, what are you on about?"

"I'm here for Evans, sir, I is. They've gone and taken him. Those brutes, there was five of them, and they knocked him to the ground before they tied his hands and feet. Coo, but they was rough with him. The biggest one dragged poor Evans through the street and then he jumped into a waiting carriage and hoisted poor Evans by his feet into that carriage. I was hiding behind a grocer's cart but I seen it all, sir. Poor Evans tried to call for help, but they stuffed a cotton hanky into his mouth so he couldn't cry out."

"Any idea where they took him? Which way they were headed?" Holmes asked in the tone of voice he reserved for the young.

"That carriage was pointed towards the Thames, sir. I heard the big man yelling as he slammed the door behind him. He said they needed to hurry or they'd have to watch for the tide to come back in." Stuckey shifted his weight from one leg to the other. His worried manner was contagious.

Thank goodness, Holmes kept his manner calm because Stuckey was on the verge of tears. "Do not fret about this, Stuckey. I shall go and see what has happened. You can count on me to do my utmost to secure Evans' freedom. But before I dismiss you, I must ask: is there anything else you can tell me? Any other clue we might find unusual? Was the carriage a growler? Or an omnibus? Did the driver wear a top hat? Did you hear anyone call another by name? Anything at all that might help us to identify those who took Evans would be useful."

A startled look came over the boy's face. "There was one thing, but beggin' your pardon, sir, it don't signify much, but here it is."

Digging deep in his pants pocket, Evans retrieved a rock about the size of a pea wrapped in a small piece of paper. With a swallow and a wholly regretful look, he dropped the bundle in Holmes' empty hand. Holmes unwrapped the paper to reveal one word: *Gravesend*. There was something else wrapped in the paper.

Stuckey said, "I was going to give it to you, honest, but I happened to forget. It's ever so pretty, ain't it?"

There in the middle of Holmes' outstretched palm, a nugget of gold winked up at us.

"Good lad," said Holmes. "You shall have this back, Stuckey. When all is said and done, I shall get this back to you, I promise."

Mollified by Holmes' pledge, Stuckey cheered up considerably. "That's very kind of you, sir."

"Watson? The game's afoot," said Holmes. "You do have your revolver, don't you? Yes, good!" Holmes went charging out of 221B and threw himself into the cab. I followed, moving as fast as humanly possible. I was closing the door behind me when Holmes shouted at the driver, “Take us to Gravesend and hurry!”

In a wildly swaying carriage, the driver prodded the horse with a crack of his whip. His effort sent us hurtling through the streets at nervewracking speeds. With the curtains drawn, I had long since given up the notion of trying to memorize our direction of travel through London. Vaguely, I recalled that Gravesend was at least twenty miles away. By my calculations, we were in for a journey lasting at least four hours. After a time, the horses slowed to an easy canter, and being ignorant as to our exact destination or the identity of our host, I worried as to our fate. But my friend’s relaxed breathing offered me a glimmer of comfort. Shortly, his snoring filled the cabin. He was asleep! I struggled to remain alert, but soon the rocking carriage lulled me off to a dreamless sleep as well.

I was slowly returned to wakefulness by flashes of brightness, then dark, as the light from a lantern crossed my face. On the other end of the lantern was Holmes. He gently shook me.

“Where are we?” I asked, stifling a yawn.

“Gravesend,” came the reply.

“Gravesend? Oh, so that’s the smell. It’s the salty air. I couldn’t place it. But how? Why?” My mind was a tumble, and I couldn’t complete a single thought. Stiffly, I stepped down from the carriage and looking ’round, I saw that we were alone.

“Holmes, I don’t like this. Where is our driver? Where’s everybody gone? This place is deserted!”

Ignoring my questions, Holmes walked to the edge of the wharf and glanced out at the water. I walked over and stood beside him, staring into the cold blackness. Finally Holmes said, “I believe we’re to be picked up by a ship. That’s the only reason the tide would matter.”

“A ship?” I lamented. “There’s nothing out there! It’ll be hours before we’re onboard. I mean, really, Holmes. Just look out there on the horizon. The only thing to be seen is that rotting hulk of a barge. Furthermore, the tide's not even in. No ship can dock until the water level rises. And who knows when that will be? Something's not right about this. Where's Evans? How can we be sure this wasn't a trick to get us out of the city?"

Holmes didn't respond to my caterwauling. His silence made me even more irritated. I groused until even I couldn't stand my own voice. I roamed the dock, angrily kicking at stones and bemoaning our plight. Taking in our surroundings, I groaned, as there wasn't a light to be seen. Every building was locked up tight. In my meandering, I neared a barrel sitting at the far end. The container gave off the stench of rotting fish. As I drew closer, a scraping sound instantly set me alert. The noise was coming from behind the barrel. I withdrew my revolver from under my coat. "Come out, whoever you are!" I shouted, cocking my pistol. "Come out, or I'll shoot!"

28

Holmes, hearing my cry, came running up beside me. "What is it?"

"There's someone behind the barrel! Come out, or I'll shoot! Stand back, Holmes!"

Without warning, a cat raced by and fled into the night. Feeling like a complete imbecile and wearing an embarrassed smile, I put my pistol away and looked at Holmes. "Sorry," I muttered. "I thought..."

However, my friend wasn't paying me any heed. Holmes kept staring intently at the barrel. "You'd best do as Dr. Watson suggests," Holmes said. "He's a crack shot, you know."

I was about to rebuke the great detective. After all, it wasn't necessary for him to make light of my confusion with the cat. But Holmes' tone was deadly. Rather than chastise my friend, I raised my revolver once again.

"Come out!" Holmes commanded.

Slowly, two tiny hands appeared in the air, and the smallest man I have ever seen stepped into view from behind the barrel. He was not much more than three feet tall. His hands were held aloft as he walked towards us. I can only describe his gait as that of a child learning to walk. He waddled with his arms outstretched and crooked at the elbows whilst his pudgy hands still pointed towards the sky. The small man's body swayed to and fro with each jostling step, until finally he stopped and stood before us. Then he smiled sheepishly.

His shabby, ill-fitting clothes suggested a life as a common beggar. And had it not been for the intelligent and mischievous twinkle in his eyes, one would have naturally written him off as nothing but an oddity, suffering through life's cruel intent and misfortune. But it was plain to see that there was more to him than that.

"Who are you?" I asked, gazing down into his upturned face. His visage could have been pleasing if it had not been planted in a head of odd proportions. His forehead was huge and bulging, making his eyes seem unnaturally small. "I could have shot you. What do you think you were doing? If it hadn't been for that cat..."

"Ah, the cat," he responded in a startling stentorian voice. "*I could endure anything before but a cat, and now he's a cat to me.*" The dwarf nodded his head in the direction that the furtive feline had fled. "Dr. Watson, I presume? Mr. Holmes? Excuse me while I light this candle."

The little man pulled a candle stub and a box of matches out of his pocket. With a quick swipe, the match sputtered and caught the wick. The wavering light that the candle emitted was enough for me to examine the face of our strange new acquaintance. His features were not ugly, but the vast size of his head on such a small body was off-putting. His easy grin held a hint of mischief and his eyes sparkled with amusement.

"Tuck your pistol away, Watson," Holmes spoke, finding his voice. He looked down at the small man. "We're in the presence of the Bard. I'm honoured, sir."

"*The heavens, through you, increase our wonder, and set up your fame forever,*" retorted the little man, bowing with mutual respect. "Please, if you will follow me, gentlemen."

"Not until you assure me than Evans is all right," said Holmes.

"Of course he is," said the small man. "We let Evans out of the carriage once we were out of sight of Baker Street. There was no reason to harm him. *Children they are heaven's lieutenants.*"

The man turned and hobbled towards the edge of the dock. Glancing back over his shoulder, he stared into the shadowy recesses of the buildings lining the area. Smiling, he bobbed his head up and down. "Dr. Watson, if you would be so kind as to tap on this pipe, three times with your revolver, we shall get under way."

I glanced over the edge of the dock and saw that the pipe ran down the entire length of the piling and disappeared into the brackish water. My wedding band glowed in the dim light from the Bard's lantern. Holmes nodded for me to follow the dwarf's instructions.

With the butt of my pistol, I produced three loud clangs by hitting the pipe. The dwarf craned his neck to look over the side of the dock, and Holmes did the same. Not knowing what to expect, or what I was looking for, I followed their example.

A low whirring of gears emanated from the dilapidated barge. My body tensed, as a sudden sharp clang and the sound of escaping air broke the silence of the deserted waterfront. As the noise died, an unusual red glow pulsed up through the darkness. A dark form moved away from the barge. This shadow in the water slowly coalesced into the shape of a fish. But it wasn't a fish. It was some sort of sailing vessel! A deck hatch opened a crack. Slowly, the arms and then the head of a sailor poked out from the aperture. With a squeal of resistance, the hatch cover was thrown open. It slammed against the deck as the sailor waved to the Bard.

The waters churned. The barge strained at its mooring. The black waters below it bubbled and roiled, producing a thick white froth. The noise was deafening!

"There!" cried Holmes, pointing to the sailor who had stuck his head out of the hatch and who was now climbing onto the deck of the vessel.

"Watch him, Watson!" Holmes shouted.

"Welcome to Stratford-upon-Avon, gentlemen," said the dwarf. Another hatch sprung open, this one on the aft end of the barge. One after another, sailors in navy blue coats and matching trousers climbed out of the red glow and stepped onto the wooden deck. My body trembled from pure excitement! I had never seen such an amazing sight.

The crew waved enthusiastically at us as they drew nearer. When the barge was almost directly below the dock, one of them scurried to grab a metal ladder. This was locked into place and extended within a foot of where we stood. The Bard scrambled to grab the handrails. With startling agility, he scampered down the ladder and into the arms of an awaiting sailor.

One of the sailors called out to us, *"The time and tides wait for no man!"*

"Remarkable," Holmes whistled, as he swung over the side and carefully made his way down the ladder. "Simply remarkable." Reaching bottom, Holmes stepped onto the deck of the barge. He turned to gaze up to where I was standing. "Be careful, Watson!" he shouted.

As I lowered myself, I realised why he'd called out the warning. The rungs were slick with damp seaweed. Many a treacherous step nearly caused me to fall headlong into the frothy waters. By grabbing the ladder tightly with both hands, I finally made it to the bottom. With an exhilarating leap, I found myself standing proudly on the deck of the barge.

I expected to feel the solid planking that a barge of this type would have for its decking. Instead, there was a little give beneath my feet. As I took my first, exploratory steps on the rubbery surface, I had the stomach-churning sensation that I was about to crash through the deck and wind up in the water with the barge slowly pressing down on me. My expression must have betrayed my chagrin.

"It takes some gettin' used to," said one of the sailors as he observed my troubles. "But in time, you'll be walkin' pretty regular." He escorted me to the hatch where the Bard and Holmes were waiting. "Mind your step," the sailor said.

The dwarf lowered himself into the hole. Looking up, he cast us a wink and disappeared into the bowels of the ship.

"After you, Watson." Holmes gestured that I should go ahead.

I wished he'd led the way, as I was not feeling at all brave. With a nod of determination, I got down on my hands and knees and backed into the opening. Once I found one of the rungs with my foot, my courage returned. I gripped the sides of the ladder but my balance was completely out of control, and I fell with a violent crash. "Be careful, Holmes," I called, my head smarting. "It's more difficult than it appears."

I watched as Holmes' shoe soles appeared. Lowering himself one rung at a time, he arrived unscathed. Upon reaching bottom, he glanced at me, shaking his head. A smile appeared, as he winked and then glanced up at the descending sailor. My head was hurting, my heart was pounding, and to Holmes this was all a grand adventure.

Once the last of the sailors joined us, there was a muffled thump as the hatch was slammed shut. More whirring of gears could be heard, and one of the sailors turned a spoked wheel. A vise-like apparatus spun outwards and clamped the hatch cover.

The air pressure confirmed what we'd seen with our eyes: We were sealed in.

The compartment was aglow with small lamps fitted with red glass orbs as their lenses. The ship reeked of sweat, oil, and other odours that I couldn't place. The temperature below deck was pleasantly temperate, surprisingly so.

I attempted to see forwards of where we stood, but a curtain had been drawn and blocked my view. On the other side of us was a heavy door with rounded corners. There was the murmur of activity on the other side, as well as the clang of other hatches being secured. The heavy clatter of metal slamming down echoed throughout the ship.

Three uniformed men stood in our presence, and each eyed us with bemused curiosity. Their nearness and unwavering glares made for extremely cramped quarters, and I became quite uncomfortable. The dwarf tugged at one of the seaman's trouser legs, and without taking his eyes off us, the latter bent at the waist and listened intently to the whispered words from the dwarf. "Very good, sir," said the sailor, straightening. The dwarf disappeared behind the door, closing it with a solid thump.

"This way if you please," the sailor gestured as he extended his arm outward. "The Bard has ordered meals to be sent to your cabin. Now, if you'll follow me, I'll see that you're settled in. I'm sure you'll want to wash up before anything else. After you've dined, you may wish to take a nap. The crew will be occupied with their duties for a while, so we would appreciate it if we were not distracted by any questions. If, however, you wish to stretch your legs, you're free to roam about the ship. But please, do not touch anything until it is explained to you. There are suitable clothes for you in your cabin. Please change into them before coming forwards."

As our guide rattled off his instructions, we followed him through a maze of cubbyholes and compartments. Finally we ended up at our cabin. As the sailor opened the door, he smiled warmly. "This is your cabin. Your meals will be along shortly. Now, if you'll excuse me, I've other duties to attend. Gentlemen."

The door closed behind us with a click.

"My word, Holmes. What have we done? Where are we and are we safe?"

His smile was tight. "I cannot say for certain, Watson, but if the intention was to murder us, why not do it at the dock or in the carriage? Why bring us here?"

"And where exactly, is here?"

"I have no idea," he said bluntly.

"This was right under our noses all the time while we were standing there on the pier! You'll have to admit that this is incredible!" I whistled excitedly, as my eyes soaked in our surroundings. The cabin, though small, was nonetheless quite comfortable. The walls, paneled with the richest grain of an unfamiliar wood, were polished to a lustrous shine. An ornately woven rug covered most of the floor. The carpet's many hues of crimson, dark blue, and gold trim, accented the heavy furniture. There were two sleigh beds against the far wall with a nightstand between them. Small velvet curtains covered the portholes.

"I admit it," replied Holmes, with remarkable aplomb, "There is much that I do not know."

Against the right wall rested an intricately carved writing desk. Its legs were filled with lifelike renderings of sea creatures, prickly coral, seashells, and mythological gods. All these were inlaid with pearls and jewels. Along the desk's sides and rear, deeply etched carvings of sailing ships and tropical islands told a seaman's story of fact and fancy. In the water closet, I discovered a washbasin, created out of one half of a giant seashell with gold spigots in the shape of seahorses.

Inside this very confining room was another narrower door. As I opened it, I could feel heat emanating from a small grill that rested on a shelf high above my head. Above the grill, sitting atop four spiraled legs, was a copper cask with a long pipe extending out of it and tilting downward. At the end of the pipe was a horn-shaped attachment with holes in it. On the right side of the keg was a pull chain with a handle that had been fashioned into the shape of an anchor.

Holmes had crowded into the room and watched over my shoulder. "Pull it," he said as he nodded at the anchor-shaped handle.

"But the man said not to touch anything."

"Argh, Watson. Go on, pull it."

I reached up and grasped the anchor. At the very instant that I pulled on the chain, a loud whooping noise coursed through the cabin.

In surprise, I let go of the chain, and to further alarm me, hot water poured onto my hand. The shock sent me stumbling backwards and I nearly tripped over Holmes' feet. He smirked at my having been startled.

"Holmes!" I grumbled.

"It's used for bathing," he said, stifling laughter.

"I know what it's used for!" I responded, huffily. "The man said not to touch anything and you encouraged me to do what I did! Must you always take delight in punishing my nerves?"

A knock on our door saved my companion from any further verbal drubbing.

"Enter!" Holmes said.

"Your dinners, gentlemen," said a portly sailor, as he carried the tray over to the desk. His double-breasted shirt had ridden up above the waistband of his navy trousers, exposing his pinkish belly. His merry demeanor was further enhanced by an impish grin and jolly blue eyes.

"What's on the menu?" Holmes asked.

"Wondrous things! Oh yes, wondrous things!" Our server sang out as he clapped his hands. With a bow, he introduced himself. "I am the ship's cook, Peabody. If you want more, all you have to do is ask me!" Bobbing his head up and down, he backed out of our cabin and closed the door.

"Strange fellow," Holmes mused, sampling the fare.

"Wondrous things! Oh yes, wondrous things!" I mimicked Peabody and set Holmes into a fit of laughter.

We sat on our beds, eating. The meal was surprisingly delicious. The fish was cooked in a lemon and caper sauce flavored with burnt sage. The rice tasted of coconut, chopped nuts, and dried fruit. A variety of steamed vegetables that I had never seen before were sliced and cooked. These were served in a buttery sauce that was complimentary and delicate. To wash all of this down was a carafe of very dry white wine. For dessert, we were served a flat biscuit studded with bits of candied ginger. When we were unable to eat another morsel, we stretched out upon our beds and fell fast asleep.

Sometime later I awoke to Holmes' baritone voice bouncing off the walls. He was singing a little sea ditty that had been making the rounds of late. His voice came hammering through the door of the shower bath.

I rolled over and tried to go back to sleep. But I couldn't because Holmes kept singing that infernal tune. The door swung open, and a cloud of steam rushed into the cabin. "Most refreshing!" Holmes exclaimed, entering freshly dressed in the same style of clothing as the cook had worn. "Most refreshing! Watson, I'm a new man!"

"Good," I said. "I was growing very tired of the old one."

Holmes ignored my barb and rubbed his head vigorously with a towel. "Hurry up, Watson. It's time to see what this ship is all about."

"Are you daft?" I asked incredulously, "Or hadn't you noticed the deplorable condition this tub is in? All about? I'll tell you what this is all about! This bucket is about to sink, that's what it's all about!"

I crashed about the room, angrily snatching the clothes from the bed and brushing past his surprised face on my way to the shower bath. My sour mood was most likely caused by the blow my head had taken when I fell down the ladder.

"Sink?" Holmes repeated. "I think we already have."

I slammed the door in his face, not wanting to entertain such a horrible fate. After disrobing, I stepped into the cubicle and carefully pulled on the chain. A soft, warm flow of water washed over me, as I leaned my aching head against the stall. There was a slight vibration in the walls. The motion was not altogether unpleasant.

Reaching for the soap, I noticed a sea sponge resting in a small cutout on the opposite wall. Before long, I was singing in full voice, as I worked up the most luxurious lather I had ever experienced. As I rinsed off the fragrant foam, I chuckled and realised that I was singing the same song as Holmes had sung.

29

Feeling completely invigorated and attired in my new seaworthy clothes, I bounded out of the shower bath with a spring in my step. I was about to say something to Holmes, but I found him sitting at the head of his bed with his ear pressed against the wall. Clearly, he was listening. His face held a contemplative look, as he pushed away from the wall. "Do you hear it?" he asked. "Do you feel it?"

"Hear what?"

Holmes pressed himself against the wall again and directed me to do the same.

"Oh, that," I replied, recalling the vibration I had felt when I leaned my head against the wall in the shower bath. "I imagine it's just the steam engine."

"You're wrong, Watson. That's not a steam engine. This sound is different. There's a curious hum to it. Did you observe any smokestack on deck when we arrived? I know that I didn't. No, this ship is propelled by some other means."

"Are you telling me that we're moving?"

"Of course we are. We have been since right after we came aboard. But there's something else."

"What?" I asked. I pressed myself against the wall and listened to the distinct humming. I also detected clicking noises.

Holmes added, "Do you hear any water lapping at the sides of the barge? Surely, a blunt-nosed ship like this would produce a pounding reaction of the water as it sloughed through the waves, but I hear no such sounds."

"What do you make of it?" I asked, hearing nothing of the kind.

Holmes' perplexed look told me that he didn't have the answer. Because our faces were pressed against the wall, we didn't hear the knock on our door. Nor had we noticed that we'd been joined by a tall, physically fit young man with coal-black hair that had been slicked back. Our visitor must have been watching us for some time, for he was completely inside of our cabin before either of us had taken notice of him.

His affable smile shone brilliantly through perfect white teeth. He asked, *"Avez-vous bien dormi?"*

"I'm sorry?" I fumbled, surprised by his presence.

"*Ah, Anglais. Pardon.* I have asked you whether you—? *Comment dit-on en anglais?* Slept well? No?"

"Yes, thank you," Holmes replied. *"J'aimerais parler au capitaine."*

The seaman's face lit up at Holmes' impeccable French.

"*Ah, oui, Monsieur Holmes. Bien entendu! Le capitaine est avant. Pour suivre moi, s'il vous plait.*"

"Merci," Holmes replied, straightening. "Come, Watson. The captain's waiting."

Holmes followed the Frenchman out of the cabin and into the narrow hallway. I took up the rear.

Holmes and our guide continued their conversation. At every opportunity, I explored the recesses of the ship. The corridor's width was ample enough to allow three abreast, but I chose to follow behind, in order to peek into the various compartments along the way. Most of what I saw were sleeping quarters and storage rooms. But two compartments held an array of strange and unfamiliar-looking equipment and machinery.

We paused when we arrived at an unoccupied reading room. The space was illuminated through the panels in the ceiling. I stepped inside to examine the titles. Many were in English, but an equal number were in French, German, Italian, Spanish, and Portuguese. The overhead light panels had caught Holmes' attention, and he and the sailor spoke at length outside the doorway of the reading room. It soon became apparent the entire ship was illuminated by a mysterious light source that was hidden behind a meshed screen near the ceiling. This light source continued the length of the ship.

"Come with me, *s'il vous plais, Docteur Watson,*" said our guide. Finally, we arrived at the door the dwarf had used when he had disappeared earlier. Our guide paused there.

"Que' est votre nom?" Holmes asked.

"Je m'appelle Michele. Vous permettez?" The sailor opened the door and gave a polite nod of his head for us to enter.

"Merci, Michele."

"Au revoir, Monsieur Holmes et Docteur Watson." Our guide bowed formally and closed the door behind us.

"Ah, Mr. Holmes, Dr. Watson," said the dwarf, smiling upon seeing us. "You are feeling refreshed, no? Why, of course you are, but you are too preoccupied with the wondrous sights to answer such a foolish question. *Such a deal of wonder is broken out within this hour that ballad-makers cannot be able to express it.*"

Holmes smiled. If he was as bewildered as I, he didn't let on. He merely looked 'round, in a casual, disinterested way. However, I've learned over the years that Holmes, when taking pains not to evince any reaction to that which was about him, was at his most heightened state of awareness. Of course, if an unsuspecting thief or murderer was the subject of this particular method of scrutiny, he would soon find himself—often when it was too late—examined, dissected, and impaled by my friend's unerring logic and astounding powers of observation.

But Holmes' casual manner wounded the Bard's pride, because the dwarf misread Holmes' expression. The little man remarked, "*Oh, to what purpose dost thou hoard thy words, that thou returnest no greeting to thy friends?*"

Holmes smiled. "I must apologize," he said. "It's not often that I am at a loss for words. Watson will attest to that, but this..." Holmes waved his arms about.

The Bard, realising his error, smiled, too. "*Oh, I like your silence. It the more shows off your wonder.*" He gestured for one of his men to step forwards out of the shadows. "Carlo will answer your questions. Please, join me when you are through. Carlo?" The little man made a motion of dismissal to his subordinate and then climbed a spiral staircase that led to the deck above. It was a daunting task for one so small.

Carlo was a muscular man with flawless olive skin. His dark, brooding eyes followed the dwarf's every step with disdain, as he absently ran his fingers through his hair. Suddenly aware that I was watching him, Carlo's eyes clouded. He turned to me and stroked his impeccably trimmed beard and mustache. His facial hair could not mask the nasty scar that ran down his right cheek, onto his neck, and disappeared into his shirt. He smiled in a most insincere way and said, "*Signori, ah, scusi,* my English, she is not so good. My name is Carlo Busconi. I am to be, *come dice questo...son guida?* Your guide, yes? *Sì? Vogliamo?*"

When we didn't respond, Carlo grinned conspiratorially at us and began speaking again but this time without a trace of an accent! "I'm sorry for the charade, gentlemen, but the captain has his reasons. His requirements of his crew are extremely rigorous. He wants only educated men. Every crew member is required to read, write, think, and speak fluently in any number of languages. I speak nine, myself—Italian, Portuguese, French, English, Spanish, German, Russian, Polish, and Mandarin Chinese. And because of our captain's—shall we say, penchant for Shakespeare—we must also be familiar with every word written by him."

As he was speaking, Carlo opened a gridded floor hatch to expose a metal staircase. "Follow me, please, and watch your step," he said, as he descended the spiral steps. "The captain also demands that we are experts at fencing, boxing, marksmanship, the Far Eastern forms of self-defense, explosives, mountaineering, close combat, and most any other discipline that assists us in quelling an attack. In addition, our crew excels in all of the sciences, including mathematics, geometry, physics, chemistry, engineering, navigation, topography, and a score of other endeavors. This, gentlemen, is the engine room."

We found ourselves standing in the cavernous, metal-plated belly of the ship. Taking up most of the area, and bolted into the middle of the deck, were the two massive engines, yoked in tandem by a fast-turning shaft of gleaming, oil-coated steel. Exiting at the aft engine, the shaft continued and disappeared into the darkness. From the size of the engines, one would naturally assume that the decibel level would be deafening, but surprisingly, they only emitted a low, powerful hum.

"These are the ship's horses," Carlo remarked proudly, as he pounded the engines with his hand. "They are powerful enough to maintain sixteen knots above and eleven below."

"And we are presently at?" Holmes asked, his eyes keenly alert.

Carlo's eyes narrowed as he stared at Holmes. Then our guide turned to glance at the gauges. "We are presently at neutral buoyancy, fifty feet of water above us, and turning at nine knots."

"Would you gentlemen mind telling me what you're talking about? Sixteen above and eleven below what?" I asked, immediately regretting my question when I was treated to their smiling faces.

"May I?" Holmes asked a nodding Carlo. "Do you realise, Watson, that we're traveling at a rate of nine knots?"

"So? What's so remarkable about that? I know of—"

"—and," Holmes continued, interrupting me, "we're fifty feet below the surface?"

"Below the surface? Below what surface?"

"The top deck is fifty feet below the surface of the water and we are traveling at nine knots. Watson, we are in a submarine boat."

"Not quite a submarine boat, Mr. Holmes," Carlo interrupted. "But you are close enough. This is a submersible ship. Most of the time, we ride the surface but we can, as we are now doing, submerge for a short period of time."

If Holmes and Carlo expected a violent reaction to this latest revelation, they were disappointed. After all, I had read about the Hunley, the so-called "fish torpedo ship" employed by the American South during the Civil War. Although the Hunley's crew met with a terrible fate, their courage proved that underwater warfare was worth further consideration. That said, I had never expected to actually spend time in such a vessel, so I was pleasantly surprised at my own calmness. "Fifty feet you say? Imagine that."

I glanced 'round with a keener interest, as my insides slowly constricted with nervousness. While chasing a supernatural fiend in an adventure titled *Sherlock Holmes and the Father of Lies,* my claustrophobia had nearly caused my heart to quit beating. Curiously, since the satisfactory conclusion of our expedition through endless underground tunnels and caves, my problem with confined spaces has dissipated to a great degree.

Carlo turned his attention to Holmes. "Mr. Holmes, how is it you knew that we were submerged? No one told you of this."

"A number of things," Holmes responded. "First, the air. I observed that the air within our cabin was recirculated through the two vents near the ceiling. It was a matter of holding a piece of paper up to each one of them. Of course, one of the vents worked to the opposite of the other. In other words, one drew the air into the duct and thus held the paper firmly against its grill, whilst the other pushed the air into the room, caused the paper to flutter away."

Carlo nodded; I listened attentively.

"Second," Holmes continued, "there had to be a reason why the air was being recirculated. If it was simply a matter of breathable air, one could always open up the portholes or hatches, but the porthole in our cabin had been sealed shut. When we first arrived onboard, one of the sailors had taken great pains to seal us in by clamping the entrance hatch closed. It didn't escape my notice that the device used to keep the hatch sealed was designed in such a manner as to keep the hatch from being forced open from within. It was as if the possibility existed that a great force would be exerted from inside—thus necessitating the extraordinary design of the hatch's locking mechanism."

"Bravo, Mr. Holmes!" Carlo said. "Is there anything else?"

"Of course. There's the matter of the headaches both Watson and I experienced upon waking."

"I didn't mention any headache, Holmes, though you're correct, of course."

"It was obvious. I saw it in your eyes."

I decided not to remind him that I'd hit my head on my way

into the barge. If he'd considered that bit of information, Holmes might have drawn a different conclusion.

"Ah, yes," Carlo offered. "It is a delicate task to maintain the proper balances. We must calculate the amount of air pressure required to equal the force and weight of the water on the outside. If we have too much pressure inside, the ship will pull apart and explode at the seams. Conversely, if we have too little, the ship will collapse inward from the pressure outside. Neither of these instances would allow one to live a long life. Don't worry, your headaches will subside, once your bodies have acclimated themselves."

Despite Carlo's fatalistic examples, I found the subject fascinating. "But how does it work? I mean, the ship can either rest on the surface or travel underwater. How's it possible that to do both? Pumping air into the ship cannot cause her to submerge."

"Very good, Doctor. Yes, of course. The laws of physics and mathematics enter into the equation. We know that sea water weighs sixty-four pounds per cubic foot. If you go down two feet, the water weighs one hundred and twenty-eight pounds. At three feet, one hundred and ninety-two pounds, and so on. So in order to float, the object must weigh less than the amount of water it displaces. If it is heavier, it will sink."

Not waiting for a reply, Carlo continued, "To put it more simply, if you have a box that measures one cubic foot, and it is submerged at a depth of one foot, a force of sixty-four pounds will be exerted on its top, while on the bottom of the box, which is two feet down, there will be a force that is doubled to one hundred and twenty-eight pounds. In other words, there would be a positive push upwards of sixty-four pounds. If the box weighs less than sixty-four pounds, it will float; if it weighs more, it will sink. If you are able to introduce just enough water into the box to equal the sixty-four pounds of the upward push, you will have neutral buoyancy, and the box will remain evenly suspended under the water."

"I see." I'd easily comprehended his explanation. "This ship is like that box. You pump in enough water to balance out the amount of water it displaces, until she is below the surface. The more water you pump in, the heavier the ship becomes."

"Excellent, Watson!" said a very impressed Holmes.

"But," I continued, "what if you pump in too much water? Won't we sink like a stone?"

"Yes, but if that happens, we expel the excess water by pumping air into the tanks."

"And," Holmes asked, "if the pumps fail?"

Carlo's eyes darkened. "We do not like to think about that, but in the event this occurs, we have other means for rising to the surface. Are there any further questions?" He smiled easily.

"Yes, I have one," I said. "What is the purpose of this ship? By your account, the crew's defensive skills, the armour plating, and the equipment... I would say..."

"This is a scientific ship—nothing more!" Carlo snapped angrily, before recovering his composure. "A floating laboratory, if you will. Of course, most of the equipment and machinery have been designed to serve mankind and are only in the experimental stage. Once they have been perfected, the world will benefit from our knowledge and toil. Please remember that and understand that what you have seen here is secret. Now, I think the captain is ready for you. This way, gentlemen."

30

Carlo's strident tone was as troubling to me as was the ease in which he slipped in and out of his Italian character. I was relieved that Carlo's curt manner was not lost on Holmes. My friend's expression soured upon hearing the terse response.

"Carlo? Perhaps you'd better take us to see the captain," said Holmes. "We're finished here."

It was barely noticeable, but for a second, Carlo's body tensed as if ready to spring. Then just as quickly, he relaxed his stance. "*Mi scusi, per favore!* This way, please."

Before ascending the stairs, Holmes grabbed my arm and whispered. "Those are the other means of returning to the surface," He pointed to the canvas and rubber suits hanging on the wall. Sitting on the floor next to each suit was a pair of heavily weighted boots and an iron helmet with a round glass faceplate on the front.

We climbed the steps up to the main level of the ship, the same level where our cabin was located. Carlo had hurried ahead of us and was talking to a group of men. It was impossible to determine his mood. He gave instructions to one of his men, who saluted and glanced back at us over his shoulder before slipping past us to race up the spiral staircase.

Holmes whispered, "We must wait here." Rather than question my friend, I stood with him there in the hallway without uttering a word. The messenger previously dispatched by Carlo came hurrying back down the same spiral staircase he'd climbed so recently. Darting past us, he whispered something to Carlo.

In response, Carlo's face flushed with anger and he barked at his errand boy, *"Cosa significa questo?"*

"It means," said Holmes, staring into the fiery eyes of Carlo, "that when you are asked a question, we expect an answer. We would like to speak with the captain without further delay. Come, Watson!"

Without waiting for Carlo's permission, we climbed up the spiral stairs. When we were nearly at the next deck, I glanced back down the stairs in time to see a very angry Carlo kick at the air in frustration.

"*I cannot fight upon this argument; it is too starv'd a subject for my sword*," the Bard recited as he noted our presence.

Forsaking his beggar's garb, the little man was now attired in a vested navy woolen suit with a blouse of the starkest white and a starched collar. He wore a navy-and-maroon cravat held in place by a tiepin studded with a lustrous, pinkish-white pearl. His malformed body nestled in a tall gold-and-bejeweled chair that swiveled as he pushed on a wooden ring at his feet.

"Please forgive Carlo his evasiveness," the Bard said. "Every member of the crew has been directly or indirectly responsible for the creation of many of the ship's inventions. Carlo, as it happens, is the inventor of the ship's engines, the twin dynamos, and a marvelously clever battery storage system. It has something to do with the minerals of iron, nickel, and an alkaline electrolyte. In fact, when it comes to the many uses of an electrical apparatus, there's no one more knowledgeable than he. Carlo also developed our incandescent lighting system. So I allow him his petulant and prideful manner. He's merely being protective of that which he has given birth. He is responsible for most of what you see." The dwarf waved his arms about in undisguised awe.

We were standing inside what would have been considered the wheelhouse, but it was like no other wheelhouse that I'd ever seen. Off to the side, a sailor deftly manipulated a series of levers. Grasping the two outer levers with practiced hands, he pulled one back, whilst pushing forwards on the other. His feet rested in sheathed pedals, which he alternately pressed down or lifted up. He managed all of this and never let his eyes stray from the gauges or the compass mounted in front of him.

"This is our navigator and helmsman, Raoul. Without him we are as blind as a bat," said the Bard.

"Even with him, you mean," I said, nodding at the forwards wall. "How can he see where we're going? He's looking at a solid wall."

"Ah, have no fear, Doctor. We have extensively charted these waters. There is no danger. We are precisely where we are supposed to be."

The dwarf spun 'round and eyed my companion curiously. "And you, Mr. Holmes. Have you nothing to ask?"

Sherlock Holmes walked closer to where the dwarf was sitting. "What happened to the Elvira Stockton? And Lieutenant Morel? Or whoever that man was who washed up in the Thames."

"Sherlock? May I be presumptuous and call you by your given name?" Seeing Holmes' nod, the Bard smiled. "You may call me by that which I haven't told a soul. My true name is Ezekiel Emeritus Marder. I would prefer Zeke."

"Fine, Zeke. Now, what of the Elvira Stockton? And the John Sebastian? And the Celestial?"

But the dwarf had no chance to answer as a sailor ran up and whispered in his ear. Meanwhile, my friend's posture slumped at this most incommodious interruption.

As Zeke listened intently to the sailor's words, a smile filled the dwarf's face. "Dr. Watson, if you would accompany the seaman below and lend a hand, Mr. Holmes and I have matters of a delicate nature to discuss before you are transferred."

"Transferred?" I asked, puzzled. "What do you mean transferred? What the devil is going on here, Holmes?"

"All in good time, Dr. Watson." Zeke's smile was forced. "Now, please excuse us." The dwarf spun 'round in his chair and turned his back on me.

Holmes spoke very quietly and without his normal forceful manner. "Go ahead, Watson. Do as he says. I'll be with you shortly."

Though I am loath to admit it, I was put off at being dismissed so handily, but I had no choice. As I left, I soon found myself immersed in the mysteries of the ship. Whatever was transpiring, a knowledge of our intimate surroundings could not help but be useful.

My escort manipulated a wheel that cause a hatch to slide open. The round metal door moved along a pair of rails and slowly revealed a spiral staircase. "Be careful, Doctor," my escort said. "The stairs are rather steep. The Bard would have my head if anything should happen to you."

He laughed as he went ahead of me and quickly disappeared below. My stomach churned as I wondered whether his laugh was sardonic or simply playful. Clearly, my escort expected me to follow him, so I did. Once I'd reached another level, I glanced 'round me to see a pool of gurgling water. "We're sinking!" I thought, and with a gasp, I backed up several of the steps, although I knew that if we were, indeed, taking on the brine, the situation was hopeless.

With a distinct click, the metal plate that separated the levels snapped into place. Looking up into the darkness, I realised the hatch was locked shut. I was trapped!

"Relax, doctor," the seaman laughed. "We're not taking on water. This is how and where we leave the ship when we wish not to be observed."

The diving preparation area was as wide as the ship and ran lengthwise for approximately twenty feet. Along the far side of the wall were ten diving suits suspended from hooks. Their companion helmets, with glass faceplates, stared at us accusingly and rested on the floor alongside a row of breathing apparatuses.

The seaman explained how everything worked, and I was his rapt pupil as I tried to absorb every fascinating detail. A series of limp canvas bags hung from hooks. Attached to them were tightly woven mesh bags. "Those are the diving bags," the sailor said when I walked over to examine them. "You slightly inflate the canvas bags with your air or another cylinder of air that you carry just for that purpose. The buoyancy makes the sack want to rise, and therefore, you can attach the mesh bag and carry anything that's heavy without effort."

What I had previously taken to be a pool of leaking water was a diving well. The sea was contained within a circular wall that rose approximately three feet above the deck's surface. Just inside the lip of that wall was the ocean. Air pressure was used to hold the water at a prescribed level. The bubbling I heard earlier was the fluctuation of the pressure that had occurred when the plate from the level above had broken its seal. The unequal balance, caused by the escaping air when the hatch opened, made the water rise from the tub and spill over into the scuppers. Once that pressure was equalized again, the sea water ceased its roiling and held at dead calm. The seaman assured me that all was as it should be. Nonetheless, I was uneasy with the realisation that we were fifty feet below the surface of an unforgiving sea.

Dangling over the diving well was an inverted V made of iron. It was attached by a cable to a spooling winch. The V-shaped device assisted the divers by raising them from or lowering them into the water.

A tap on my shoulder startled me. Holmes appeared at my side. "Being a good pupil, are we?" he asked, eyes keenly alert and mischievous.

"I've seen that look before, Holmes. We're about to be in it, aren't we?" I asked, when we were out of earshot from my escort.

"Ah, Watson, you know me all too well. Yes, as you have so succinctly observed; we're about to be in it."

31

Holmes glanced at the sailor walking towards us. "Will you excuse us?" asked Holmes, stopping my escort in his tracks.

"Right, Mr. Holmes. I'll be above, should you need me. Just press this lever to open the hatch when you're ready to leave."

"Thank you."

The sailor climbed the stairs and we watched as the hatch rolled along the rails and sealed itself closed.

"Holmes, this place is incredible!"

"That it is, Watson. That it is. But we have other things to discuss."

We spotted wooden crates pushed to one side. Without discussion, Holmes took one and I took the other. As usual, he crossed his legs to relax. I leaned against the wall of the diving room. Admittedly, it lacked the comfort of our sitting room at 221B Baker Street, but there was still a sense of the congenial atmosphere our friendship seemed to engender.

Holmes spoke of his conversation with the dwarf. "Our primary target is an important scientist who threatens the

Royal Navy with an invention that is sinking our ships. The goal is to plunder the gold and any munitions on board."

"The Elvira Stockton —" I began.

"Yes, and the others as well. Watson, I've never worked a case so vexing. If it goes wrong—and I fear that there's a very strong possibility that it will—we shall soon be in the midst of fighting at close quarters. Under the surface of the sea. Zeke told me that we're about to spring a trap. If you feel more comfortable with staying on board rather than coming with us, I'll understand."

"How dare you, Holmes! I've not asked for you to protect me like I am a little child! Why do you...?" I sputtered to a stop. Holmes' brow had knit in such a manner that my anger evaporated. The pain on his face suggested he was powerfully worried. I asked, "Who is the trap for?"

"A French scientist who wishes to rain total destruction on our country. He has nefarious plans that must be thwarted. It seems this man has built a warship unlike any ever known to man. He has been practicing its destructive skills on individual ships in our navy."

I nodded. "The Elvira Stockton, the John Sebastian, and the Celestial."

"Right. His treachery runs much deeper. I believe he is also behind the trouble in Aldershot. After all, building a new type of warship is a costly endeavor. Not being independently wealthy, he needed funds for his dastardly endeavor. Remember that foreign dignitary who was kidnapped in Aldershot? When the munitions were stolen?"

"Yes, and when twenty-three men were killed. I remember what you told me. Go on."

"It was not exactly as I was told at the time." Holmes used the toe of his shoe to scuff the floor.

I became enraged. "Of course, it was not as you were told.

Nothing about this mess is what it seems! We are surrounded on all sides by liars! So there was no foreign dignitary? Come on, Holmes. This is no time to play coy! Tell me everything you know! Do not attempt to hold anything back. I won't stand for it. I won't!"

Holmes' sigh was long and low. "The foreign dignitary was Prince Wilhelm of Prussia, the Queen's grandson."

"My word!" I tried to remember the last picture I'd seen of the boy. It had been in *The Times,* as an illustration to an article on the Queen's Jubilee. As I recalled, he was a very good-looking young man. "But he is only, what? Fifteen? How could this have happened? Why was it kept secret? Who does the Bard work for?"

Holmes stared at me.

I said nothing. I waited.

At last, with a sigh, he admitted, "The last question first. My brother."

"Does the Queen know Her grandson is missing? Or have they kept that from Her?" Given her age, and the fact she'd only recently returned to public life, the subterfuge might have been deemed necessary. Although sooner or later, She would find out. Frankly, I couldn't imagine how they would keep this news a secret from Our Queen.

"Yes, of course She knows. She is beside Herself with worry." Holmes scuffed the toe of his shoe. An internal debate was raging within the great detective. After all these years, I could tell when he was arguing with himself.

"You may as well tell me, Holmes. Out with it."

"According to the Bard, or Zeke, as he prefers to be called, the Prince was held hostage and taken from Aldershot. Mycroft had a choice to make: the thieves held Prince Wilhelm hostage as they moved the munitions through the country and loaded them onto a ship. Then they offered to exchange the young

Prince for a considerable amount of gold. Only, the Frenchman tricked my brother. He was told the boy would be transferred to the Celestial."

"The ship that was destroyed?"

"Yes. The transfer was to happen before the ship docked in Liverpool. But if you recall, the Celestial had a sister ship, the Clarity. A pirate ship that looked like a twin to the Celestial in every way." Holmes paused to massage his temples. "The Frenchman took the gold and loaded the Prince onto the Clarity, which was sailing under the guise of the Celestial. That's why the Celestial was destroyed! The Frenchman wanted Mycroft to think the transfer had taken place. But as we know, the Celestial didn't dock as planned. In fact, if it had docked, Mycroft would have known the Prince was missing weeks ago. No, the Frenchman let my brother think the Celestial was still out there and it had the Prince on it."

"That drowned lieutenant whose corpse we examined," I said slowly.

"Was the first mate on the Celestial." Holmes shook his head. "I only found out from the Bard. My brother would have recognised the man's true identity when Berthold reported the tattoos."

I was staggered. "They destroyed the Celestial? All of those British seamen lost their lives in service of that foul gesture? And it happened after the ransom was paid? By all that is holy, this is deceit most foul." I gathered my wits enough to ask, "Is the Prince dead?"

"No, according to the Bard, he is out there on the Clarity, which is the lead ship. Two other ships, heavily fortified with armour and artillery, follow in its wake." Holmes pinched the bridge of his nose. "So many of our seamen have already been sacrificed. I'll give them this: Mycroft and his ilk have done a splendid job of attributing this to sea monsters and the like. It's truly amazing."

My eyes swept the breadth and depth of the diving room. The helmets, the suits, the oxygen tanks, and the other gear lined the walls. I wondered what they would be used for, but that was only one of many questions: What were we doing here? What was Holmes planning?

It seemed to me that the damage had already been done. This ship, the Stratford-Upon-Avon, was only a submersible barge. How could we hope to catch up with the Clarity? I doubted that we could rescue the Prince, and of course, the gold and the munitions were long gone.

Or were they?

32

"Where did Ponsonby come in?" I asked. "Was he a sacrificial lamb, too?"

Holmes clapped me on the back. "Good old Watson. As keen as a knife's edge. You are right, old friend. Mycroft has been quietly seeding all of her Majesty's ships with spies. One never knows when there's a plot afoot or a mutiny being planned. Ponsonby was, of course, one of Mycroft's spies. The Frenchman and his crew left Ponsonby for dead after his keelhauling. As we both know, Ponsonby survived. He told Mycroft about the double-cross, and how the Clarity was substituted for the Celestial. That's the real reason Ponsonby had to be falsely charged with treason and hanged. Mycroft couldn't risk the Frenchman knowing that he, Mycroft, knew about the trick with the twin ships. Mycroft needed time to marshal an appropriate response and come up with a plan to rescue the lad."

"I see," I said, tentatively. "Let me make sure I understand all of what you've said. There's a mad French scientist who has been boarding English ships and robbing them of the gold that's been mined in Australia. Essentially, he's a pirate, although a highly skilled thief of the seas. Once the gold has been transferred, the Frenchman uses the lethal powers of his scientific vessel to destroy the ships. In an even more daring maneuver, he dispatched men to attack the troops in Aldershot, robbing the garrison of munitions and kidnapping Queen Victoria's grandson, Prince Wilhelm of Prussia. In an attempt to secure the young man's life, Mycroft allowed the pirates safe passage as long as the young Prince was unharmed. Negotiations have been ongoing. Rather than resort to warfare and bloodshed, Mycroft paid the pirates off, ransoming the Prince for yet more gold and allowing the French ships keep the munitions. But instead of transferring the prince to the Celestial as promised, they put him on the Clarity, a twin of the Celestial in every way. Meanwhile, they destroyed the Celestial and her crew. Thus far the Frenchman has managed to destroy four of Her Majesty's ships, steal gold from all four, rob Aldershot of munitions and gold, kidnap the Queen's grandson, and collect a sizeable amount of gold for a pretended ransom. Is that about right?"

Holmes smiled wanly. "Mycroft does not want to go to war with France. We are the superior naval force, it is true, but we are stretched to the snapping point because we have troops in all the colonies. Furthermore, there are rumblings that the Reichstag will pass legislation to fund the building of a German fleet later this year. We cannot risk a fight with the French that will leave us depleted and unable to protect ourselves from the Germans. It's too risky."

"And we are now here to do what?"

"Mycroft has charged the Bard—Zeke—with procuring the Prince and sinking the ship of the mad scientist."

I shook my head. "Come now, Holmes. The scientist must have a name! This is ridiculous."

"Verne. Jules Verne," said Holmes.

"The author? But his fantasy was published nearly thirty years ago! And that's exactly what it was, a tall tale!"

Holmes shifted his weight. The crates were not comfortable seating. "At the time, he tried to raise money to build a ship such as the one in his book. I distinctly recall that he spoke passionately about it to Mycroft after a lecture at the Diogenes Club. Of course, Mycroft and his fellow members thought that Verne was daft. They paid him very little serious attention."

Holmes cleared his throat. "That seems to have been a mistake. A very, very costly mistake."

"So Jules Verne is the mastermind behind all of this?" I asked. "How does the Bard expect to retrieve the Prince?"

"According to the Bard," said Holmes, "the divers will slip aboard the Clarity, the lead ship, grab the boy, and remove him. Mycroft has a spy on the Clarity, and this spy has told him where the boy is being held."

"I see. So the Bard's men are going to bring the Prince here?"

"No, not here." Holmes got to his feet. "We are on course to rendezvous with three British warships, the fastest ships in the Royal Navy. The Bard's men will sneak the Prince off of the Clarity and onto a ship from the Royal Fleet. They will sail as fast as possible towards a predetermined spot where the Prince will be transferred to land and taken to his parents. As you might imagine, they are incredibly angry and upset that their son was kidnapped on British soil."

"A warship," I said, thinking that only a warship could safeguard this young man who was being tossed about like a badminton birdie.

Holmes agreed. "Three warships, actually. At least the young Prince will escape with his life."

"And then, what happens to the Clarity? Will the Bard fire on it? What about the missing munitions?"

Holmes nodded his approval that I was following his explanation. "The gold and weaponry are divided among all the ships in the convoy. Mycroft told me that he's decided to let the ships go."

"Go!" I jumped up. Involuntarily, I'd balled my hands into fists. As a soldier I could not conceive of letting anyone get away with taking the lives of my countrymen, much less of fellow service members. "But they've spilled British blood. They've plundered our gold and our weapons! They've attacked our ships and our garrison. Those are acts of war!"

"True, but they are also the acts of a rogue genius," my friend said, "and not of the French nation. Mycroft has been reassured repeatedly that if the French catch Verne first, they will destroy him. And, think about it, Watson. Fighting a ship filled with ordnance and weapons would be extremely risky. The Stratford-Upon-Avon is not a fast ship, although she is a versatile one. We would, more than likely, die in the attempt to destroy the three ships." Holmes stood up and stretched. Then he linked his arms behind his back and walked back and forth. His feet made a hollow sound on the metal deck. "No, we must let them go."

I was astonished. "That ship and its two companion ships are nothing but pirates. The crew of the Clarity killed the men on the Celestial! They are pirates and kidnappers and murderers."

Holmes smiled at me sagely. "And they are French. Firing upon those ships would hurry us into war. The French people don't know that their pirates have repeatedly targeted British ships. They wouldn't believe it if we told them! No, my friend, we cannot retaliate. Tensions in the Sudan are mounting between our government and the French. Mycroft hopes to keep the fighting there, and not let it come to our shores, because if it does, then surely it will expand throughout Europe.

Mycroft would rather have casualties on a distant shore, thank you, than to involve our fair green island."

Holmes paused and added, "Firing upon the Clarity and her two escorts would be an act of war. It's one thing for a rogue French element to commit piracy, kidnapping, and murder. Remember: They attacked our ships one at a time and did it anonymously. It is quite another for the highest echelons of the British government to sanction letting British warships open fire on a ship flying the French flag. Furthermore, Mycroft has gone through diplomatic channels to discuss this matter. The French swore to Mycroft that they did not approve of Verne's mission to kidnap the Prussian Prince and are horrified to learn about his plans. As a matter of fact, they're eager to wash their hands of the whole mess. No, all three nations involved—the United Kingdom, the French, and the Prussians—want this to be brought to a speedy and bloodless conclusion."

33

"All right, but where does Mrs. Morel fit into all of this?" I asked. "And what about the sailor with the gold in his gut? Was he her husband?"

"I don't know...yet." Holmes looked away.

I persisted. "Mrs. Morel and the sailor must figure into this somehow. Also, why was it important that you be drawn into this skirmish? Someone went to a lot of trouble to call our attention to this nasty bit of business, didn't they? And why? To wit, someone played the part of a grieving widow, played the part of her maid, played the part of a family friend who was a decorated sailor, and pointed us to a drowned sailor. Why?"

I stopped short of pointing out that we had no reason to assume the worst of Mrs. Morel, at least not yet, but I knew my protestations would fall on deaf ears. Even so, Holmes must have suspected that I was biting my tongue. He responded with a sideways twitch of his lips, holding back a smile.

"Good old Watson," Holmes said. His eyes took on that faraway look they often get when he's in the midst of a case. I knew that his comments to me were cursory while his mind was moving quickly in a dozen different directions.

"Why were we brought here?" I asked again. I was not about to quit asking until I had a reasonable answer. Even if I had to shake him out of his reverie, I would.

My friend gave me a guarded smile. "Word of my visit to the Queen got back to Mycroft. He decided that I would never be content unless I saw this adventure through to the end. To be precise, he doubts I would believe the young Prince had been transferred from one ship to another. He decided he doesn't want me hunting down a handful of French pirates and causing trouble. And of course, he was right. So rather than simply tell me what Zeke was doing, he decided I should see it with my own two eyes. Zeke would explain my brother's decisions to me. That way I would be satisfied."

"How is Zeke to accomplish this mission?" I asked. "You've handily skipped over the details."

"This is where Zeke's men come in. Once the barge pulls alongside the Clarity, we're going to come up to a depth of twenty-five feet. Zeke's men will leave from here and swim for it. Their goal will be to board that ship and recapture the young Prince. Once the divers have left the Stratford-Upon-Avon, the barge will drop back and submerge to fifty feet and wait to make sure the British ship is allowed to safely sail away with the Prince on board."

"And the pirates will not interfere?" I asked. "They will let the Prince go with no trouble?"

"Right. No trouble and a bag of gems as their reward. They'll get the gems after the Royal Navy ship signals the Prince is safe. The gems must be hidden here, somewhere."

This confounded me. "My word, Holmes! They've already gotten our gold from the ships they've plundered and the munitions from Aldershot. All of this and gems, too?"

"Think of it this way, Watson. It is much cheaper to pay them off than fight with them."

Perhaps Holmes was right. Perhaps Mycroft was, too. Having seen war close up, I should be fine with seeing this one lonely spot remain peaceful. I spoke my mind. "I must say, Holmes, the idea of letting these pirates kill my countrymen, rob us, and kidnap the grandson of our wonderful Queen angers me. But I, of all people, know what the alternative looks like. I know how men suffer when politicians act recklessly."

"Yes," Holmes continued, "At the worst, the Bard will fire a warning shot across the bow of the Clarity to prove he has the firepower to blow it out of the water."

"Then what do we do?"

"We are here as witnesses. Zeke says we'll report back to Mycroft, and possibly to the Queen."

"And the Bard is confident that his men can grab the young man, move him to another ship, and get away from the Clarity without a fight? Even if that ship only has a skeletal crew, that's a tall order."

"I asked Zeke the same question, and he only chuckled. When I pressed, he said that I would find out soon enough. His exact words were, *Men at some time are masters of their fates."*

"That's from *Julius Caesar."* I added, "Just what are we to do, while all of this is going on? Sit by and stay out of the way? If there are gold nuggets on board the Clarity, that might explain where our drowned seaman was when he was tortured and killed. I didn't come this far just to be an observer!"

"Nor did I, Watson. Nor did I." With that, he rose to his feet. Holmes walked to the diving suits hanging on the wall and ran his fingers along the canvas. His arched brow told me what he had in mind. "Watson, do you know how to work these?"

"Not entirely," I replied, hesitantly. "The seaman told me the rudiments. Why do you ask? You're not suggesting—"

"Well," he said, smiling, "if we're going to board the Clarity, we had better learn how these work, wouldn't you say? An education not utilized is a wasted education." Holmes tapped the glass viewing plate on the helmet.

"You're daft, Holmes. I'm not sure I know where to begin."

"You said so yourself, Watson. We didn't come this far to sit and watch." A thin, deadly smile fell short of his eyes, as he envisioned the liberation of the Prince. For a few moments, we stood in awkward silence.

The noise of a clanging bell roused us.

34

"What's happening?" I cried, covering my ears.

"We must be nearing the Clarity," Holmes said, glancing up at the hatch as it opened.

Mercifully, the bell stopped pealing but the sound reverberated through the ship for a few seconds.

"How can we be sure of our location?" I wondered. "Don't forget we're fifty feet under the surface."

"Not anymore. I'd say we've been rising at an angle of four or five degrees for the past few minutes."

Of course, Holmes was correct. We had both leaned slightly into the incline without becoming fully aware of our adjustment.

"Mr. Holmes, Dr. Watson," a voice called through the hatch, "you are needed above."

Entering the main room from below deck, we came upon Carlo and a grim-faced and determined crew. One by one, the men's eyes turned towards the staircase leading to Zeke's control room. Carlo, standing at the foot of the stairs, glanced up. Zeke's tiny feet appeared on the top tread.

As the Bard made his way down the stairs, it became

obvious he had dressed for the occasion. By the time he reached the bottom, the entire crew was all smiles. There, in all his glory, stood Ezekiel Emeritus Marder. The little man was dressed in an impeccably tailored uniform. Later we were told it was an exact replica of the one Admiral Nelson wore during the Battle of Trafalgar in 1805.

The valiant leader called the men to attention, and they immediately responded. They stood as rigid as tin soldiers. Their eyes stared straight ahead.

With both hands clasped behind his back and staring at the floor, Zeke paced up and down the line of men. Their neutral expressions turned dark and worried. When the diminutive captain passed in front of me, his head tilted upward to reveal his face. Given his men's scowls, I expected to see a troubled expression on Zeke. But I was surprised to see him smiling. As our eyes met, he gave me a wink and spun 'round to face his men. Looking at his crew, he smiled broadly as they remained at attention.

"Men," Zeke began, "the hour is at hand. We have fallen in behind the last ship's wake and are quickly overtaking them. In a few minutes, all of your training and sacrifice will be put to use. *In God's name, cheerily on, courageous friends, To reap the harvest of perpetual peace by this one bloody trial of sharp war.*"

Carlo stepped forwards, extended his hand, and wrapped it 'round the dwarf's. Zeke shook his hand gratefully. The two exchanged the sort of wordless communication so often seen in friends and colleagues. They were of one purpose.

"And what of the Nau...?" Carlo, his face ashen, turned to see if we had overheard.

Zeke, noting that we had overheard, smiled wickedly. "Don't worry, Carlo, she's where she's supposed to be. Now, take your men below and prepare to disembark. Be sure the extra suit is checked and taken with you. It wouldn't do to have our target swimming on the surface, now would it?"

Carlo spun on his heels and led his men below.

Holmes and I followed Zeke down the steps to the diving room. The three of us watched the preparations. The men climbed into their diving suits. In the crook of their arms, they held their breathing helmets. Extending from the rear of the helmets were hoses that disappeared into a cumbersome-looking box that was sheathed in a canvas sack. These boxes, we were told, allowed the divers to breathe whilst under water. The boxes were then strapped to the men's backs. Around their waists, the divers wore web belts carrying an odd assortment of tools and weapons. One of the latter was an ingenious and lethal-looking crossbow. Its size and shape was the same as a small revolver. Instead of bullets, it could fire small deadly darts that were secured to the sleeves of the diving suits by thin straps. Last of all, the men grabbed diving bags.

The divers inspected their gear, whilst the other sailors located three wooden crates and dragged them into the diving area. Each crate was carefully opened to expose two round metal objects. Each object was approximately a foot in diameter and six inches deep. Oddly, these disks reminded me of tarnished serving tray covers. In the center of each disk was a lever that spanned half the width of the device. Inside each lever was a dial clearly marked with the numbers zero through eleven.

The divers watched the other men with great concern as the sailors meticulously set each disk inside a case made of hardened rubber. Once all of those cases were safely packed, the entire crew noticeably relaxed.

But there was more to be done. Sailors worked in pairs to assist the divers by lifting the newly loaded circular cases chest-level. There was a tension clamp on the back of each case and when the clamp was opened, it would neatly slip through rings sewn on the front of the diving suits. Once the case was in the correct position, the clamp was snapped closed.

Carlo carried the extra diving suit and helmet over to another rubber case shaped more like a valise. He placed the apparatus inside and snapped the lid closed. Then he lifted the case and rested it on the lip of the diving well. He gave a nod to Zeke and smiled before saying, "Helmets!"

Each sailor approached a diver. The diver handed over his helmet, and the sailor responded by lifting the helmet and lowering it gently until touched a metal collar ring. Next the helmets were twisted slightly to the right and locked into place. The assistants spun their divers 'round and twisted the valves that extended out of their backpacks. A gentle, hissing sound emitted from these air packs.

Carlo's broad smile filled his faceplate, as he balanced the valise he was holding on the lip of the well. He saluted us with his gloved hand and then lowered himself over the lip of the diving well. The water roiled, and he was swallowed up by the cold, murky depths. One by one, his men followed, until all of them were gone.

"This way, gentlemen," Zeke said, gesturing for us to follow whilst the rest of the crew made themselves busy. A surprisingly silent Holmes and I followed Zeke to the control room. We watched as the small man climbed into his chair.

"Will they be all right?" I asked Zeke.

"My men know what they're doing. *Things done well —And with a care, exempt themselves from fear.* Don't worry, our plan will succeed."

"Holmes?" I said, staring into his grey, expressionless eyes. "Why don't you say something? You've been too quiet. What have you going on in that machine you call a brain?"

35

"I'm sorry, Watson, but something has been troubling me." Holmes paused to look at Zeke, who was now paying close attention to the both of us.

"All right, Mr. Holmes," Zeke remarked, spinning in his chair. "What is your concern?"

At first Holmes didn't say anything. Instead, he closed his eyes and reviewed what he had seen. Suddenly his eyes snapped open. "Those round circles! I thought they were weights, but they weren't. They're explosive devices, aren't they?"

"Oh, ho!" sneered Zeke, his tiny legs dangling over the chair of his seat. "You haven't the stomach for what we're about to do, do you? *Thus conscience does make cowards of us all.*"

Holmes clenched his fists, as he barely contained his rage. "You speak to me of conscience, as if it were a weakness, an infirmity! *Every man's conscience is a thousand men, to fight against this guilty homicide*. Tell me, Zeke, just who do you work for? You know why this is a bad idea."

I couldn't hide my surprise. "Holmes, what are you talking about?"

My friend raised his hand to silence me. "Watson, we are about to become accomplices. Of course! Don't you see? Zeke wants us to bear witness and thus become unwitting collaborators in this act of war! He is delivering munitions and gold to the French scientist!"

"Because the British government's policy is all wrong and unfair." The dwarf sneered. "The officers are chosen by social status and rank rather than by skill. They see themselves as superior beings and their troops are cannon fodder. Raised to such lofty thrones, they decide who is promoted and who will be sent to the front lines to die."

"I rather suspect this is more personal than that," Holmes said, his voice taunting.

"All right!" The little man slammed his fist down on the arm of his chair. "Perhaps it is! They won't accept me into the military hierarchy. They say I'm of low birth and deformed. I ask you, have you ever seen a more capable commander? No, you have not."

"But Mycroft—" Sherlock Holmes began.

"Your brother refused to help me. When the Royal Navy decided I was unfit to join its loftiest ranks, I went to him at the Diogenes Club. I begged, I pleaded, and I showed him my accolades. My preparation for the admiralty is sterling! Without peer! But he refused to override the Royal Navy's decision. Mycroft said I could do my part, but I would have to remain in the shadows. Hidden away! He said I was far more valuable to the Crown if I remained a secret weapon. Do you know what it's like to be tossed aside like rubbish? Well, I do! I decided that I would make him regret that he did not secure an admiralty for me. Using the Queen's money, I built this barge. I assembled the finest crew in the world. But I don't look like a naval officer, do I? Nor do I speak with a plummy accent. And so I was expected to serve others—less talented but highborn men—with a smile but never to gain the approbation of the English people! How dare they!"

I felt my own face redden as I listened. Mycroft's decision didn't surprise me. After all, he had to keep both the Royal Navy and the Queen happy, and challenging centuries of history would definitely be disruptive. As a nation, the British believed that one's hereditary station in life was a prognosticator of exceptional talents and abilities. Of course, I had seen that theory exploited and fail on the battlefield, but I had endured an experience most men had not. Furthermore, the Crimean War had proven how dreadfully inept British leadership could be. But the mythical advantage conferred by birthright endured.

Instead of going against our national beliefs, Mycroft chose to pacify Zeke, giving him money and a purpose, but keeping the little man in the shadows. Mycroft Holmes' charge was the British Empire, and not just one disgruntled citizen. Mycroft had managed to exploit the Bard's skills whilst keeping the small man in a subordinate position. Until now...

The Bard continued, "We shall see who is fit for high command! Mycroft has sent me on countless missions, risking my life and the lives of my crew, and for what? To stay forever hidden? Enough I say! *Time's glory is to calm contending kings, to unmask falsehood and bring truth to light.* To Mycroft Holmes and his ilk, my men are a lower caste of humans, a subordinate species, but I saw the courage in them! The talents! These men have heroic hearts. They wanted to serve Queen and Country. But She does not care if we live or die! Then die we shall, but our blaze will burn bright and hot before it is extinguished."

Sherlock Holmes was shaking with rage. His body actually trembled, which is a state I've seen so rarely that at first I thought I was imagining it. Had Mycroft realised this little man would be so bitter? And so dangerous? I doubted it.

"Perhaps my brother was right all along. You are inferior. See how you turn on the hand that fed you? I relish the thought of being done with you," Sherlock Holmes spat out. "If death is to be our lot, then to quote from your friend the real bard, *Death unloads thee.* But putting our fates aside, I take it that you have other plans for the shipment on those three ships, the Clarity and the two that follow her."

Then in a moment of eureka, Holmes said, "Oh, ho! You have sold the arms, right?"

The small man in the fancy uniform chortled with glee. "Ha! You are smarter than I thought you were! Yes, I have sold the arms to the French so that they might have a chance against British imperialism in the Sudan."

"British imperialism?" I scoffed. "What about French imperialism? Are we really that much different?"

The small admiral lifted his chin defiantly. "I have been promised that the French, with their history of *Liberté, Égalité, Fraternité,* will treat the colonists differently. They are truly a government of the people, by the people, and for the people. Furthermore, I will not be forgotten. I recently posed for a statue that will be erected in my honour as a valiant admiral whose brave sacrifices paved the way to a free Sudan," said the dwarf. His chest puffed up with pride.

"I see," Holmes said in a cold voice. He cast me a sideways glance, and I understood that I was being entreated to hold my tongue. Reluctantly, I agreed with Holmes. It was far too late to convince Zeke that he was on the wrong side of history.

The little man continued. "To me, attacking the British ships is nothing more than a sound business decision. We confiscated the arms shipment and we will divert it to the highest bidder."

"What possible difference can that make if you are dead?" I

asked. The question made perfect sense to me. Both men turned to stare in my direction.

"We are delivering the arms to Mr. Verne, and he shall distribute them to the appropriate French forces. In return, he has promised me that if I survive, I shall be named an Admiral in the French Navy. If I do not survive, the French Navy shall honour me and pay a bounty to my sister, a good-hearted woman who raised me as her own after our parents neglected me and left me to die."

Inwardly, I swore a series of oaths on this very subject. The abandonment of deformed infants was a common practice that I had worked assiduously to curtail over the course of my career. I found it especially reprehensible in those families where there were resources to take care of a child, but their fear of social disapproval mattered more than Christian charity. Zeke's bitter tone reminded me of the many imperfect children who had been cast aside.

"What do our deaths accomplish?" asked Holmes, in the most conversational of tones.

"Ah yes, your deaths. A letter has been sent to *The Times* stating that you've been captured and are being held prisoners by the French for spying. Of course, there are enough details provided to make them assume—with some effort, mind you—that your brother is a turncoat." At this pronouncement, the small man grinned with a wicked sort of happiness.

"You're mad!" I laughed. "The British government will never go to war over the lives of two civilians, a handful of munitions, and a boy Prince."

"You are correct, Doctor, but she will go to war over the sinking of some of her ships. As we speak, three of the Empire's fastest ships of the Royal Navy, out of Portsmouth, are being readied to intercept those up there." Zeke pointed towards the ceiling.

"B-b-but," I stammered. "How do you know where the ships from the Royal Navy are headed?"

"Because, Watson," Holmes answered, "that's the way Zeke has it planned."

"Very good, Mr. Holmes. Go on."

"If I'm correct, you will have sent a message to the Prime Minister, suggesting that we be rescued. Of course, the credentials must prove to be impeccable as to leave little doubt of its authenticity—perhaps our clothes?"

"Excellent!" the dwarf clapped. "Your clothes and a letter sent by you."

"Hah," I laughed aloud. "That's where your plan falls apart! The Prime Minister is sure to show the letter to Mycroft. He will notice that it is not in Holmes' hand!"

"Mr. Holmes?" Zeke prodded.

"Most probably, the letter will explain it away. An injury of some sort?" Sherlock Holmes said.

Zeke nodded, enthusiastically. "Splendid! What else?"

"It wouldn't do to be interrupted by news about the Fleet," Holmes said. "So I would surmise that the information would be delivered at a predetermined time—with enough of a delay to allow you to accomplish your traitorous plan without interference."

"Quite correct," the dwarf said. "We will be lying in wait, submerged, with our eyes open like a crocodile." Zeke smiled malevolently, rubbing his hands with glee.

"What's a crocodile have to do with this?" I wondered out loud. All of this subterfuge was exceedingly hard to follow. "Lying in wait with open eyes? How is that going to work?"

"Where are my manners?" asked the dwarf with a laugh. "Of course, you haven't seen one of my favorite toys." Zeke jerked his thumb upwards, towards a shiny, metal cylinder that protruded from the ceiling.

"The scope, please," he called out to one of the crew.

The sailor walked over to Zeke and pulled down on a lever. Suddenly, a soft hiss of air escaped, and the cylinder raised up until it came to a quiet stop. Zeke released the catches on either side of the cylinder and snapped two arms into place. Once the arms were locked down, Zeke spun the cylinder 'round whilst turning the handles. Satisfied with the set-up, he nodded at our curious expressions. We could see two eyepieces protruding from the center of the shaft. The dwarf peered into the lenses, twisting the handles slowly. Giggling, he gestured for us to move closer and look for ourselves.

Holmes peered into the eyepiece and backed away disinterestedly, making room for me. Turning the handles in the same manner as Holmes, I brought the lenses into focus and was surprised that it was well past dawn already, judging from the grey light of the faraway horizon.

"A periscope!" I cried, staring at the surface of the water. Of course, I had read of such things before, but I had never expected this. Rotating the tube, I could just make out our divers bobbing up and down in front of a dull metal wall. That wall, I realised quickly enough, was the hull of a boat, the Clarity. As the ship crested a wave that lifted it higher out of the water, I saw that the divers had attached those six round devices to the hull of the ship, just below the waterline. Knowing this to be important, and that I was not meant to see it, I had to make Holmes aware without arousing the suspicions of Zeke and the crew.

"Holmes," I said excitedly, "come take a look. This is incredible! You can see the divers working!"

"I've seen enough."

"I do not want you to miss this fantastic sight," I persisted.

Holmes' eyes flashed angrily, as he nudged me aside. Whilst he positioned himself, I continued, "Take a good look, Holmes.

Who knows if we shall ever have a chance to see the sun rise again?" I noticed by Holmes' tightening grip on the handles that something had caught his eye.

"The good doctor is correct, Mr. Holmes," remarked the dwarf, as he turned to busy himself with his charts. "It may well be the last time you will ever see the surface. Or the sunrise or the horizon. I'm sorry, but it has to be this way."

"Hmm, you may be right," Holmes did his best to sound resigned. "Although you do realise that by killing us, you're no better than those whom you seek to destroy?"

"That's just it, Mr. Holmes. I do not pretend to be anything but what I am," said the dwarf, as he ran a finger down his charts. "I'm not a zealot, believing my cause is just. I'm simply a very talented sailor —nothing more, nothing less. I created all of this as a means to an end. Admittedly, an ending sadder than I had hoped, but your brother is to blame for this."

Holmes swiveled the periscope slightly to the left and refocused the lenses. His body tensed. "You do know, Zeke," Holmes said over his shoulder, "that your plan will never work."

"Of course it will, Mr. Holmes. Of course it will."

The dwarf was distracted by his charts, and he hadn't noticed how my friend continued turning the scope ever so slightly, as if he were following the movement of someone or something. Finally, he stopped, and I saw by his manner that whatever it was, he could barely contain his excitement. Holmes shifted his weight to the balls of his feet. His hands tightened on the periscope. Just as Zeke looked up from the charts, Holmes spun the periscope back to its original position as he continued to look through the lenses.

"That's enough," Zeke said, snapping the grips back to their vertical position. He pushed the lever forwards, and the periscope rose into the ceiling. "Well, what do you think, Mr. Holmes?"

"I think my brother wasn't worried about your stature. I am convinced that he didn't promote you because you are insane," said Holmes in a tone filled with conviction.

"Take them below!" bellowed Zeke, rubbing his neck. "If they cause trouble, into the water with them! *Vengeance is in my heart, death in my hand, blood and revenge are hammering in my head!*"

36

"What are we to do, Holmes?" I whispered. The door to our cabin had slammed shut after the two men charged with moving us had left. Our escorts had not been gentle, so I rubbed my elbow where they'd banged it against one of the doorways.

"Give me time. I must think," he said. The words were heavy and pained.

Though there appeared to be little hope of escape, I was struck by Holmes' expression. After what he had been through, one would expect the light in his eyes to be filled with doubt and recrimination, but this was no ordinary man—and his vibrant intensity could leave little doubt as to my companion's mindset. Holmes' close-set eyes locked onto mine, and I felt their hypnotic power. "Watson, what did you see when you looked through the periscope?"

"Why, let me see. I recall the divers in the water. And, oh, yes, those things attached to the hull of the ship. I assume they are explosives. Are they, Holmes?"

"Yes. But did you see anything else?"

"No. I wanted you to see the explosives and where they

were attached. I spotted them and turned the periscope over to you."

Ignoring my question regarding our next move, Holmes told me what he had observed. "I saw the divers and the explosives, of course, but I also saw a man climbing down the ladder of the ship. Very reluctantly, I might add. From what I could see, I would say that he was being forced to cooperate. Carlo had his weapon trained on him, and after some heated words, the man pulled on the diving suit and swam away from the ship. Another diver swam alongside of him. But what was interesting was that Carlo did not swim with the other divers. He slipped beneath the surface a good distance away and to the left of them. The other divers just watched the reluctant diver and his companion go. That's all I was able to see. Zeke was no longer distracted, and I felt him turning to watch me."

"But who was the man?" I wondered. "Was he the missing Prince? And where did he and Carlo go? What's going on?"

Holmes sat down on his bed, resting his back against the wall. "In answer to all of your questions, I don't know who that first diver was, or the identity of his escort, although I have my suspicions. I am nearly certain we watched the young Prince swim away. But we haven't the time to find out. The other divers should be returning shortly, and we have to get off this ship before they do."

"Get off the ship? What? Holmes, you're mad! Just how do you propose that we do that? The hatch is locked from above, and there are too many of them to overpower anyway."

Sherlock Holmes smiled. There was a light in his eyes that suggested what he was planning.

"You are indeed mad!" I protested. "Even if we were able to get out, where would we go? You heard Zeke—he's going to destroy the ships. We'd only be postponing the inevitable."

However, Holmes had made up his mind. "Would you

rather sit here and be part of the maritime forces that start a war? And kill an heir to a throne? Hmm?"

I scoffed. "Of course not. I would rather go down with a sword in my hand than sleeping in my cot!"

"Good. Then grab hold of anything you want to keep, although I cannot imagine what that might be."

I looked regretfully at my newly cleaned topcoat. It would be hard to replace but honestly, what difference did it make? I was probably a dead man who would never wear a topcoat again. With a jerk of my chin, I pointed towards the hall. Holmes smiled and slapped me on my shoulder. Together we padded silently down the hallway and the length of the ship. I held my breath and followed Holmes down the metal curling stairs and into the diving room.

"I hope you were paying attention when they dressed in these," my friend said. He was now preoccupied with the task of climbing into a diving suit. Reluctantly, I struggled into one myself. As I did, Holmes bounded about, examining this and that, turning things over and over thoughtfully. When he had touched every article scattered about, he rummaged through the crates and lockers in the diving compartment. Meanwhile, I took off my socks and turned them into saps. I filled each one with nuts and bolts before tying off the necks. As a weapon, it was not elegant or fancy, but I knew from personal experience that a well-placed blow could bring a man down.

Holmes attached various items to his belt. Wordlessly, I handed him a sap. He rewarded me with a quick, "Well done." I noticed that he'd selected a lantern, a flat piece of black material that resembled a child's chalkboard, a loop of rope, and other sundry things. Meanwhile, I sat on the lip of the diving well, mulling our predicament.

"Watson," said Holmes, "see if you can find anything to wedge into that rail that guides the hatch up there. Something to jam up its movement. They mustn't be able to open that hatch from above or from here. Hurry, man, our lives depend on it!"

After a quick scan of our environment, I grabbed a length of metal tubing and climbed the ladder. Remembering the hatch slid to my right to open, I wedged one end solidly between the wheel and the rail. Once it was jammed there, I pulled down on the tube until it broke with a snap. I did the same with the other rails and wheels, until I had blocked all the ways to open the hatch. By the time I turned 'round to see what Holmes had been up to, he had an assortment of weapons and gear piled in the center of the floor. We'd both tucked our saps into pockets on our suits.

"Come on," he said. "We haven't much time. The divers should be returning. Grab a couple of those crossbows and all the darts you can."

"I still don't know what you have in mind." I tucked the crossbows into the waistband of my diving suit. The darts went into a pocket.

"It's simple, really. Unless Zeke has a means of communicating with the divers out there, they are unaware of our present circumstances."

"I see where you're going, Holmes. Since they don't know what has happened here, they'll be expecting to return to a friendly environment." My heart quickened as I readied myself for a surprise attack.

Holmes nodded that I'd understood his plan. "Exactly. We must act as if everything is normal. We'll assist them into the ship and render them unconscious. When we have them all, we'll pitch their helmets and breathing tanks into the diving well. The apparatuses will sink into the sea. Of course, we'll do the same with the extra diving suits and equipment. That way they can't come after us."

Breathing heavily from the exertion, Holmes was busily tearing strips of cloth from a pile of oily rags he'd found stuffed in a bin.

"Watson," he said, tossing me the rags, "finish ripping up these rags, while I see what else we can use to slow them down."

His exuberance was contagious, although the thought kept running through my mind, *Where do we go from here?* I had ofttimes placed my trust and my very life in his hands, before I knew that he had a plan. Was this particular adventure any different? The gurgle of water coming up through the divers' well suggested it was. This time I could not run away and seek shelter, not that I ever would.

"Hullo, what's this?" Holmes remarked, looking into a small leather pouch he'd found.

His eyes twinkled as he tossed me the bag. Catching it with one hand, I spread the neck of the pouch apart and emptied the contents into the palm of my hand. "Diamonds!" I said.

"These will be put to good use," Holmes said, taking the gems from my hand and dropping them back into the bag. Pinching the leather closed, he tucked the bag in his web belt and was about to speak when he grabbed my wrist tightly. With a silent word, "Look," he directed my attention. His eyes stared into the diving well, as a canopy of bubbles floated to the surface.

"Here they come," he whispered. "Watson? I'll help them out of the water and maneuver them so that their backs are to you. It's your job to deliver a blow to their heads. Get ready."

✤ 37 ✤

I grabbed my sap and hid it behind my back. My blood raced with anticipation, and then with sudden dread.

"Holmes," I hissed. "Their helmets!"

"Don't worry, I've already thought of that. Now, get ready—here he comes."

The water was a roiling mass of bubbles as the first diver's helmet broke surface. Holmes loosened the chain so that it lowered the lifting bar. The diver grasped the bar with both hands, as I held him out of the water. Holmes turned the lever locks on the collar ring and prized off the helmet.

Placing the man's helmet on the floor, Holmes pulled on the opposite chain so that the diver rose from the water. Holmes assisted the man in stepping over the lip and, just as my friend had indicated he would do, Holmes turned the man 'round so that his back was facing me. I raised the sap and brought it down on the back of the diver's head. The man collapsed in an unconscious heap, and I dragged him out of the way and out of sight. Repeating the scene with little variation, all the divers were neatly stacked in a pile off to one side while Holmes and I made short work of binding them hand and foot and stuffing cloth gags in their mouths.

We had little chance to savour the success of our work, because a loud, clanging sound reverberated throughout the ship. Holmes pointed to the hatch that I had jammed closed. I noticed the slight rise and fall of the plate as it strained to open.

A thin smile of satisfaction crossed Holmes' face. He tossed the divers' helmets and tanks into the diving well. We watched the apparatuses sink. Everything we weren't going to use was thrown into the hole. The pounding from above grew desperate, and this time, it was I who smiled proudly. I'd done an excellent job jamming the hatch shut.

My friend gathered a number of buckets and filled them with sea water. "Watson, stuff some rags in the scuppers of that trough over there. Then fill it with water." Pointing towards a compartment with connections to the engine, Holmes told me, "We want the batteries in there to be completely immersed. Move!"

I did as instructed and soon had the batteries covered with salt water. The results were immediate. The lights began to flicker, as the corrosive salt water began reacting with the batteries' plates.

Holmes raised his head to study the flickering overhead lights. "Excellent job, Watson. Come here, I need you, and bring a rag."

I walked to the rear of the compartment to where Holmes was standing next to the round fitting that held the spinning propeller shaft in place. On the top of the metal ring, a funnel had been hammered into the oil hole. Smiling, Holmes poured the diamonds into the funnel. Then he reached for the rag in my hand and stuffed it down the throat of the funnel. As the diamonds cut deeply into the revolving shaft, they made a piercing, grinding shriek.

"The strongest mineral known to man," Holmes said. "With any luck, this bit of sabotage will cripple the Stratford-Upon-Avon."

The lights dimmed. Sparks flew out of the batteries. "It's time, Watson," Holmes remarked, surveying the compartment. "We've done all that we can. You have the crossbows and the arrows? Attach them to your belt. Good. It's time to leave the ship."

My claustrophobia came roaring back with a vengeance. My mouth went dry while my palms turned wet. The pounding of my heart caused a loud sound inside my head. I felt my fear growing, as Holmes handed me the helmet and placed the tanks on my back.

"Don't worry," he said in a soothing tone. "We won't be in the water long. But you must listen to me now." Holmes looped a coil of rope and tied it 'round my waist, then tied the other end 'round his. "This will keep us together," he continued. "When we go in, I'll go first. I noticed some hand grips in the water as I helped the divers. I believe they run the length of the barge. I'll hold onto them until you're in. Then, as soon as you can, I'll move aside and you must grab onto the handles. Don't let go of them until I signal like this." He clenched a fist, then opened it quickly, as if releasing something.

I nodded. My helmet was heavy as I held it under one arm.

"Remember, don't let go of the handles until I signal. The speed of the ship and the water's current are going to pull on you heavily. As long as you hold on, we'll be fine. Just grip the handle until I find it."

"Find what?" I asked. My voice cracked with agitation.

"A cable. It has to be there," he responded. "Once I've located it, I'll signal you to let go of the handles so we can follow the cable to its end. I'll tap you on the shoulder when we've arrived at our destination. That's a signal to have the weapons ready. I'll go inside first, and you follow right behind me. Do you understand?"

I nodded glumly. "I guess so, but go in where? Where are we going? What cable?"

Holmes said, "Don't worry, Watson, all will become clear to you. Are you ready?"

My eyes must have been wide with alarm. Holmes gripped both of my shoulders with his hands and repeated in a sonorous tone, "All will be well. All will be well." Since he'd hypnotized me numerous times, my body quickly responded. It was like falling asleep with my eyes open, because I felt all of my anxiety loosen its hold on me.

Holmes noticed and said, "Good. You are going to be all right."

A little voice inside me reminded me that we were probably going to die, but I still felt calm. Holmes continued, "Do your best to breathe normally when we are in the water. Don't be alarmed at the lack of visibility. At this depth, we won't be able to see too far. Remember this won't take long. Ready?"

I nodded. Holmes lifted my helmet over my head, aligned it with the top of my canvas suit, and used a set of locking clamps to secure my headgear. I did the same for him. He motioned for me to turn the valve of my air supply, and I did as instructed. A soft hiss affirmed that the gases were flowing into my helmet. Through the small glass window of his helmet, Holmes' eyes shone with steely determination. Stepping awkwardly in our weighted boots, we strode to the diving well. Holmes climbed over the lip. Looking up at me, he lowered himself into the water. I saw that he had a firm grasp of the handles that lined the sides of the well.

As I lowered myself over the lip, I took one last look at the diving compartment. A small, bluish fire had broken out next to the batteries. An eerie glow filled the room, and the fire jumped to some of the oil-soaked rags. Seconds before my vision was obscured by the metal wall of the diving well, I saw the hatch to the upper deck as it sprang open. Right before I was submerged, I glimpsed the soles of a sailor's shoes while he raced down the stairs. The chase for us was on!

38

Panic nearly overtook me as I descended into the water, moving lower and lower, hand over hand. Just as Holmes had warned, once I came out of the tunnel that was actually the diving well, I was buffeted about by the current. I struggled against my own fear, as my breathing became fast and shallow. Reaching out for the handles that ran along the bottom of the barge, I became dizzy. Fortunately, Holmes got a grip on my hand. His gloved hand guided mine until my fingers were tightly wrapped 'round one of the handles. Once I had that tactile reassurance, I concentrated on consciously controlling my breathing.

Holmes had been right: in those black waters, I could barely see his shadowy form. But my eyes slowly adjusted, and I realised he was staring at me. His expression was concerned. I bobbed my head up and down in an exaggerated fashion to let him know that I was fine. And I told myself repeatedly that I was just that: fine.

The pull of the water strained every muscle in my body. I struggled against it in the current. Holmes faded in and out of my view. I assumed he was searching for this mysterious cable that he had mentioned. Suddenly, his hand popped up, right in front of my face. I watched with giddy fascination, as he balled his hand into a fist then snapped it open repeatedly. Placing my trust in Holmes and God, while silently blessing the rope that leashed us together, I let go of the metal handle I was clutching.

At first, I had little sensation of movement, perhaps because I was no longer fighting the current while holding onto the moving ship. Slowly, I drifted along. Then I looked up in time to see the hulking mass of the ship's bottom glide by. Suddenly, I was tossed around violently. The tethered rope tied about my waist snapped taut. My arms whirled around my body. My breathing was more gulping than taking measured breaths. I was caught in a vortex, a nightmare of gigantic proportions because my body was out of control, my vision was gone, and my head was spinning.

I was caught in the wash of the giant propeller's vortex of water. That explained why I was spinning. Once again, panic bubbled up inside me. What had we done? Was I going to die, alone in this watery grave? But in the midst of all this chaos, I heard the words of Horatio Nelson, our brave naval commander who fought and gave so much to our nation: *I thank God for this opportunity of doing my duty.* With the realisation that whether I lived or I died, I was serving my country, all my fears suddenly vanished. At that very moment, a sudden tapping on my helmet made me aware of another presence—Holmes! In my confused state, I actually talked to him, as if he could hear me! Shaking his head from side to side, he reminded me how foolish I was.

I would have laughed if I hadn't been so embarrassed.

Though the water was black and murky, I could see Holmes' face clearly through his faceplate. It took some moments before I realised that he had lit his lantern, and it provided some visibility as he held it aloft. With his free hand, Holmes grabbed my shoulder. He rotated, turning the lamp left and right. My eyes followed the light, but I had no sense of what Holmes was trying to accomplish. Finally, he let go of my shoulder. The rope tethering us tugged me along as my friend swam with me in tow. We followed the narrow thread of lantern light, until I finally saw what Holmes had been seeking—it was the cable!

Holmes grabbed for it. He crawled, hand over hand, along its length. It took effort for me to master the art of rope climbing in water. My impulse was to grab the cable with both hands at all times, but one hand at a time was much more efficient. Holmes took to the rope climbing immediately, as if he had done this a thousand times before.

As my mind and body bent to the task, my heart rate slowly returned to normal. So did my breathing. I mimicked Holmes' one hand at a time movement, although with less agility. Slowly I came to realise that the cable, rather than being taut and straight, was actually bowed. Once I understood that, I was able to modify my motions to be more effective.

"Of course!" I thought. "The cable is attached to something on the other end! Zeke's barge is keeping pace with whatever that is, and the bend in the rope is caused by the weight of the water as the cable is dragged through the blackness."

I should have been pleased with my ability to deduce the solution, but a sickening thought intruded. The cable we were dependent upon would snap as soon as the diamonds Holmes had placed against the propeller's shaft did their full measure of damage. With that sudden realisation, I quickened my pace. Soon I found myself nipping at my friend's heels, literally and figuratively.

I struggled to grab hold of Holmes' foot so I could warn him. When he turned 'round, I draped my left arm over the cable and locked it in place under my armpit. As I tapped the cable with my right hand, I drew my fisted hands together and twisted them down, as if breaking a twig in half, and again tapped the cable, after pointing back towards the barge. I repeated the pantomime several times.

Praying that Holmes understood my frantic gestures, I mouthed the words "move faster" when he shone the light in my face. Holmes' eyes went wide as he bobbed his head up and down, and without a moment's hesitation, he did as instructed.

Racing our way along the cable, I became aware we climbed an incline. Again, I quickly took its meaning. We had passed the center of the cable and were no longer heading away from the barge, but rather we were drawing closer to whatever was on the other end.

Frantically, I glanced back and saw, rather than felt, a slight tremor inching along the cable. The cable twitched and vibrated, transferring its tension into my gloved hands. I watched as Holmes yanked his hands off the line, removing them as though they had been shot with a bolt of electricity, only to regain his grip at the precise moment the cable began to run straight.

The cable vibrated wildly. It beat a froth of bubbles and went rigid. Holmes stopped his climb. I held on for dear life. Holmes pulled on the rope 'round my waist, and I drifted next to him. The eight-foot tether drooped lazily between us. Working quickly, Holmes tied a bowline round the cable and pulled my body against his. He demonstrated how to lock my arms round the cable, and as we secured ourselves, we nervously waited for whatever the Almighty had planned.

A low groan came from the direction we had just traveled. Turning to check out whether Holmes had heard the same noise, I was puzzled to see him looking in the *opposite* direction. The pressure of the water against our bodies, as we were being dragged and pummeled, was colossal. I thought that we would surely die!

The sound grew louder. It had to be coming from the barge. The shaft must have given way. Without any means of propulsion, the barge was buffeted by the crushing weight of the water even as it was being dragged behind something unknown.

Again, I turned towards Holmes, but he continued looking the other way. The gyrating cable, unable to withstand the tons of enormous stress placed upon it, snapped with the sound of a rifle's report. Fortunately, the cable broke about a hundred yards behind us. However, the resulting reaction whipped us through the water, as if we were flies being swatted by a horse's tail. Just as suddenly, we were pulled through the water in the opposite direction from where we'd come. Holmes untied the knot he'd made, and we resumed our hand-over-hand trek into the unknown.

Proceeding at a comfortable pace, I had the opportunity to calm myself, but my comfort was short-lived when a dark shape loomed up ahead! Holmes had seen it too, and he stopped dead in the water. Pointing at the immense shadow, he nodded his head. As he turned the lamp towards me, I was surprised to see him smiling. He pointed towards the shadowy bulk and pulled me along with him.

As we drew near, a shimmering form slowly took shape. It was mountainous, so large that it filled my limited field of vision. Approaching the hulk from the rear as we were, it was impossible to make note of any specific details. Then without warning, the huge shape changed direction and made a wide turn to the left.

There was another pause. The cable again took up its slack. This time it swung us into a straight line, so that we faced the front of the behemoth.

My mouth fell open in terror. My eyes blinked repeatedly as I tried to make sense of what I was seeing. Dead ahead was the sea monster! The very one that so many people had described in their reports!

The beast's stare—cold and dead—glowed red. Ethereal green-black forms flittered in and out of its two enormous eyes. The creature's snout was long, and it tapered to a spiraling point with large jagged scales running the length of both sides.

I fought a scream of terror. The cable suddenly changed direction once more. This time it swung us alongside the gigantic body of the monster. Desperately, I tugged on Holmes' suit. With an angry motion, he shrugged off my hand. My whole body went weak and I gasped in shock.

Then, surprisingly, Holmes pulled me right up to the glass window of his helmet. When the lamp illuminated his features, I realised he was speaking. It took a few tries, but I slowly understood what he was saying. "Everything's fine," he mouthed. "It's not a monster. It's another submarine!"

Holmes twisted around and shone the lamp, so that the beam illuminated the creature's dull, scaly body. My eyes followed the thread of light. At last I saw what Holmes had been searching for! At the very rear of the vessel was one word, lettered in gold: *Nautilus*!

After wrapping one arm around the cable to secure his position, my friend raised the flat board that dangled from a cord on his belt. Reaching into a hidden pocket of his diving suit, he withdrew a long, shiny item that resembled a candle. Next he scribbled on the board and held it up to my face plate.

"Going inside," he had written. "Follow me."

I nodded that I understood. He wiped the slate clean and wrote something else. Turning the slate towards me, he showed me these words: "Do as I do. Danger inside!!!"

I nodded. Holmes gestured with an open hand and I unfastened one of the two small crossbows from my belt. He wrapped the lanyard round his wrist and drew the cord tight against his gloves. He nodded for me to do the same. Once I had accomplished this, I watched as he drew the strings back and clipped them to the safety switch. I did the same. Holmes removed two arrows from his pocket. I hadn't seen him storing them on his person, but I was glad he had. Placing the arrows notched ends onto the strings, he locked them in place by an elastic catch. I followed his actions with my own crossbow and completed the task with little effort.

Grabbing me squarely by the shoulders, Holmes bobbed his head up and down. Raising one of the crossbows, he dramatically mimed the act of releasing the safety before firing the weapon. I nodded that I understood. "Be careful, my friend," he mouthed, his eyes searching mine in our dark underworld.

I nodded.

Holmes crawled along the cable with me close behind. The nearer we drew to the Nautilus, the more powerfully we were batted around by the force of the propeller wash. We struggled mightily to keep going. Yet every muscle in my body cried out with pain. The exertion had been overwhelming. But we were saved by the sudden way the cable dipped beneath the ship's hull. This moved us out of the direct currents caused by the engines. With renewed vigor, we pulled ourselves to the centre of the ship's underbelly. Holmes strapped his crossbow to his diving suit. I did the same.

Pointing to the metal handholds fixed to the monster's hull, Holmes released his grip on the cable. Free from all the security we had, Holmes swam away, dragging me with him. He kicked furiously and clasped onto the metal protrusions with both hands. I was still tethered to Holmes, so I swam towards my friend, but my strength had started to ebb. My limbs felt wooden and heavier than I could ever recall. I did not think I could go on.

Sensing that I was in trouble, Holmes released his grip on one of the rungs and pulled me forwards. And I, aware that he had little reserve left, did my best to assist his efforts. Even as I did so, I prepared myself to die. Surely, all was lost!

39

With a last herculean attempt, Holmes clutched my sleeve, the one without the crossbow, and pulled me through the water, guiding my hand until I felt my glove bump against the rung. Through his faceplate, I saw Holmes grimace in response to the strain. I could not let my good friend down! With renewed determination, I grasped the metal handhold. Seeing that I was secure, he gave me a pat on the shoulder.

We had only a few handholds yet to conquer until we reached the ship's diving well. A soft glow of light emanated from inside the Nautilus. Holmes gestured with his thumb, pointed to the ladder's rungs, and stepped onto the lowest one. Keeping his legs bent, he raised his head slowly until it broke the surface of the water. He placed a foot on one rung, then the next, and finally Holmes rose out of the water and disappeared. After a few tortured seconds, his hand appeared in the water and he waved me up.

I climbed up the ladder and out of the water before crawling over the lip of the well. Holmes helped me to my feet. Exhausted, I stooped over, dropping my crossbow and placing my hands on my knees as I attempted to catch my breath. I heard the snap of the clamps popping open as Holmes undid my helmet and removed it.

"Quiet," he whispered, pulling me with him as he scuttled along the wall. Our target was a large crate. Once we were behind it, we were hidden. "Get out of the diving suit and into those clothes over there." Holmes pointed to the uniforms hanging on wall hooks. We hurriedly dressed and stashed our diving suits and gear in an empty crate. Then we tossed a tarpaulin over it. Behind the crate, I found a pair of fresh stockings and an unusual looking pair of rubber-soled canvas shoes that fit my feet quite comfortably. I handed Holmes his crossbow as I tucked mine into the waistband of my trousers. He did the same. He'd also located a pistol and appropriated it. That went into one of his pockets.

"Are you all right?" I asked. I was embarrassed that my incompetence had taken such a horrible toll on my friend.

"I'm fine," he replied. "How about you—are you all right?"

"Yes," I replied sullenly. "I'm just sorry to cause you..."

"Come now, Watson, we're here. We've made it and we're alive. That's all that matters."

"Speaking of here, did I read the ship's name correctly? Is this the Nautilus? Like in the book."

"That it is. This is the ship built by Jules Verne. According to the Bard, he plans to use it to fire upon Her Majesty's fleet after they transfer the young Prince. The barge might also have some firepower, but I doubt it was built to attack another ship."

"From what I saw, all of its weaponry was committed to saving herself," I agreed, as I looked around. Whereas the Stratford-Upon-Avon looked as if it had been built from salvaged parts, the Nautilus was a thing of beauty. She was sleek, fast, and capable of plumbing the depths of the oceans, if Verne's books were to be believed. I could not help but wonder if the actual ship had been patterned after the fictional submarine or if the fictional submarine had been patterned after this ship. "I never imagined that it was real. I thought it was just a writer's fantasy! What came first? The story or the ship?"

"I don't know, and we haven't the time to discuss the matter," Holmes said. "Right now, we have to worry about who's running this ship."

Holmes paused, listening to the sounds of the oncoming footsteps. He peered around the corner of the crate and raised the crossbow. After a few seconds, the sounds receded. Breathing a sigh of relief, he lowered the crossbow. In a hushed voice, he asked, "Did you by any chance read the novel?"

"Which one?"

"The one about the Nautilus, of course. Did you read it?"

"No, I can't say that I have. That book was all the rage years back, but I'm afraid fantastic stories are not my cup of tea," I said.

Holmes found my answer amusing. After a few seconds, he turned serious. "Watson, listen to me carefully. We must move forwards. We can't allow Zeke's plan to succeed. He can't sink those ships from the Royal Navy and murder all of those men. Not to mention the young Prince."

"But the Frenchmen in the other three boats are pirates! We must allow Zeke's men to blow up those ships. After all, what about our ships that they sank?" I replied, surprised by Holmes' misplaced loyalty.

Sherlock Holmes clucked disapprovingly. "My immediate concerns lie with Her Majesty's Fleet and Her gallant men. If Zeke is allowed to blow up the French ships, a war will follow. I trust the British warships to take care of themselves, but another war between England and France will cause all sorts of bloodshed. And the conflict could spread to the entire continent. Do you understand what I'm saying?"

"Of course, I do, Holmes." I sighed. "It's just the old warhorse in me. I hate seeing those pirates sail away with our gold and our munitions. That aside, I'm with you, no matter what."

His questioning glance troubled me.

"No matter what!" I repeated, forcefully.

Holmes nodded.

Although his prodding seemed unnecessary, I understood my friend's hesitation to believe my resolve. Having seen battle and its gory aftermath firsthand, I have no desire to repeat the experience. But Holmes feels differently. It's always been his way to take measure of a man's heart. He observes the troops and their leaders keenly as events unfurl.

Despite my declaration of unswerving fealty and commitment to the cause, the undeniable truth was that we were at the mercy of fate's often whimsical nature. More than likely, we would die here, a lonely death at the bottom of the sea.

"Are you ready?" asked Holmes. He patted the pistol in his pocket.

"Ready." I removed my weapon from my waistband and handed the second crossbow to Holmes. He followed pointed his lethal crossbow straight ahead of us.

With our weapons drawn and half-expecting at any moment to be found out, we crept towards the doorway. Thankfully, we were able to enter the nearest corridor unobserved. Taking opposite sides of the hallway, we inched our way slowly forwards with our backs pressed flat against the walls. As we came even with a door, Holmes gestured for me to turn the handle and peer inside. I shook my head vigorously and motioned for him to keep going. Anger flashed across his face, as he sidled up next to me. "What's the matter?" he whispered nervously, staring down the corridor.

"Why don't we keep moving forwards and do what we came here for?" I responded in hushed tones.

"Because," Holmes replied stiffly, "I do not wish to fight a battle on two fronts. If we fail to check the compartments for occupants, the possibility arises that someone within may exit and sound the alarm. Then we'll have the enemy forwards and aft. We'll be sitting ducks, caught in the middle."

"All right, Holmes. Have it your way." With my free hand, I pressed down on the handle and edged the door open whilst standing to one side. Holmes pointed his crossbow through the narrow opening on the hinged side. Once satisfied, he craned his neck to look through the aperture. Finally, he placed his palm on the door and pushed it wide open. Holmes took one last look down the corridor before entering the cabin.

"Stay here," he whispered. His eyes were wide with heightened anticipation. "If you hear anything, signal me. I'll be but a moment."

True to his word, after disappearing behind the door, he exited the cabin a few seconds later. His face was clouded with disappointment.

"Nothing at all," he grumbled. "All quiet?"

I nodded. We moved cautiously to the next cabin, holding our crossbows at the ready. This cabin was on the right side. I reached for the handle to repeat our previous movements, but Holmes' hand wrapped round mine before I could exert any downward pressure. I stopped immediately, feeling my pulse quickening. Holmes' nostrils twitched, as he tested the air. Pressing his highly disciplined nose against the door frame, he sniffed it. He smiled and pressed his ear flat against the door.

"Two men," he mouthed. "Heavy smokers."

Holmes leaned back, resting the crown of his head against the wall and closing his eyes. Feeling exposed and certain that at any moment we would be seen or heard, I could only watch and wait as he mulled over the situation.

"Wait here," Holmes commanded as he handed me his crossbow.

Before I could voice my objections, Holmes took the gun out of his pocket, ran down the corridor, and disappeared into the cabin he had previously searched.

A crewman at the far end of the ship walked into view. I was standing next to the wall. My heart sank. I could only pray that my uniform had transformed me into someone wholly expected and not an intruder. I shielded the crossbows by tucking them against my far side and pretended to study the nearby door. Preoccupied as the crewman was with a stack of papers in his hands, he moved across the width of the corridor. Without ever raising his eyes, he disappeared behind the wall on my left.

Hearing the hiss of my own breath as I exhaled, I gazed down at my hands. I was startled to see that both crossbows had the safety catches off! How easily I could have killed that strolling seaman! I quickly secured the catches.

"Good job, Watson," Holmes whispered in my ear. "You did not catch his attention." Holmes was not empty-handed. He carried a silver serving tray with a white cloth draped over it. "Tuck away the weapons," he ordered me.

As I jammed the crossbows into my waistband, he placed the tray on my shoulder and instructed me on how to enter the room.

"Be sure to enter so that the tray is the first thing they see rather than your face," Holmes said before he nodded at the door. "Every second is critical. You must provide me with enough time to assess the situation and act. Ready?"

"Ready," I replied, smiling determinedly. Holmes took one last look down the corridor both ways, and exhaled deeply.

Tapping on the chamber door with the butt of the pistol he

had purloined, Holmes turned the handle and pushed the door open. I hid my face behind the tray and entered the room. "Dinner, gentlemen," I called, disguising my voice. By the time I had fully entered the room, the two men were rising from their bunks.

"What the...?" I heard one of them begin, just as Holmes' sap knocked the first man to the floor. The second man, though slightly quicker than the first, fared no better. Holmes whirled. On his way round, he once again used his sap to good purpose. The second man went down.

40

Holmes tossed me a length of rope and a length of torn rag. He bound and gagged one seaman while I did the same with the other.

"What's next, Holmes?" I asked.

"We mustn't let anyone find these fellows," he responded, hoisting one of the men onto his shoulder. I did the same with the second. Seeing that there was no one in the corridor, we ran back to the diving room and tossed the bodies into a crate. We then used a short length of rope to tie the crate shut.

We returned to the empty compartment. Sherlock Holmes walked to the bedside table and lifted a still smoldering cigarette out of the ashtray. Putting it to his lips, he drew on it. Inhaling deeply, he blew the smoke out of his nostrils and permitted little wisps of grey to filter through his puckered lips.

"Curious," he said, rolling the cigarette in his fingers and studying its glowing tip, "a new species to add to my tobacco listings: seaweed. Quite satisfying, really."

"We were fortunate, Holmes," I said, bringing his attention back to the matter. "A seaman crossed from one side of the corridor to the other. He could have seen me as he walked by."

"But he didn't," he replied. "Fortune favours the bold." Holmes grabbed the ashtray and stubbed out the cigarette. Rising and turning to face me, the great detective shrugged his shoulders. "Do you have any suggestions as to how we should proceed?"

"None," I replied sadly.

Holmes collapsed in a chair and ran his fingers through his hair. With his head bowed, he massaged the back of his neck in nervous agitation. Gradually, he leaned back, stretching his neck to allow the back of his head to rest on the wooden chair.

The result of achieving such an awkward position was that the skin of his neck was stretched taut, and his Adam's apple bobbed, as he clucked his tongue inside his mouth. His eyes stared vacantly at the grill work of the ceiling. He continued this most strenuous stretching exercise, until he had the front legs of the chair off the floor as he leaned further back. Then with a thud, the chair returned to its normal upright position. Holmes proceeded to bend over and hug his legs. Exhaling loudly, he remained in this position for some time. I can only assume these strange gyrations are the result of a book he's been reading on the practices of swamis in India.

In a matter of seconds, Holmes rose from his chair with an obvious air of determined purpose. "It's time to put it to them, Watson. Let's see what they're up to."

"But how? We can't just walk in and ask them!"

"True enough, but we can find out what's happening, just the same."

Walking about the compartment with his eyes examining the ceiling, Holmes, found what he was looking for. He pointed to a nearly invisible hinge in the ceiling's grill, near the corner of the room. Standing on a chair, he slowly moved his fingers away from the hinge in search of the release that he knew had to be nearby. Holmes' hand hesitated over a recessed lattice, and he smiled down on my upturned face. He gripped the camouflaged piece between thumb and forefinger and applied a slight pressure. The panel swung down.

Standing on his toes, he raised his head above the grid and into the blackness above. "Hullo," he said, retracting his head back into the light. "It's just as I suspected, Watson. If you recall, the barge's floor was a series of grids that concealed the pipes, cables, hoses, and so on, underneath and out of the way."

Holmes stepped down off the chair. "This ship has it reversed. Everything is in the ceiling and covered by a grid. All we need do is climb up and into the gridwork, and we can roam the ship, undisturbed and unobserved."

"That sounds too easy, Holmes," I said, gazing up at the opening. "What do we do once we're up there? Your plan sounds vague at best, and if we are found out, we've nowhere to go."

Holmes was about to snipe at my caution but thought better of it. "It's the best we can hope for, but we won't wander aimlessly. If we remain here, we run the risk of being captured. Surely, these two men will be missed in time. Help me straighten up this room, then we'll be on our way."

We erased all signs of our deed and climbed up into the ceiling. The crawl space reeked of machine oil and stale odours, but what was most worrisome to me was the possibility of our crashing through the ceiling and into the hands of the enemy.

"Grab hold of my feet," Holmes whispered, as he dangled back down into the room. While I held his shoes, he reached down for the chair we had used and moved it into its original position, which was away from the opening. After taking a last look round the room for any signs of our occupancy, Holmes shimmied back into the grill work. He pulled the lattice panel over the duct and locked it securely.

"All right," Holmes whispered. "Stay close behind and be

sure to stay on the beams. Under no circumstances should you lean on the grids, understand?"

I nodded. Of course, I did. The beams could support us, the grids might not. Though it was dark, there was enough light filtering in from below that we could see each other clearly. We crawled along. I found that with each movement, the pattern of the grids' shadow moved across our faces, as if it were a living and a never-ending series of puzzle pieces, racing to keep abreast of a changing landscape. With my active imagination, I found it somewhat disquieting.

We moved inexorably forwards at a snail's pace. We two—our bodies sprawled, our hands and feet guided by the beam—crawled ever onward. As we traversed the inner veins and skeleton of the ship, I marveled at its complexity. But fearing to let my mind wander, I recalled that the purpose of this monster was to sink Her Majesty's Fleet and bring England into war with France. That spurred me to action.

Holmes stopped and waved me forwards, putting his finger to his lips and cautioning me to silence. As I crept forwards, I could hear voices coming from below where my friend was now crouched. I leaned forwards and stared down into the cabin.

"I don't like it," said one of the men who was out of my view, but apparently not out of Holmes', for my friend was following the man with his eyes, as the fellow paced the floor below.

"What don't you like?" retorted another voice. "Jaeger said that as soon as we make the Fleet strike its colours, we can have anything we want."

"But, what if...?"

"What if, nothing!" the voice interrupted, carping angrily at the other. "We got our orders. We attack the British ships, get 'em to surrender, and take all the plunder. Then we climb aboard the barge and blow up this monster. Don't forget, that old fool, Captain Verne, already saw his sister and watched us pour that laudanum down her gullet. He knows that if he don't do what Jaeger wants, she'd a dead woman for sure."

"Argh," the other replied, disgustedly, "I don't want to be lookin' after her, while you gets all the gold. What's the use? I should do her in now and get it over wid."

"Ha! But she's a lovely girl. Don't see many of them, do ya?"

"No, but who needs the trouble? She put up a rare fight, she did. Ain't worth the trouble, if you ask me. Besides, having a woman on a ship is bad luck. We need to get rid of her, throw her off the side of the ship and be done with her. Besides, I want to get my share of that treasure Jaeger promised."

"That's me ol' mate talkin' again! Right, bash the skirt, and have done with it. Don't matter to me none whether she's the loveliest bit of jam or not. Go ahead and get the job done. I'll wait here. Do it right, and come meet me back here. Knock twice when you're finished, and I'll let ya in."

Holmes and I looked at each other. Even in the dark, we could see the shock in each other's eyes. This brutal turn of events had alarmed us. A woman here on this ship was about to be murdered!

"Wait here," Holmes whispered, hearing the door open below. "Have you your sap? And your crossbow? Good. Give me mine, please. Keep an eye on the man in the cabin. If he tries to leave, stop him. I'll take care of our other friend."

Holmes inched his way backwards and disappeared into the shadows without a sound.

After shifting my position, I readied my crossbow and pointed it through the grid at the man pacing below. Keeping the pirate in sight was a difficult task, for he would wander in and out of sight as he walked about the cabin. Finally, he perched himself on the end of his bunk, and I held him in my sight, pointing my *fléchette* at his lower leg. I could not bring myself to kill him in cold blood, but if I crippled him with the crossbow, I could finish the job with the sap and knock him out cold.

Although it seemed as if hours had passed since Holmes disappeared, in actuality only a few minutes went by. But I drew back in fear when I heard the two distinct taps on the door below. I felt a horrible hollow feeling in the pit of my stomach. The man had returned! Holmes couldn't save the poor woman's life! And the rogue was now knocking on the door to gloat over his deed.

"It's about time!" said the man I'd been watching as he walked out of view. "Keep ya knickers on." I listened as he undid the lock. I cursed my helplessness, as he opened the door. "Well," he said, "that didn't take—" But his voice ended with a muffled groan.

41

My finger tensed on the trigger, as the man in the cabin below me staggered backwards into view. Holmes had taken the sap to the sailor's head and knocked him unconscious. Deftly, Holmes used rope and a makeshift gag to keep the fellow under our power and silent.

Holmes glanced up to where I was crouching and whispered, "Watson, go straight along the beams for another twenty or so feet. You'll see the open panel. You will find a woman there who requires your medical expertise. I'll join you as soon as I get rid of this man. Now, hurry. There's no time to lose."

I followed Holmes' instructions and crawled to the open panel. I lowered myself into the confines of a small, dimly lit cabin. A woman was lying on her stomach on a bed with her face turned to the wall. Her hair was undone, so it fell over her features like a thick veil of dark silk. I immediately took her pulse. It was a tad fast, but strong. From the rise and fall of her back, I could see her breathing was regular. Her skin was cold and a bit clammy to the touch. On the bedside table next to her was a brown glass bottle half-filled with laudanum. The label did not share the patient's name.

Holmes walked casually into the room. "Tend to her," he said.

"Without my kit, there's nothing I can do, Holmes. It's plain to see that she's been abused by some drug, but her heart is strong and her pulse, though rapid, is steady. The best I can hope for is that she'll come out of it on her own."

"All right," Holmes whispered, "but if she comes to, make sure she remains quiet. We don't want her to scream and give us away."

"Right," I replied, taking pity on the woman. "Perhaps I can rouse her slowly."

I found a glass and a tumbler of water. Setting it on the floor, I propped myself up next to the woman on the bed so I could move her more easily. Holding her by the shoulders, I rolled her over. As I did, her dark hair fell away from her features. Holmes gasped.

"Maria Morel!" he said.

I was equally shocked.

"By Jove, at least we'll be able to tie up one end of this tangled thread. Right, Watson?"

"I hope so, Holmes," I said.

Slowly Mrs. Morel became lucid. I asked her if she knew her name.

"Maria," she mumbled.

"And where are you?"

"I-I-I am with Jules, my brother, on his ship." Mrs. Morel buried her head in her hands. "Oh, no! What have I done! My brother! His life is at risk! Jaeger has him!"

I turned to Holmes. "Jules Verne? The author who wrote..." and then I stopped. I gawped at Holmes. He nodded and a wry smile twitched his lips. Inwardly, I grumbled as I suspected Holmes had known who this lady was all along.

Holmes took my hesitation as a chance to intervene. In his

most cordial voice he said, "We are honoured to see you again, Mrs. Morel, or perhaps I should call you Maria Verne?"

She sighed. "As you wish. I don't care."

As usual, Holmes had a plan. "I want you, Watson, to escort, Missus—"

"Miss Verne will do." Her voice was brusque.

"Do you know if any of the crew is loyal to your brother?" Holmes asked.

"Yes, five men. They are being held captive in a room, but if they hear that my brother is safe, they will overpower their guard and join us. They will be enough to safely pilot the ship. Jaeger keeps most of his men near him in the control room."

"Good," Holmes said. "I'll be right above you two in the ductwork, and if my plan goes right, above Jaeger. When you hear my signal, you must strike down the two of Jaeger's men who are closest to you. That will leave just one more, plus Jaeger, their Captain. Ma'am, it is too much for me to ask of you. I know this is a tremendous burden for you to bear, but I'm afraid there is no other choice. And Miss Verne? Should the opportunity present itself, it may fall on your shoulders to eliminate the third man. Or at the very least, cripple him. I say this because Watson and I overheard their plans. You are to be disposed of." Holmes handed the woman his crossbow and three *fléchettes*.

"Are you mad, Holmes?" I protested, feeling shocked by his request. "Surely, you're not asking this delicate woman to do this? There has to be another way!"

I turned my eyes to the woman. I expected to see her similarly disgusted by my friend's plan. But she surprised me. She flashed a determined smile whilst narrowing her eyes and nodding silently. "*D'accord.* I shall do what I must, Doctor. My brother's life is at stake, and I will not let him die because I am lacking in courage. There are four entrances to the control room. Jaeger has locked three of them. This hall ends at the only entrance that's unlocked."

"Good to know. Keep your weapon hidden in the folds of your skirt," said Holmes. Turning to me, he said, "Please make note of the safety latch. Watson? Are you prepared? Make it look as if she is your prisoner and you are marching her to the Captain's helm. Miss Verne? Let me loosely bind your hands. You'll be able to slip out of the rope easily, but this might improve your chance of deception." Holmes wrapped the rope loosely around her hands and she held the ends together.

I had my sap and my crossbow, so I nodded and asked, "What's the signal?"

"You'll know," Holmes replied, turning his eyes to me. "Are you ready? Don't forget—do not leave this room for thirty seconds. I must have enough time to get into position."

"Understood," I said.

Holmes climbed up into the crawl space. After a few seconds, his face appeared over the opening, as he sought out my eyes. Then he was gone.

As soon as he disappeared from view, I counted to thirty. Maria Verne twisted her hair into a knot and bound it into a bun at the back of her neck. Even disheveled, she was glorious. Reaching my goal of thirty all too quickly, I faced Miss Verne. "Are you ready?" I asked, feeling my pulse quicken.

"Oui."

I opened the door and checked the corridor. Seeing that it was clear, I sucked in my breath and looked to my weapons. I found it strangely exhilarating that we were about to confront the enemy full-on.

I allowed Miss Verne to position herself in front of me. I rested one hand on her shoulder as though frog-marching her. Without hesitating, she stepped across the threshold and into the corridor. I followed her with my head slightly bowed. The clatter and clanging of the machinery drowned out any possibility of the crew hearing my wildly beating heart. All along the corridor, the seafarers were working on various projects. Their backs were towards us. Their duties made them too preoccupied to pay us any notice. Chancing a look over Miss Verne's shoulder, I glanced ahead. About twenty feet from us, there was an open door, leading to the control room. Clusters of men in navy shirts and matching trousers stood around a chart table.

Thankfully, they were facing away from us. We escaped their notice because they appeared to be listening to someone who was hidden by the bulk of their bodies. Suddenly, two of the men shifted and I saw the Captain. Jaeger! The illustration in the newspaper had been accurate. There was no mistaking who the man was. He was the one they were listening to!

Miss Verne stiffened slightly and nodded her head to the right imperceptibly. At first, I did not understand the import of her signal. Then I noticed a man sitting in the shadows. He was bound hand and foot and tied to the periscope tube. His head was tipped down.

"My brother," Miss Verne whispered so that I would hear.

I was shocked by her revelation and even more worried by the calmness with which she spoke. I whispered to her, "Keep moving. We must get closer."

A single nod was returned by the courageous woman.

"Still no contact with the barge?" Jaeger asked his men, as we drew near enough to hear.

"Nothing, sir," came the reply. "Something must have fouled the dwarf's engine. If we had known in time, we could have stopped to reduce the drag, but the cable snapped, I'm afraid."

"All right, thank you. As soon as Monsieur Verne explains the guidance of his torpedoes, we'll bring the Nautilus to periscope depth. Perhaps Zeke will have the acumen to do the same. Where is Mr. Klarner with the woman?"

Miss Verne and I had arrived at the outer edge of the circle of three officers, just as Jaeger questioned our whereabouts. I managed to position myself so that her head blocked Jaeger's view of mine.

"Ah, there you are," Jaeger said, noticing us for the first time. Fortunately, he focused his attention on my faux captive. "Miss Verne, if you would be kind enough to take your place by your brother's side, we will dispense with the unpleasantries straightaway. Stand to the right of him, please." Jaeger pointed to a small dark space next to Mr. Verne.

She took the spot he indicated, holding the ropes loosely in her hands the whole time. I kept my head lowered, but I noticed her right hand had dropped the rope and was moving beneath the fold of her skirt. Suddenly I understood! She was readying the crossbow! She would kill her captors if she had the opportunity!

I stepped to the side, positioning myself for a clear shot at Jaeger, and recalled that Holmes had instructed me to kill Jaeger's men. However, I thought that if I had the chance and took on Jaeger, the other three would panic without their leader.

"Monsieur Verne, I ask you one more time. How do your torpedoes work? Explain the guidance system to me." Jaeger sounded irked and his small eyes shone with ferocity.

Jules Verne lifted his upper lip in a sneer. *"Non."*

This infuriated Jaeger. He bellowed, "Are you willing to die for what you believe in?" It was clear that Jaeger's question was not of a rhetorical nature. He expected an answer.

"Oui," came the reply, full of anger.

"I see. I believe you, but are you willing to watch your sister die in your place?"

"*Oui,*" was the answer and it was delivered with a smile.

42

Miss Verne flinched at her brother's cruel tone and I, being completely unprepared for his answer, felt my breath catch in my throat. My reaction caused one of the men to notice me.

At that very instant, a loud clanging noise was heard, far forwards of where we were. Reflexively, everyone turned towards the sound. I raised my weapon in that direction. A ceiling panel came swinging down and crashed violently into the back of Jaeger's head, sending him sprawling to the floor. Above the din of confusion, Miss Verne fired her weapon and pinned a guard's foot to the floor. I let loose of one of my own arrows and followed her example with the second seaman. Once my man was immobile, I used my sap to bring him down, flat on his face.

Holmes dropped from the blackness above, landing on his feet. With his sap, he knocked down the last of Jaeger's men. Miss Verne hurriedly tossed her rope around the man she had pinned to the decking and with surprising industry tied him to a post. Whipping a handkerchief out of her pocket, she gagged him. Only then did I realise he'd been whimpering.

When our work was done, we faced each other in shocked silence. Our plan had worked! The quickness that had exploded in a fraction of a moment held us spellbound.

Holmes recovered first. Walking over to the prone figure of Jaeger, Holmes turned him face up with the toe of his shoe. "Is everyone all right with you, Watson?" my friend asked, bending down and tying Jaeger up with a length of rope.

"Yes," I managed.

Miss Verne ran to her brother and untied him—and, to my surprise, lovingly embraced the man who just moments earlier coldly offered to sacrifice her life. "Jules!" she said as she threw her arms around his neck. "I am so sorry that I dragged you into this!"

Monsieur Verne jumped to his feet and moved past her. He unlocked the remaining three doors into the Control Room before speaking into some sort of sound system. *"Attendez!"* he shouted and then he told them that the mutiny had been quelled. As he explained that he had regained control of the ship, crewmen came running. He ordered his crew to disperse and go about the duties of inspecting the ship for other intruders.

"How can you tell which ones are your crew?" I asked.

Miss Verne gave me the faintest of brave smiles. "I chose their uniforms myself. They are the men in the striped shirts, the navy trousers, and the flat caps with a red kerchief at the throat."

A particularly imposing sailor arrived and spoke to Monsieur Verne in urgent but hushed tones. At the conclusion of the conversation, the seaman dragged the groggy Jaeger to his feet and shoved him rudely down the hallway we'd used earlier.

"Monsieur Holmes, Dr. Watson, please follow me," Verne said. "We have much to prepare for."

Verne was an austere-looking gentleman, with a receding hairline made more obvious by a large forehead. His hair color had once been black, but now was threaded with gray and white. His brows were still black as coal. They met at the center of his face and undulated in wild abandon over darkly penetrating, intelligent eyes. Monsieur Verne sported a beard and mustache showing signs of maturing into salt-and-pepper. His features couldn't help but convey an eerily intense expression.

His bearing and demeanor declared Verne to be a man whom I would have avoided at any cost. Under normal circumstances at least. Without regard to civility, he spun on his heels and left us standing there. One would have thought he could have spared a few words of appreciation for freeing him and his sister. Certainly, he should have asked after his sister's welfare. But he did none of this, and I was shocked. Glancing at me, Miss Verne pleaded with her eyes to excuse his coldness, before following her brother.

Sherlock Holmes squinted after them and shrugged his shoulders. "Come, Watson," he said, dramatically. "We have been summoned."

"Tell me, Holmes," I whispered, as we followed the disparate siblings. "Would he have let her die under such terrible circumstances?"

"No. He may be poor excuse for a brother, but he knew I was above him."

"Oh? And how did he know that?"

"Miss Verne signaled him with her eyes. From your vantage point, you couldn't observe her, but I was in the perfect position. She's a remarkable woman, Watson."

Before I could respond in the affirmative, we entered the Captain's suite. There we found Verne sitting at a massive ornate desk. Miss Verne was nowhere in sight.

"Ma soeuror est malade. Ce n'est rien de grave," said, the man, stonily.

Recalling my early days of language courses during my schooling, I struggled with the translation. Then it came to me what Verne had said. He'd just said his sister was sick, but we shouldn't worry about it. "I am a doctor!" I responded, a little too harshly. "Perhaps if I could see your sister, I may be of help."

Non!" came his angry reply. Monsieur Verne's face went red with the threat of a tantrum. *"Ce n'est rien de grave!"* For emphasis, he pounded his fist on the desk's surface.

"You ungrateful fool!" Holmes glowered at the fiery man. "We nearly died saving you from your folly! And we risked our lives to save your sister. But you don't seem to care! You and your cursed ship were about to commit an unspeakable crime!"

Monsieur Verne jumped out of his chair, kicking it and propelling it against the wall in a fit of anger. The Captain's face played a symphony of emotions before eventually settling on one—despair. *"C'est plus qu'un crime, c'est une faute,"* he responded with a ragged edge to his voice.

"What do you mean worse than a crime? What mistake?" asked Holmes, translating instantly.

Verne collected himself and righted his chair. Gesturing with his hand, he motioned us to take up the chairs that faced his desk. "This ship—" he replied to Holmes' question, "—it was a mistake to ever create it. Twice the Nautilus has brought us to the brink of a calamitous war. It was built for science, not for fighting! And now! *Je vous prie de m'oxcuser*! I must apologize to you for my—how did you phrase it? Ah yes, my folly. But it is not over. Do you accept my apology?"

I ached to ask what part his sister played in all of this, but some instinct told me that was a tale for another time. If we lived that long.

Holmes nodded impatiently. *"Yes, yes, but revenons a' nos moutons."*

Again a momentary flash of anger crossed Verne's face but it quickly dissipated. *"Ainsi soit-il*—so be it. Of course, you're correct. Apologies can wait. At least, the Nautilus is under our control, although the barge is still out there. And that should be your primary concern. What the dwarf doesn't know is that the barge is in all actuality a bomb. I have made sure there are enough explosives built into her to destroy the entire fleet. So you see, gentlemen, all of your actions have led to failure—it's all the same."

"But," I said, "the barge is loose. She's no longer tethered to the Nautilus."

Holmes sat slouched in his chair, making a steeple of his fingers. He was deep in thought.

"It does not matter," replied Monsieur Verne. "The cable is not what controlled the explosives. It was nothing but the means for the crew to travel back and forth from the Nautilus and the barge without getting lost. Jaeger installed it. That was before I knew of his treachery! I take it that that is how you arrived here—by following the cable?"

I nodded.

Holmes asked, "What triggers the explosives on the barge?"

"Percussion. When the charges placed on the last ship detonate, a concussive wave will result. The ensuing shock wave, spreading outwards from the dying ship, will apply a calculated amount of pressure on a series of plungers built into the hull of the barge. These plungers, collapsing in on themselves, will pierce a thin diaphragm, creating an electrical charge. Once the circuit is open, the entire barge will explode."

"What kind of man are you?" I said with a scowl. "You are willing to kill untold numbers of men, for what? Did Jaeger promise you gold?"

"Not now, Watson!" Holmes snapped. "We'll leave the recriminations to the Almighty."

"Think of me what you will," Verne responded, indignantly. "But they had my sister! Despite what you have recently seen, Monsieur Holmes and Docteur Watson, she means everything to me. She is in this predicament because I demanded that she come with me to meet your Queen. Her Majesty was very taken with the book I wrote and requested an audience. Once that loathsome Prince Bertie saw Maria, he would not leave her alone. He wooed her, made promises, and broke her heart. The loss of his affection made her mad with grief. Since then, she has done things to get back at the Crown—and her mistakes are my fault, I fear."

43

Holmes plunged ahead. "Are we safe? How many men did Jaeger bring aboard? We trussed up two in the diving room and two who held your sister. That's before we met you in the control room."

"Then I believe you have almost all of them. They are of no consequence," said Verne. "My men are loyal to me. Now that my life and that of my sister are no longer at risk, my seafarers will dispose of Jaeger's thugs."

"Let me see if I understand you correctly, Monsieur," said Holmes. "The barge will detonate when a ship on the surface explodes. Those were the charges attached by the crew members who work for Zeke, the Bard. Am I right?"

"I did not see the devices," said Verne. "*S'il vous plait,* describe them to me."

Holmes did, estimating their sizes and mentioning their magnetic manner of attachment.

"Mais, oui," said Verne. "One of them alone is not enough to cause the sort of percussion to set off the barge. But any two of them? *C'est fini."*

Holmes frowned. "I assume they would be set for a predetermined time?"

"Yes. I believe the Bard calculated approximately how long it would take the Royal Navy to set sail and arrive in these waters. He has his spies, *n'est pas?* A note with news of your kidnapping was delivered to the Prime Minister along with a separate message regarding the Queen's Grandson. The young Prince was taken off of the Clarity with an escort for his safety."

"But how?" I asked. "How was he removed?"

"One of my trusted men left the barge using diving gear. He boarded the Clarity and used another invention of mine, an inflatable boat. You see, Jaeger removed all the lifeboats from his vessels so that none of his men could cut and run. But this invention of mine starts as the size of a small trunk and expands. Once you get it into the water, you can row to your destination. That escape from the Clarity allowed ample time for the discussion of the note's contents with the proper naval departments so the Prime Minister could issue orders for the Fleet to intercept us. The arrival of the Fleet has been calculated. The last ship in the convoy is the Collier, and it will explode in four hours' time."

"To be so precise is impossible," I argued. "If the Fleet doesn't arrive in that four hours timeframe, then that barge will explode and kill the Bard's crew and those on the ship."

"I wish it were so," Verne replied, grimly. "That variable, of course, was taken into account. Jaeger's trio of ships—the Collier, the Curzon, and the Clarity—will maneuver into position to intercept the Fleet, one hour before the rendezvous. According to the plan, Jaeger's three ships will allow themselves to be seen. They will run for a little while—always losing ground, mind you. At precisely one hour after being observed, the ships will stop all engines and allow the Fleet to move in. It is then that the explosives will detonate."

"All those men will die!" I said.

Holmes took a deep breath and clapped a hand on my shoulder. "Remember, old friend, if they were brought back to England, there's little doubt they would be hanged for piracy or thrown in jail for the rest of their lives. Perhaps it seems heartless, but I would rather go out like a lighted match, wouldn't you?"

He had a point. But I couldn't stop, "What about the Queen's Fleet? We must save those men. They are loyal to the Crown."

Rather than answer, Holmes said, "Four hours doesn't give us much time. Oh, one more question. Where will the barge be positioned when the Fleet arrives?"

"The barge is to be one hundred meters on the port side and amidships of the triggering ship, the Collier, the last ship in the line-up. That's the one with the six explosive devices on the hull, thanks to the Bard's men," said Verne. "The barge will be precisely sixty feet below the surface. Why do you ask?"

Holmes ignored the question, drumming his fingers on the desk. Speaking more to himself than to us, he muttered, "I must find a way of disarming those explosives on the Collier, and a way to stop the barge from moving close to its target."

"Impossible," argued Verne. "Even if you could get to the Collier, the explosives are not accessible to you. They are attached to the outside of the hull beneath the water line. As you described them to me, they are magnetized. And the only way to stop the explosion is to physically turn the timers off. Also, there is no way of knowing where the barge is right now. We can't risk moving the Nautilus alongside Jaeger's fleet. One of his ships might hit the barge and cause it to explode. That's why we have gone lower than the barge can go. We can only hope to pick up any survivors after it is all over. There is nothing else we can do."

"There is something we can do!" I said. "We have to turn the Nautilus around and intercept the Fleet. They have to be warned that they're sailing into a trap."

"Good thinking, Watson!" Holmes smiled, clapping his hands together. "Monsieur, how fast will the Nautilus go?"

"She is much faster than the barge. She will do twenty knots submerged. We can cut the distance in half, and I..." Verne paused, with a curious look upon his face.

Holmes and I glanced at each other, realising that the engines had stopped. In fact, we hadn't moved for some time.

"Why are the engines stopped?" I asked.

Surprised by my question, Verne leaned back in his chair and felt the wall for vibrations. "This is impossible," he yelled as he jumped out of his chair.

"What is?" I asked.

"There is nothing, nothing at all! This is impossible!"

"Sir!" Holmes said loudly and firmly. "Will you tell us what is wrong?"

Before he could respond, one of the crew burst into the suite. It was the same imposing sailor who had taken Jaeger away. His navy-and-white striped shirt was stained red with blood. His head had a nasty gash. After an animated and whispered conversation with Verne, the sailor looked at us sheepishly and left the room.

Verne's face had turned the colour of watered milk when he walked back to his desk. Shaking his head, he collapsed into his chair. *"Laissez-moi tranquille."*

"My good man," Holmes chided, scornfully, "now is not the time to be left alone. What did that man tell you? Why aren't the engines running? Come on, out with it!"

"All hope is lost! Jaeger has escaped the ship! He killed one of my men and accosted the other. That is why my crew member was bruised and covered in blood. I am told that Jaeger has also damaged the engines. One of the diving suits is missing, so he must be out there! There is no hope of warning the Fleet!"

44

Verne's news rocked Holmes. I, too, felt positively ill.

"What incredible incompetence," I spat out.

"Never mind, Watson," Holmes remarked. "It is of no importance. We should be..."

"Of no importance?" I asked, shocked at his acceptance. "Are you mad? What about the Fleet? They're sailing into a trap, and you say it is of no importance!"

"What I was about to say," snarled Holmes, "is that we waste an extremely limited commodity to go about casting blame—I mean time, of course. Since there's no way of warning the Fleet, then we must make sure the pirates fail in their mission."

"But Monsieur, the ship..." Verne began.

"Take me to the Engine Room," said Holmes.

Verne led the way while Sherlock Holmes and I followed closely. The great detective's face was a harbinger of doom as he asked, "Monsieur Verne, Jaeger spoke of mysterious torpedoes of some sort. Would you be so kind as to explain what he was talking about?"

"Certainement," Verne responded. He launched into an intense conversation with Holmes. The men came to a pause as Verne opened the door to the engine room. Judging by the size of the two mammoth engines, the compartment should have been an area of intense heat and deafening noises, but the only sounds were the swearing of the men, as they attempted to repair the damage Jaeger had caused.

Upon seeing us, an oil-blackened man of undetermined age came forwards, wiping his grease-stained hands on an equally dirty rag. The sailor smiled good-humouredly. "Nuttin' we can't fix," he said, looking at us all. "It'll take some doin', but she'll be hummin' her favorite tune in a few hours—give or take. Providin' we don't find nuttin' else wrong with her, that is."

"That's not good enough," Holmes admonished.

The smile instantly disappeared from the workman's face. Verne stepped between the two men, Holmes and the worker.

"Monsieur Holmes and Docteur Watson, this is Thomas Rollins. He knows everything about the Nautilus and how she works. There's no one more qualified than he. If he tells me it will take a couple of hours, then it will take a couple of hours."

Rollins extended his ham of a hand for Holmes and me to shake. Holmes glanced down at Rollins' palm, then into the engineer's mischievous eyes. The man was having sport with Holmes, knowing full well that a gentleman would never accept the oily-blistered hand from such a dirty character. But Holmes was never put off by honest labor.

Laughing, Holmes grasped Rollins' hand and pounded the startled man on the back. "Now let me ask you..." Holmes commenced, leading Rollins out of earshot with his arm draped casually over the engineer's shoulder. Verne and I watched the curious partnership of brain and brawn being formed. It wasn't long before the two men were chatting like they'd known each other all of their lives.

"D'accord. I will go and tend to my sister," said Verne, leaving me alone to watch Holmes weave his magic.

45

The animated faces of Holmes and the engineer turned serious as the conversation wore on. At times, their exchanges became quite heated, as they scribbled and sketched on pieces of paper, only to discard the scraps one after another, leaving crumpled balls on the floor. They enthusiastically delved into a myriad of schematics, diagrams, charts, and visited the actual torpedoes themselves, comparing the missiles against one another and the drawings they created. When their conversation ended with confirming nods, they smiled and offered each other congratulatory slaps on the back.

"Mr. Holmes, I'll say this," Rollins said, "if this is what you want, then that's what you'll get. Criminy, if this don't beat all! I'll get somethin' out of the engines. It might not be much, but the Nautilus will be maneuverable."

"That's all I ask," Holmes responded, handing the drawings back to Rollins. "Let me know when everything is ready. If you will point us towards the Captain's office, I'll inform Monsieur Verne of our plans. Come with me, Watson. We've much to accomplish and so little time."

Following Rollins' directions we arrived at a pair of huge

doors carved with marvelous scenes. "Indonesian," said Holmes. After a single tap on one, we were bade to enter. To our left was an enormous desk made of the same wood as the doors. To the right was a library, an upholstered sofa and two cushioned arm chairs. Monsieur Verne had taken a spot on the sofa, and I was cheered to find the courageous Miss Verne sitting at her brother's side. Thankfully, she seemed recovered from her earlier ordeal.

"Monsieur Verne," Holmes began, "I've spoken with Rollins, and we have come up with a plan. I will need some of your men."

"Of course. What can I do to help?"

Sherlock Holmes took a chair. I did, too. My friend recited the most daring and clever scheme that I had ever heard. "At present, everything depends on Rollins and his crew. Until they're ready, I'll explain to all of you what I hope is a way out of our perilous predicament. Spending my eternity down here does not sit well with me at all."

My companion's words sent a shiver down my spine! It hadn't occurred to me that Jaeger's damage to the Nautilus's engines meant the possibility of us never seeing the sky again. Death does not frighten me, but I did linger over all that I would miss when I was gone. The sunrises, the sunsets, the heather, and the sound of songbirds. A fresh pillow under my head, Mrs. Hudson's candied ginger scones, and a pasty from the corner vendor.

I shook my head to clear it and smiled. "Tell me of your plan, Holmes. You can count on me."

"Good. Now where would Jaeger go? Would he seek out the barge? No, I think not. If it were me, I would head for the first ship in the convoy and make my escape. I'm positive that that is precisely what he is doing."

"And why would he do that, Mr. Holmes?" queried Miss Verne. "Surely, the barge is closer?"

"Perhaps, but Jaeger has no way of knowing what damage Watson and I inflicted upon the barge. It is currently incapacitated. He has to know we managed to break the cable. That's no small feat. It would make sense for him to wonder what other sabotage we inflicted on that vessel. Besides, why would he go to the barge when it is a ship that he knows is rigged to explode? Furthermore, he doesn't know whether the barge is navigable. And lastly, would he risk seeking out the barge since it is underwater with a limited air supply? No—my hypothesis is correct. He will get to the surface as quickly as possible and swim for the first ship, the Clarity."

"Why not one of the other two?" I asked.

"Think, Watson! The last ship, the Collier, has explosives on it, and the second, if you recall when looking through the periscope, was riding low in the water. That suggests she's weighted down with cargo. That leaves the first ship, the Clarity, which is undoubtedly faster than the second vessel."

"I see," I responded. "So that means Jaeger will climb on board that first ship and escape whilst Her Majesty's Fleet sails into a trap?"

"Not if my plan succeeds. I believe that you have ten torpedoes on the Nautilus?" Holmes directed his query to Verne.

"That is correct; but they are useless. We have no way of knowing where the barge is. We have no power to steer a course away from here. If we just fire those torpedoes blindly, they could possibly hit the barge, but she may be very close to us. If we do manage to hit her, she might explode and sink us along with her. No, Monsieur Holmes. Those torpedoes may as well be made of stone for all the use they are."

"Ah, but they do have a use!" said Holmes, jubilantly. "As we speak, three of the torpedoes are being modified to serve us just the same."

"Please explain, Monsieur." Verne sounded genuinely curious.

Before Holmes could respond, the Nautilus vibrated to life. Holmes smiled. "Excellent! Whatever you are paying Rollins, Monsieur, it is not enough."

A tap on the door informed us of a visitor.

"Qui est là?"

"It's Rollins, Captain. I need to speak with Mr. Holmes."

"Entrez!"

I didn't think it possible, but the man was even dirtier and grimier than before. However, now his face beamed with satisfaction. "The first one is ready, Mr. Holmes. And, oh yes, Captain, I got one of the engines running. She'll do no more than a few knots, but it's enough for what you have in mind. My men are still working to bring the others back to specs."

Holmes rose and gave the burly man a clap on the shoulder. "And the volunteers?"

"That was a problem, Mr. Holmes," Rollins said. His face was suddenly glum. "I could only get sixteen men."

Sherlock Holmes stood there looking perplexed.

"Cause that's all the crew there is!" Rollins roared with laughter. "Down to a man, they said they wouldn't miss this for all the tea in China. Even if it doesn't stand a chance of workin'."

Smiling, Holmes turned back to us. "Shall we see the results of Mr. Rollins' labours?"

We followed Rollins to the engine room and observed only a few men present, as we strolled into the main area. I wondered where the others had gone. My curiosity was satisfied upon entering the area, as it brimmed with the smiling faces of the rest of the crew. Surprisingly, they stood at rigid attention and gathered round an obviously modified torpedo. All were dressed in diving suits and waited anxiously for Holmes to come to the center of the group.

"Here she is—the first of three," Rollins said, slapping the blunt nose of the torpedo sharply.

"Be careful!" I cried. "Do you want to kill us all?"

"Argh, I'm sorry, doctor. I thought you knew. The explosives were taken out of her."

"Taken out?" I asked, looking at him incredulously. "Then what good is it?"

My accusatory tone hurt Rollins' feelings, and he looked to Holmes for help.

"Perhaps I should explain," Holmes offered, diffusing the situation. "Rollins and his men have acted upon my orders. He was instructed to remove the charge from the torpedo. For what I have in mind, the explosives are not necessary."

"Go on, Monsieur," said the inventor, stepping forwards to examine the torpedo more closely. "What are these for?" he asked, tapping a loop of rope in his hands.

"You will notice that there are a total of four such contrivances on the torpedo attached to the cleats," Holmes answered, allowing us to move forwards for a better view. "These will allow us to hold on as we are carried through the water." He paused to allow his words to register.

"Are you saying," I asked, as calmly as I could, "that four men are to be dragged through the water on this?"

"Five. The fifth will be at the rear, steering the torpedo to its destination."

"That is impossible!" Verne laughed mockingly. "You cannot steer the torpedo. It will only go... *Comment dit-on ga en Anglais?"* The inventor, looking at his sister, raised his hand and slowly extended his arm out in front of him in one fluid motion. *"Tout droit?"*

"Straight ahead," she translated.

"Not anymore, Captain," said Rollins, stepping forwards. "I think you'll want to take a look at this. It's Mr. Holmes' doin', and if it does what it's supposed to, there's no tellin' where it'll end. It's goin' to change the way we explore the oceans. Mr. Holmes?"

"Go on, Rollins, you're doing fine."

"Right, well, here goes." Rollins brought a number of different lengths of tubing from behind his back, while one of his men placed an assortment of wedges or triangle-shaped pieces of hammered sheets of metal, on a table.

"You better finish, Mr. Holmes. I'm not sure I'm up to explainin' it proper."

"Very well," Holmes acquiesced. "You and your men have done a splendid job, Mr. Rollins. I'll take it from here." The crewmen beamed at my friend's recognition.

Holmes continued, "My idea was—" all eyes studiously watched his every move, as he assembled the parts and attached them to the torpedo—"to have Rollins and his men manufacture parts that would allow the torpedo to be maneuverable even while it is running. I asked Rollins for the schematics of the Nautilus. Providing me with the same, he explained in exquisite detail the workings of what he called the bow planes and rudder. It occurred to me that, with a little creativity and the crew's excellent craftsmanship, we might be able to fashion similar parts for the torpedo. These parts would mimic the ship's steering mechanisms."

Whilst my friend was speaking, he continued to assemble the parts, threading the different lengths of tubing into the prebored holes of the torpedo and attaching the various hand-rolled and hammered triangles to the newly completed assembly.

By turning a specific tube in one direction or another, Holmes changed the angle, determining whether the triangle pointed up or down. This, he noted, would cause the torpedo to run flat, go up, or go down, according to how he turned the controls. As for turning port or starboard, Holmes showed us that merely moving the rear-attached tube along a series of notched grooves would turn the rudder accordingly. Thus, the torpedo was now capable being turned right or left.

Monsieur Verne took advantage of the ensuing silence, as I knew he would, but I was surprised by his words. "It is sheer genius!" he marveled.

The crew burst into applause and an embarrassed Holmes smiled.

"Excellent!" I said, shaking my friend's hand. "But now that the torpedo can be controlled, where do you intend to take it?"

46

"First things first. It hasn't been tested yet. Rollins? Please wheel her to the diving room."

"All right, men," Rollins ordered. "Put your backs into it and lift!"

Using the hoist, the men lifted the torpedo and lowered it onto a dolly. As they rolled it out of the engine room, the Verne siblings wished us well and left, as did the other extraneous crew members.

"You?" I asked, when I was alone with Holmes. "You're going to test it?"

"Yes. Oh, please, Watson, I can't ask the men to do something that I wouldn't do. Besides, this is the easy part."

By the time we reached the diving room, the torpedo was already in the water. Holmes stepped into a diving suit. I assisted him attaching the canisters of air. There were two, one hooked up and a second in readiness. Holmes also requested a rubber satchel. For what purpose, I did not ask.

"Here you go, Mr. Holmes," said Rollins, handing my friend a key like one of those used to wind a clock. "Remember, all you need is a half turn to the right, and she'll be good. And mind the propeller. Even though we took out three of the batteries, that torpedo can still slice you up pretty nasty-like."

"Thank you," Holmes replied, shaking the man's greasy paw. "Don't waste any time. Prepare the other three torpedoes. If there are any changes to be made, I'll tell you what they are when I return."

"Right, Mr. Holmes. We're already workin' on 'em. Good luck."

Holmes glanced back with a nod to us. "If everything goes according to plan, I'll return in fifteen minutes. Watson, please retrieve my helmet for me."

"I don't like you going out there alone, Holmes," I protested. "What if something goes wrong?"

"Nothing will go wrong."

But something in his manner told me that he was worried. I was about to argue further, when he did something completely out of character: he changed his mind.

"I wouldn't mind having a little company, if you're up for it," he said. From the very first days of our having roomed together, I have never known Holmes to temper his words, but these carefully chosen ones told me that he was indeed having second thoughts.

"Won't be a minute," I answered as I plastered on my cheeriest face. While I laboured into the diving suit, Holmes shuffled over to where I was struggling to dress. His diving boots were not made for traversing a normal surface. "You are truly a remarkable friend, Watson. Thank you." He slapped me lightly on the back.

"We're in this together, Holmes."

"Just the same, thank you."

"Here you go, Mr. Holmes," said Rollins, joining us. He handed Holmes his helmet and a lamp. "This is magnetic and attaches to the top of your helmet. Just switch it on here. It'll work in the water with no worries. Is the doctor going, too?"

"Thank you, Rollins. Yes, Dr. Watson will accompany me for the testing of our brainchild. He'll need a lamp for his helmet, too."

The engineer glanced at me with an expression of surprise that quickly changed into a smile. "Good show, Doctor. I told Mr. Holmes that you would never sit still, leavin' him to go out alone. I'll grab another one for you and get you your helmet."

Rollins left us alone.

"All set, Watson?" Holmes asked, as he was attaching and re-attaching the lamp to the helmet in his arms. The magnet worked perfectly, allowing Holmes to position the light as he thought necessary.

"Ready."

Rollins came back with several men and a helmet for me. They strapped the twin air tanks onto my back, just as they'd done for Holmes. They also strapped an extra set of air tanks onto the torpedo. Once that was accomplished, Rollins and his crew members assisted Holmes and me by lifting our helmets, positioning them, and locking them in place. Holmes stepped over the side of the diving well first and lowered himself into the water. His rubber satchel briefly floated to the surface until it filled with water and drifted down. I followed Holmes with one final glance at the crew. Rollins gave me a nod of approval.

Our diving suits were watertight, but we were deeper than we'd been when we left the barge, so the water was much, much colder. Our lightweight canvas suits did little to shield us from the bone-chilling temperature. Immediately, my teeth began to chatter. The shock of the cold numbed my senses.

My hands firmly clasped round the handle attached to the bottom of the ship whilst I watched my friend manipulating the rods on the modified torpedo. With each movement of his hands, the rudder and diving planes responded in kind. The torpedo stayed in its harness, as Holmes continued to practice. His confidence grew with each movement. Finally he was satisfied enough to gesture for me to take hold of the rope handle in the middle of the torpedo. Reluctantly, I released my grip on the metal handhold and took possession of the rope.

47

Holmes released the catch on the harness, and the torpedo immediately started to sink. As the torpedo cleared the last strap of its harness, he turned the key to the right. Instantly, the torpedo propelled us both through the water. I held on for dear life.

Surprisingly, and in very short order, we were tearing through the water under full control. At first, we didn't venture too far from the Nautilus. We merely ran a straight course down the length of the ship and back. A number of divers had since joined us in the water. The lights on their helmets illuminated their faces, making them bright with excitement as they watched us return to our starting point. The beams of light from their helmets afforded us an excellent view of our surroundings. Holmes maneuvered the torpedo closer to the exuberant men.

Before long, Holmes had us heading out and away from the safety of the Nautilus and her crew. I glanced over at my friend who was guiding the torpedo from the back of the underwater missile. He was smiling broadly. His fingers played with the rods. Soon he had us flying through the water in a lazy pattern that reminded me of gulls playing, lifted by invisible hands, and supported by moving currents of air.

Suddenly, a loud tapping sound came from behind me. I turned towards Holmes and saw him pointing to starboard. My head turned in the direction that Holmes was pointing and—I saw the barge! The Stratford-Upon-Avon loomed malevolently in the water.

Holmes headed us towards the barge. When we were about a hundred feet away, Holmes steered us to the right, sailing us past her bow. We continued until we were clear of her, and then we turned left. Even under water, we could hear the furious blows of hammers. The men inside the barge were attempting to undo Holmes' handiwork. The diamonds he had dropped into the engine must have caused a tremendous amount of damage. We circled the barge four or five times before heading back in the direction of the Nautilus.

I knew we were getting nearer to our home base when I noticed watery beams of light from the crew of the Nautilus. Holmes maneuvered the torpedo towards the submarine. As we neared the harness, he turned the key to the off position and the torpedo fell lazily into its cradle.

Rollins' face filled my faceplate, as he clapped me on the back enthusiastically although sluggishly. Holmes motioned for the crew to climb back into the Nautilus. One by one, we watched the men disappear into the ship. When our turn came to climb inside, the men assisted us. They also helped us remove our helmets. When the headpieces were safety off and to one side, the crew gave Holmes a thunderous ovation. At their urging, Holmes explained our adventure. The crew was all smiles as my friend explained the nuances of handling the torpedo. It wasn't until Holmes mentioned our sighting of the barge that the mood turned heavy. Men spoke among themselves about what this might mean. While they did, some of them, who had been singled out by Rollins, took turns riding the torpedo.

With everyone so busy, Holmes took me off to the side. "We need two more men to take the controls of the other torpedoes. I'd like for you and me to be on the lead torpedo. I suggest we put Rollins with us and have him select the leaders for the other two torpedoes. Do you agree?"

I nodded.

"Very good. I think it's time to tell everyone of my plan."

"It's about time," I said, with mock anger. "I was beginning to wonder whether or not you had one."

"You may not feel the same after you hear the details. I must admit that, even to me, my plan sounds desperate."

Holmes' scheme was incredibly complex and detailed. He patiently answered a litany of questions. At length, the crew and I seemed satisfied that we knew every element necessary for us to do our individual parts. Monsieur Verne voiced his displeasure at not being amongst those included to go with us on the mission, but as Holmes pointed out, it was vital that he, along with the remaining crew, stay with the Nautilus, should the plan go awry. It would be Monsieur Verne's task to somehow warn the Fleet, if Holmes' plan failed. As he bade us good-bye, Verne said, "*Alors,* if you can destroy the rudder of the Collier, steering it would be *impossible*! You would render it helpless in the water. That alone might be enough to save the Royal Fleet."

"We shall do what we can," said Holmes.

The three torpedo teams were organised. Rollins gave us specialized instructions regarding the timing devices we would be disarming. He explained the timing levers and how we needed to adjust them. Whilst he gave us this short tutorial, those who were not accompanying us on the mission readied the weapons and gear we would need on our mission.

The modified torpedoes were lowered into the water and into the waiting hands of the torpedo drivers. As each torpedo crew descended into the cold water, they had to wait until their respective drivers circled back to pick them up. Holmes was the last to accept his underwater craft.

The first two teams were circling with their full complement of crew by the time I latched on to Holmes' torpedo along with the other men. Our helmet lamps glowed weakly as the beams tried to penetrate the greenish-black water.

Finally, Holmes steered us to the lead position and the others fell dutifully behind. We circled the Nautilus a number of times to acclimate ourselves to our situations. As we crossed her bow for the last time before heading away, I was surprised to see Verne and his sister. They were standing in the area that I had previously mistaken as the eyes of the sea monster.

I recalled the chilling moment of seeing the black forms flit in and out of the creature's eyes, when Holmes and I had first come upon the Nautilus. Of course, I now realised that the "eyes" were actually windows for underwater viewing. I chuckled to myself at reaching another startling revelation. Those mysterious, flitting forms I'd seen were the silhouettes of the crew members, as they walked past the Nautilus's viewing windows. All of these thoughts filled my head, when I took one last look at the Nautilus and the figures of Monsieur Verne and his sister waving to us from the window, as our underwater caravan passed by in review.

There were still so many questions I wanted to ask Miss Verne. Did she ever have a husband? Did she know the sailor whose body had washed up? Why had she sent for Holmes? Who played the part of the friendly maritime officer who supported her claims? When did she realise—assuming she did realise—that the Bard was nothing more than a pirate? Why hadn't she made a straightforward approach to Holmes? What was the scheme her brother had worked out to avenge her? Had he abandoned that scheme after retrieving his sister from Jaeger? If not, why was he helping us warn the British Fleet? Was it possible he would kill us and blow up the fleet with the remaining explosives from the torpedoes?

All of that would have to wait while we sped away in the direction of where we had seen the Stratford-Upon-Avon, the Bard's barge. My apprehension grew, as we searched the waters but found nothing.

Holmes tapped on the torpedo's metal skin to get my attention and, with exaggerated movements, gestured for me to join him at his position. After a few harrowing seconds of moving around, I exchanged places with the young seaman nearest Holmes. Rollins watched as he continued to hold fast.

Placing his helmet against mine, Holmes shouted, "Can you hear me?"

Though muffled and distorted, his voice was nevertheless understandable. I nodded that I understood.

"Excellent!" he cried. "Write this down on your writing board."

I grabbed the board floating on the end of its tether and nodded for Holmes to continue. "Tell Rollins that he and the rest of the men are to return to the submarine and prepare for a possible attack by the barge. Monsieur Verne does not know it can sail under its own power again. We'll have to go it alone. It's up to us to find and disarm the Collier."

I looked into Holmes' eyes, questioningly.

"I know," his voice boomed, hollowly. "It's a huge task we'll undertake, but we can't risk having this many torpedoes in the water all at once. We're bound to attract attention to ourselves and then draw fire."

I scribbled Holmes' directive on the board and handed it to Rollins. After reading what I had written, he bobbed his head up and down. After all, the barge had changed positions. That must mean their engines were repaired. We could no longer assume the barge was incapacitated, and therefore, the Nautilus needed to be warned. The two other torpedo teams pulled alongside us. Rollins handed the writing board to the next torpedo leader. Awkwardly, the men transferred extra breathing tanks, other gear, and rubber sacks in preparation to return to the Nautilus.

48

Waving our good-byes, we watched as the beams from the helmet lamps of the two other torpedo teams grew dimmer. Seeing the last beam flicker into the black oblivion, Holmes steered us towards our objective. It was uncanny how Holmes, with no obvious points of reference, could set a course directly to the three pirate ships, but that is precisely what he did.

As we traveled, the enormous pressure against my chest eased, a sign we were climbing slowly towards the surface. The prearranged three taps on the torpedo's casing signaled me to switch off my helmet lamp. I watched with growing excitement as the water became clearer and brighter as we neared the surface.

At first, the hull of the Collier appeared as a wispy shadow in the distance. When we drew near, the massive, barnacle-incrusted hull filled my faceplate entirely. It was like being face-to-face with a wall. Suddenly, the nose of our torpedo broke the surface. We skimmed the final twenty or so yards on top of the water. I glanced up at the sky and marveled at having never before seen it so clear, or so high! Never again would I take it for granted, if we lived through this adventure!

Controlling the torpedo on the surface of the water was a monumental task, what with the waves cresting well above our heads. But with the precision of a surgeon conducting a delicate operation, Holmes guided us skillfully. He inched our craft alongside the ship's hull, with nary a bump or scrape.

Holmes had instructed Rollins to fashion a rope circlet. I adjusted this makeshift lasso and looped it around the nose of the torpedo. This rope would act as a tether, connecting the torpedo to one of the explosive devices that had been attached to the Collier by Zeke's crew. Without the rope leash to control it, the torpedo would quickly sink to the floor of the ocean whilst we went about the business of disarming and moving the deadly mechanisms.

As Holmes and I traveled the length of the ship, I counted the six explosive devices set at intervals. As we changed direction and retraced our path, I heard a loud tap, which was Holmes's signal for me to release my grip on the torpedo.

I turned to face the ship as Holmes sped past it. Unconsciously holding my breath, I timed my release of the torpedo as we came close to the first device. With shaking hands, I reached out and grasped the timing lever of the explosive, using it to steady myself against the water currents. With exaggerated slowness, I pulled the lever until I felt a click, exactly as Rollins had taught me to do. Next I carefully turned the dial until the red line pointed to zero.

When my task was done, I exhaled and turned to look for Holmes. He had made his circuit on the torpedo and was coming my way. I waved my hand and waited for the rope he would toss to me as he neared. The whirring of the torpedo's propeller could be heard as Holmes lined up for another pass. I grabbed the trailing rope as he motored by. When we'd gone twenty feet or so, I turned loose and kicked. With outstretched hands, I reached for the second explosive device—and grabbed it. Once again, I repeated the sequence to disarm it.

I needed to latch onto Holmes on his next pass to move to device number three. Holding on to the second device to keep my place, I watched and waited for my friend. What Holmes was attempting to do was nearly impossible. He had to control the trajectory of the torpedo, toss the rope to me, and shut down the torpedo's motor as the rope grew taut. But my friend was Sherlock Holmes, and to Holmes, nothing was impossible. He deftly coordinated all three actions, as if he had practiced them all his life.

Holmes tossed the rope, and I caught it as he passed by. I draped the noose over the lever of the third device and watched the knot cinch close. The rope snapped rigid, just as the torpedo's motor died. As we had anticipated the levers made perfect hitching posts!

By now I'd grown more confident with each repetition. As I rode along with Holmes on the torpedo, he tossed the rope over the lever of the fourth explosive device. The rope went tight, I crawled along it, making my way to the flat disk mounted on the side of the vessel. Repeating Rollins' instructions in my head, I moved the lever until I heard the satisfying click of success. Four down and two to go!

I joined Holmes at the torpedo. Once more we motored around to the next explosive device. My friend tossed the rope over the fifth lever and let it pay out through the gloved fingers of his hand. The nose of the twelve-foot, four-hundred-and-fifty pound torpedo disappeared into the murky depths, but it couldn't go far. The twenty-foot length of rope snaked down into the water until it went taut with the full weight of the torpedo. Just as the others had done, this fifth magnetic explosive device held firm, anchoring the torpedo to the side of the Collier.

My friend swam to my side and clapped me on the back exuberantly. Rather than waiting for me to reset the timer, Holmes pointed upwards. I realised he was suggesting we rise to surface. Swimming side by side, we rose through the depths. The colour of the water lightened as we rose. Once our heads were above the brine, Holmes motioned for me to remove my helmet. I undid the clamps and as the seal broke, I heard a rush of air. Holmes did the same and turned off the air supply to both of our tanks. Filling my lungs full of delicious fresh ocean air, I wanted to cheer our accomplishment. But my friend's drawn face cautioned me to remain silent.

"By my calculations, our first tanks are nearly spent," he said. Holmes undid the buckles of our air supply apparatus. Each of us carried a fresh tank of air in addition to the one we'd been breathing. First Holmes swapped out my fresh tank for my spent one. Then I did the same for him. We let the old ones slide into their watery grave, as we put our helmets back on and breathed in a new supply of air. The waves battered our bodies, causing us to bob around wildly. My friend touched his helmet to mine and spoke loud enough for me to hear, "Splendid job! Did you by any chance notice how much time remained on the four devices before you disarmed them?"

"No!" I said in reply. "I'm sorry, Holmes. I didn't think to look." My jubilant mood of but a moment ago was replaced with disappointment. Of course, I should have made note of the time remaining! Of course!

Seeing my splendid mood turn sour, my companion patted my shoulder. "Don't worry. You can check the time on the next one." But I knew we were straining the graciousness of Madame

Fortune. We needed to work quickly if we were to escape with our lives. Even as we'd been manipulating the explosive devices on the ship, the sea had turned increasingly rough. White caps crested the swells. One of our infamous storms was brewing.

49

As if we needed a reminder, the sky darkened ominously, and the sound of distant thunder rolled over us in a continuous, violent symphony. Taking a cue from the tympanic onslaught, the wind howled in a frenzied chorus. Marble-sized drops of rain pelted us. The noise of them hitting the metal echoed in my helmet. A crack of thunder boomed overhead.

"Watson, we're out of time!" Holmes shouted, over a second monstrous thunderclap. "The ships will be pulling up anchor to flee the storm. We have to abandon this particular plan. We don't have time to attach an explosive to the rudder of the Collier."

That had been the final step in our set of goals. First we had disarmed all but one of the explosives, to render the ship less likely to set off the percussive devices built into the barge. Second, we had planned to attach the final explosive device to the rudder of the Collier. This would render the ship helpless in the water, destroying the steering mechanism.

"We did all that we could!" I shouted, above another thunderclap. My heart sank, thinking of how close we had come.

Holmes and I locked eyes. My animalistic impulse was to flee and save myself. Yet another emotion triumphed. Duty. That was all I had left to give to my country. Duty. How could I turn my back on the men in those ships? I couldn't. "All those lives," I said. "How can we stop now?"

Holmes leaned his faceplate against mine, so I could hear him speak. "No, Watson, you are right. We're not leaving here until there is no hope. Listen carefully. Follow my hand. Keep your eyes peeled in that direction." And he pointed at the horizon.

I squinted and turned my face into the horizontal biting rain. "What am I looking for?"

"On the horizon—it's the Fleet!"

I stared into the rain and saw nothing. The driving rain pelted my faceplate. My eyes narrowed as I tried to see. Between the drops from the heavens and the splashing of the sea, I could barely see my hand in front of my face. I shook my head, angrily.

Holmes kept pointing. This time when I stared out at the horizon, I saw the faint wisps of smoke from the Fleet's funnels and the small silhouettes of the ships themselves.

Excitedly, I grabbed Holmes' shoulders and nodded my head. He faced me and opened my faceplate again before shouting, "We can't risk Jaeger escaping in this weather! I think his ship will be the first to run. Do you think you can take the controls of the torpedo?"

I nodded.

"Fine," Holmes continued. "Close your faceplate and lock it. You won't have to take the torpedo down far, just dive lower to escape the weather. Stay here and keep your eye on the Fleet. I'll try to disarm the sixth explosive whilst we're here and tethered to the fifth."

Before I could reply, he closed his faceplate, locked it, and sank below the water. A moment later, he bobbed up to the surface and held out a length of rope. One end was tied round his waist. I took the free end. Again, he opened his helmet so he could talk to me.

"This rope still secured to the lever of explosive number five. I'm going to swim to number six." He pointed towards the front of the ship. The last device was also the farthest away.

"When I give you the signal, you might have to pull me back with the rope. It'll act as my tether. I don't think we can risk using the last bit of thrust that's left in the torpedo. We'll need it to escape the storm. Are you clear?"

"I think so, but..."

"There are no buts, my friend. This's all we have left." He paused, handing me the key to the torpedo. He was obviously contemplating his next words and my reaction to them when he said, "If something should go wrong, get as far away from this ship as possible. Head for the Fleet. You won't have a lot to work with, but I think it'll be enough to see you safely away."

Holmes closed his faceplate, turned on his air supply, and grasped my gloved hand in his as a last farewell. As I watched, he slipped beneath the surface. I concentrated on playing out the rope as Holmes swam away. I let the line play out at a steady pace even as I was being battered mercilessly by the waves.

I saw no sign of Holmes for some time. With each passing second, my heart sank. Suddenly, the rope went rigid. The horrifying truth hit me. It was too short! There wasn't enough of it to reach the device! Holmes was not close enough to that last explosive to remove it. As if attempting to stretch out and find more length than it had, the rope went taut. It sliced through the air with a singing sound. The noise continued as Holmes tugged at it futilely.

Suddenly, the line went slack.

For a moment, I believed that Holmes had found himself unable to proceed any farther and had turned round. But when I tugged on the rope, my heart went cold! I could tell by how easily the rope moved through the water that my friend was no longer on the other end.

"Holmes!" I opened my faceplate but kept my helmet on. My voice competed with the howling winds. "Holmes!"

Frustrated beyond all reason, I thrashed about in the water. Still not seeing any sign of him, I recalled Holmes' parting words, "Should anything go wrong..."

I stared at the horizon. The Fleet had moved closer. The ships were still dots on the water, but those silhouettes had grown larger.

"So many men," I thought. "So many men sailing towards their deaths."

50

Without wasting more time, I inched my way along the hull towards that sixth explosive. The waves smacked me into the side of the ship in a titanic show of force. Thankfully, I had my helmet on, as my skull would have cracked under such a brutal assault. As saltwater washed into my helmet and over my face, I spat it out and kept on going.

My unending battle against the powerful ocean was quickly sapping my strength, but I pressed on with resolve. By following the rope that held tightly to the torpedo, I reached my first objective. I made it to the far end of the ship. After closing my faceplate, I slipped beneath the surface. Again, following the instructions I'd been given earlier, I disabled the explosive. Five were now disarmed. This time I made note of the time remaining: fifty-three minutes! When I surfaced, I opened my faceplate, shut off my air supply, and sucked in fresh air. My aim was to prolong whatever air was in my tanks.

My teeth chattered uncontrollably. Whether my jaw was responding to the frigid waters or the strain on my sanity, it mattered not! All that mattered was getting back to that last explosive device and repositioning it. I nurtured the hope that somehow Holmes had managed to accomplish his mission. As he struggled to do his part, so would I do mine.

Swirling winds splattered rain in my face. I blinked back the sting of the salt. As the waters crashed against me, the sea splashed over the seam where my suit connected to my helmet. Cold ocean water trickled down into my canvas coverall. Fearing the weight of the water would drag me underwater, I hurriedly closed my faceplate and clamped it in the locked position.

A thousand thoughts ran through my head, each replete with varying and often gruesome outcomes of my death. I pushed my way along the side of the hull, half-heartedly swimming and crawling towards the sixth explosive. The waves grew to mammoth proportions as the storm gathered its power. Relentlessly, I stayed true to my objective. My right arm kept in contact with the side of the Collier's hull, assuring me I was on course. But the waves fought my every motion. They tried to drag me out and away from the ship. Struggling to stay afloat and feeling my stamina draining away, I gave one last kick of my feet. I was rewarded with a sharp metallic clang as my helmet bounced off the side of the ship. My head grew dizzy. My lungs burned. My last breath! My last breath?

Unconsciousness licked at my brain. I gasped for air. Was this the end? It had come too soon!

That's when I realised I'd forgotten to turn my air supply back on! "You fool!" You blathering, old fool!" I scolded myself as I turned the valve to my air supply. Immediately, I inhaled huge gulps of delicious air. My head cleared and I felt invigorated. "Wait until I tell..."

No.

This was not the time to indulge in sentiment. I turned my attention back to the charge attached to the ship. The timer indicated that I had precious little time—twenty-four minutes, to be exact. I reset the dial on the detonator to zero and then I looked for the hidden switch that would reverse the polarity of the magnets. I was cold and weary. My hands, shrouded in their bulky gloves, had a difficult time of it. The canvas was too cumbersome to detect any variation along the outer rim of the device. To make progress, I would have to remove one of my gloves.

Pressing my back against the ship's hull for support, I tore at the elastic wrapped round my wrist, the material that sealed my suit against the water. The covering came loose as I unwound the material. Instantly, upon removing my glove, the icy water splashed over my skin and numbed my fingers. My entire body wanted to cramp up, but I recalled my purpose for being in this predicament and forced myself to spin 'round to face the ship. My bare fingers groped along the edge of the device, feeling for the switch that I knew had to be there. I quickly reached my limit. The pain was overpowering, I was about to give up. But a voice in my head shouted, "Once more! Try once more!"

51

I ran my fingers over the freezing, circular metal casing of the explosive device. Concentrating every last ounce of willpower, I located and reset the timer. Next I located the tiny switch and released the bomb from the side of the ship. Balancing the explosive between my legs, I pulled on my glove, wrapping the elastic as best I could. Wearily, I made for the ship's rudder, the place where Holmes had earlier instructed me to place the device. The magnet, switched on once more, held the explosive firmly in place, and I set the timer.

Using my hands to propel me, I crawled back to where the torpedo still dangled at the end of the rope. I pondered my next course of action. There was a lull in the storm. I floated to the top and scanned the waters for Holmes. I was about to surrender to the inevitable, when I spotted him waving, frantically. He was at the bow of the barge, directly ahead of me and holding on for dear life!

"Holmes!" I cried, not caring whether he heard me or not. I flailed my arms, hoping that he could see me, but he disappeared into a valley of another mountainous wave.

An idea came suddenly to mind. I switched on my helmet lamp. Then I switched it off, then on again, rapidly. Repeating this procedure a number of times, I saw Holmes' lamp blink back at me in acknowledgement.

I was giddy with excitement. "Holmes is alive!" I sang to myself, as I slapped the water in a playful fit of joy. His lamp flickered with alternating frequency. It took some time for me to realise that he was trying to tell me something. He appeared and disappeared in the valleys and crests of waves, making his gestures difficult to see, much less understand. Ultimately, I realised what he was telling me and I turned my lamp on and off to affirm my receipt of his message.

I sank below the surface and used the rope to pull myself deeper. Slowly, hand-over-hand, I reached the torpedo. I placed the key in the slot. Then I had the sudden realisation that the missile would plummet to the sea bottom before I could slip the noose over it and start the engine. Without the noose, there would be no way to stay tethered to the torpedo!

I rose to the surface. Feeling frustrated, I searched for the light of Holmes' lamp. But I couldn't find it. I knew I needed to hurry. "Hurry!" I thought. The desperation within me rose, and I slipped once more beneath the waves. "Think, man!" I shouted to myself, as I traveled along the taut line, going deeper into the briny water. "How would Holmes do this?" I rummaged through the pockets of my canvas suit for any inspiration and pricked myself with the point of a knife.

"That's it—Holmes' rope!" I decided and hurried to the surface. I lifted the rope off the lever that Holmes had tied to himself. I made my way back to the torpedo, where I lashed the rope to a cleat on its side. Feeling the cold beginning to slow my responses, I held the blade of my knife against the hemp that secured the torpedo to the ship. *This has to work,* I told myself and exhaled deeply.

Sensing my resolve beginning to wane, I turned the key. The propeller on the torpedo turned. Its thrust pulled my hands away from the missile. I fumbled as I manipulated the controlling levers. The torpedo, nose down, strained at the rope and gyrated out of control, swinging me in an arc. The knife was knocked out of my hand!

Thankfully, the blade was on a lanyard attached to my suit. Quickly, I had it back within my grip. I pressed the blade of the knife against the rope and closed my eyes. With one quick swipe, I severed the straining line. The torpedo, no longer tethered, propelled me like a shot straight down! I pulled back on the lever and the torpedo gradually started to climb. Moving the levers ever so slightly, I gently turned it. The torpedo and I moved steadily towards the surface.

As the torpedo breached the water and my head rose with it, I caught a glimpse of Holmes' lamp. I headed straight for the light. He waved frantically as I drew nearer. Not having completely mastered the delicate touch of handling the controls, I sped past him right as he lunged for my missile. Holmes' desperate attempt to grab hold ended with him disappearing beneath the choppy waves. I cursed my incompetence as I watched him thrashing and splashing behind me. At first, my trajectory continued past him. Then, slowly, I manipulated the controls and managed to retrace my course. This time as I maneuvered closer, Holmes timed his leap perfectly. He grabbed one of the rope handles nearest me on the right.

Unfortunately, his added weight set the torpedo off course. We were turned back towards the barge. I fought the controls, frantically throwing my own weight to one side in an effort to compensate for my friend's additional burden on the torpedo. Coming precipitously close to the bow, I finally managed to avoid our certain death.

Holmes gestured with his hand. He still had the rubber

satchel slung over his shoulder. He wanted me to do something, but I couldn't tell what. Holmes opened his faceplate and motioned for me to do the same. As I glanced over at him, I noticed two devices protruding from under the flap of the bag. He had taken two of the six explosive devices and stuffed them into his satchel!

"To the ships!" Holmes boomed. "We have fifteen minutes to disable them."

I nodded that I understood and aimed the torpedo in the direction of the second ship's rudder. Holmes pushed off as we came upon the colossal fin. He waved his arm in the air in a circular motion, signaling for me to come round again. When I returned, he pushed away from the Celestial, the second ship. Holmes attached an explosive device to the vessel's rudder. As he had done earlier, he grabbed the rope handle as I came 'round and waved his hand for us to proceed.

I steered us to Jaeger's ship, the Clarity. As we approached, Holmes slipped off and swam for it. I continued on past, leaving him to secure the final explosive to the last ship's rudder. As I circled back, I heard a thumping, clanging noise. It was the sound of a ship pulling up anchor!

Suddenly, I was bombarded by noise. All three ships weighed anchor in perfect unison. The propellers were already turning on them. We only had seconds before Jaeger's ship did the same. I turned the torpedo to align it with Holmes and edged ever closer.

The ship's giant propeller churned the waters, frothing furiously. The motion caused me to miss our rendezvous. Holmes, caught in the wash, was tossed about violently. With a mighty effort, he dove for the torpedo as I drew near. I saw a look of horror on my friend's face. The propellers were sucking Holmes under!

"Holmes!" I screamed as my torpedo sped away from the ship and its deadly propeller. "Holmes," I cried out again. I was sure that I had lost him, and there was no hope of his survival!

52

Suddenly, I felt a drag on the torpedo. The missile struggled to remain right-side up. I twisted my head around as I searched for the cause of my problem. Something was skimming along the surface behind me. At first, I didn't comprehend what I was seeing. Then I realised—it was Holmes! The rope I had secured to the torpedo had played out. The long "tail" followed the current caused by the ship's propeller. It had been sucked along the same direction as Holmes, and somehow, he had managed to grab hold of the rope!

His arm waved at me, gesturing for us to continue away from the Clarity. I did as instructed and headed towards the Fleet. Once we were clear, I again turned round to check on my friend. I saw Holmes release the rope and motion for me to come 'round to pick him up. My turn was erratic, as the motor on the torpedo was now running in fits and starts. I reached my friend as the motor sputtered angrily, threatening to fail, and fail quickly.

Holmes latched onto the rope handle at the side of the

torpedo, just in time to hear the troubled engine's cough. The sea swells from the storm had weakened, although the thunder and lightning rumbled and flashed off in the distance. Now and again, the world was clearly black and white, bad and good, and the differences were striking. Holmes, understanding what was happening to our torpedo, reached for the extra air tanks that had been strapped to the torpedo. He managed to grasp them right as the motor died. "Let go!" he commanded, opening his faceplate. "Get off of the torpedo! Let it sink!"

I did. We watched in silence as our makeshift watercraft sank. Our tired, pain-wracked bodies treaded water to keep ourselves supplied with air. I gasped as I said, "Holmes! It's a miracle you're alive!"

"Thanks to your quick thinking, Watson," Holmes replied, as he bobbed up and down. "If you hadn't secured that trailing rope, I never would have made it."

We watched as the three ships—the Clarity, the Celestial, and the Collier—raced away at full speed. A salvo of cannon fire echoed over the water, as the Royal Fleet advanced on the pirate ships. The first shots from the Royal Navy flew over the bow of the middle ship in the pirates' fleet and fell harmlessly into the sea.

"They're getting away, Holmes!"

He said nothing, but I saw his lips move as he counted to himself. "Any second now," he whispered softly. "Any second."

The first detonation occurred on the Collier where I had placed the charge. That explosion destroyed the hinge pin that held the rudder vertical. From our vantage point, we could see how that steering mechanism tilted at an angle. Her captain, unaware of the damage, continued to run the ship at full steam. Having lost its ability to steer in a straight line, the ship orbited slowly, turning on its own pivoting bow.

"Good show, Watson!" cried Holmes, as the two other ships

simultaneously experienced crippling explosions. Their rudders were destroyed!

The Fleet, seeing the distressed targets turning round like the hands of a clock, fired another salvo. These came much closer than the first but still did not hit any of the ships.

"They found the range," Holmes remarked, his eyes focused on Jaeger's ship. "Let's hope the enemy understands that their cause is lost."

"Look there, Holmes!" I shouted, pointing to the white flags running up the lines. "They've given up!"

He narrowed his eyes suspiciously. "Look on the deck! There, do you see them?"

I squinted and stared in the direction Holmes had indicated. I noticed a lot of activity on the ship, as the men scurried around like mice. But soon, the crew members disappeared from view as they crossed over to the port side. "What's going on?" I asked.

"There! Look over there!" Holmes pointed to the other two ships. "Of course!" he pounded the water angrily. "A ship laden with arms would have ample reasons to believe they could repel any invasion. They're drawing the Fleet into a trap! The decks are loaded with cannon and artillery!"

To present as small a target as possible, the pirate ships, though crippled, had timed the dropping of their anchors and the shutdown of their engines so that their bows were directly facing the Fleet. The enemy formed a wedge and surprisingly, Jaeger's ship was at the forefront. I didn't think him capable of making such a heroic stand—as misguided as his decision was.

Her Majesty's Fleet maneuvered into position to train their guns on all three of the enemy ships. In order to do so, the Fleet would have to slip alongside the ships by entering the wedged formation. It would be like leading lambs to slaughter.

Holmes and I treaded water, waving our arms and trying to

warn the unsuspecting Fleet. But we were mere dots in the water. "They don't see us!" I wailed. "They'll be butchered in a matter of moments!"

I turned towards Holmes to see his reaction, but he was staring steadily at Jaeger's ship. "Holmes! Forget about him. It's the Fleet! We have to warn the Fleet!"

"Hullo," he said, smiling thinly. "So that's your game." Following Holmes' eyes, I saw what had caught his attention. A lifeboat was clearing the bow of Jaeger's ship, and I could clearly see the man. He laughed as he waved at us. Clearly, he had spotted us in the water and recognised who we were. With a whoop of amusement, he leaned over the side of the boat and took a hammer to an iron pipe that had one end dipped in the water.

"Watson, keep your eye on our friend. I have an idea. Let's hope Her Majesty provided a keen-eyed lookout."

Holmes switched on his helmet lamp and sent bursts of long and short flashes to the Fleet. In a matter of a few precious minutes, a reply was returned. A moment later, the Fleet altered course and steered away from the enemy and out of range.

"You've done it, Holmes!" I turned my attention back to Jaeger's boat. Incredibly, the men had disappeared! The boat bobbed up and down in the calming sea, with nary a person on board!

"Holmes!"

"I see," he responded, laconically.

"A wave must have washed them overboard."

"Not quite," he replied, pointing to a spot of churning sea. "The barge! That's what he was doing with that pipe. He was signaling the barge. Remember how the Bard had you knock on the pipe to call his crew?" The last ripples from her wake eddied out weakly, until the water was once again calm. We scanned the water in silence.

"I knew it!" Holmes cried, pointing over my shoulder, "We're too inviting a target for him to pass up his chance."

53

Like an island rising from the sea, the barge broke the surface about a thousand yards away. It was heading straight for us! My arms, weary with pain and cold, finally reached their limit from treading water. I yearned to give in. The waiting caress of death beckoned to me. All I wanted was to slip beneath the surface and let the pain and ache of fatigue go away. My friend pulled me up by the hair and held me afloat.

"We will look death straight on with no regrets," he said calmly, as the barge loomed, ever closer.

Jaeger, standing on the bow, waved his fist, laughing maniacally. Covering half the distance between us in what seemed seconds, the barge drew closer. I glanced at my friend and with a last spurt of energy, churned my legs to keep my head above the waves. I said, "No regrets, Holmes. If we are to die now, then I go to my grave knowing that Jaeger's plan has failed, and that, because of our actions, we have saved the lives of hundreds of young and gallant men of Her Majesty's Fleet."

I mustered as courageous a smile as possible and clasped his hand in mine, waiting for the inevitable. A whoosh of water lifted our bodies and tossed us into the air. We came hurtling back down, crashed with a thud, and then fell back into the sea! Sputtering, I spat out water as I surfaced. Holmes was only a foot away and he, too, shook his head to clear it. What had happened to us? Had we been hit? Had Jaeger missed? I squinted and waited for the chance to catch a glimpse between the cresting waves—and then I saw it. The barge was still a distance away! I looked at Holmes for an answer. His laugh filled my ears.

"The Nautilus!" he shouted, "It has to be! What else could affect a rescue so daring?"

In response to his joyous proclamation, the Nautilus rose to the surface. Water roiled off of her sleek surfaces. First her spine crested, then her bulky tapered form, and of course, those yellow-tinted eyes glowed through the mist, the sea spray, and the water. She arose like a phoenix amid a broiling sea and then waited quietly, blocking the path of the barge. Her grotesque, but nonetheless beautiful, sea-serpent features beckoned to me with all the welcome comfort of a soft blanket, offering warmth and safety.

Rollins was the first to scramble out of the hatch. From a crouched position, hanging onto the ship with one hand, he tossed out a line that Holmes caught. I was fading quickly and Holmes sensed it, so he tied the rope round my waist. Then he flipped me onto my back and wrapped an arm under my shoulders so he could support my head. With his free hand, he hung onto the rope, all the while yelling for Rollins to bring us aboard. Crew members had followed Rollins' lead and joined him on the deck. In practiced unison, they dragged us through the water and alongside the submarine.

The men worked as a team to haul us up and out of the water. Once I had clamored up the blackened skin of this mysterious creature and onto its deck, I fell to my knees, exhausted. I thanked the blessed heavens above for our deliverance. When I caught my breath, I gazed up at my friend's smiling face, as he assisted me to my feet. Rollins stepped forwards, draped my arm over his shoulder, and walked me to the hatch. "Glad to see you again, Doctor. Thought you were done for, hey? Well, not with old Rollins round!"

Before I disappeared over the collar of the hatch, I saw Rollins impart the same greeting on a very startled Sherlock Holmes. Helping hands passed the two of us along like we were ungainly sacks of potatoes. Before I knew what was happening, my feet rested on the sturdy deck of the Nautilus. With a metallic thunk, the hatch was slammed shut and the pressure lock put in place. Never was a man so happy to hear such a solid noise!

Holmes and I leaned on crewmen as they ushered us to the Control Room.

"Plonger, one hundred feet, if you please," Verne commanded, as we arrived.

"Diving to one hundred feet, Captain," answered the crewman at the controls.

Verne smiled, as the angle of the Nautilus told us we were well into our descent. Turning his attention to the tube above his head, Verne spoke into it, *"Où a accosté le chaland?"*

A muffled voice answered in reply, "The barge is fifteen degrees to starboard and leveling off at sixty feet. Her range is three hundred feet and moving away."

Holmes and I stood shivering in our dripping diving suits. A crewman brought us warm blankets, towels and steaming cups of coffee. I consumed mine eagerly.

"This way," said one, as he motioned us to a chamber off of one of the four doors. There we were able to step out of our diving suits, shower quickly, and dress in the same uniform worn by the other sailors. Feeling somewhat refreshed, we went back into the Control Room. While I had appreciated the chance to clean up and change, I nevertheless thought Monsieur Verne's inattention to us was rude and unbecoming. Directing his intense eyes at us, he said, "I am aware that you are both tired to the bone, but I am not ignoring you. I thought you might wish to observe my response to this treachery. Jaeger and the Bard have endangered my sister, my crew, my vessel, and my guests. Not to mention their mercenary and treasonous plots were designed to provoke war between two, or possibly three, nations."

Swiveling his head to the side, he spoke to the helmsman in a curt tone. "Pilot, steer a course to intercept the barge broadside on her starboard. Get no closer than five hundred meters. *Vous comprenez?"*

"Oui, Captain. *Je comprends.* No closer than five hundred meters on her starboard side."

Rollins entered the control room and whispered in Monsieur Verne's ear. A cruel smile escaped the Captain's lips, as he nodded. Rollins, walking away, winked at us, playfully.

"Monsieur Holmes," Verne weighed his words, "you will have the honour of firing the torpedo that will destroy the Stratford-Upon-Avon and her crew. We will be far enough away that you will both have time to move to the viewing window and see the unimagined power and wrath of the Nautilus. As soon as my helmsman places us in the proper firing position, you will have your revenge!"

Verne's eyes glowed like the Devil himself, and I wondered whether he was mad!

"I do not need to slake upon revenge's plate to be satisfied, Monsieur Verne," Holmes replied, his tone was scornful. "It is enough to know that Jaeger has failed. You and your instrument of death are best left to the makers of war. I will have no part in it!"

Holmes continued as he waved his hand in disgust. "This ship of yours presents the opportunity to serve humanity, but instead you choose to inflict death and destruction? And you have done so before, have you not?"

"When your brother so instructed me," said Verne. "After all, he paid for the building of the Nautilus. Our agreement was that this ship was his to command whenever necessary."

"Mycroft," I said.

"I am not, nor will I ever be, my brother. If you must unleash your dogs of war and satisfy your blood lust, then do as you will because we are powerless to stop you. But leave Watson and me out of it. That is not the sort of men we are." Holmes stormed out of the area, leaving the Captain and crew to stand there in shocked silence. I followed him.

Miss Verne was waiting for us outside the door. "Come with me. You must bear witness so that if you are asked, you can put an end to this madness."

"You do not approve?" I turned to her.

"No. Not any longer. At first, I wanted to see the monarchy toppled. I wanted to hurt Bertie as much as he had hurt me. And his mother? She said I was not worth destroying the monarchy for, which was what would surely happen if Bertie left Alix and married me. So I sought my revenge. But today, seeing a battle so close, having been held captive myself, watching the courage you two employed..." She paused. We were outside the viewing cabin. Holmes opened the door for her.

"I have had enough," said Miss Verne. "For ever and ever and ever. I am sickened by what my brother has become. Whatever pain I endured, I cannot wish it on all those other mothers. This must end, here and now."

Miss Verne took a seat on the cushioned bench of a divan. She patted the empty spaces to her left and right, inviting us to sit next to her. The three of us huddled there, in sadness and despondency. We stared straight ahead into the darkness of the sea. I shivered, thinking of how close we'd come—Holmes and I—to making that blackness our watery graves.

"It will do no good, *mes amis,*" she said, placing her delicate hand on Holmes'. He flinched as if she'd burned him. She ignored the silent rebuff and reached over and took mine. "My brother is not an evil man. He is the eldest, and he sees himself as my protector. When Bertie spurned me, I lost the will to live. Jules became so angry! *Non,* he is not bad; he is simply lost. Jules does not have a friend like Doctor Watson to keep him clearheaded."

54

She squeezed my hand tightly as we stared out the window. Holmes' eyes narrowed, speculatively. He seemed somewhat amused by the woman's desire to hold fast to us as the pace of the ship's pulse quickened. Orders were barked and answered instantly, in return. Bells clanged, and crew hustled outside our doors. "What's going on?" I asked.

"There," Holmes answered and pointed. "The barge."

The Nautilus, positioned exactly as the Captain had ordered, was on the starboard side of the barge and I would guess precisely one-hundred-and-fifty meters away. We were slightly below the barge, and the bow of the Nautilus was adjusted accordingly so that we were pointing up at the flat-bottomed ship.

Though the Stratford-Upon-Avon was almost seven hundred feet away from us, curiously, we could see the barge as clear as day. A shaft of light, coming from somewhere behind us, penetrated the darkness in a silent and somehow sinister manner. The barge, completely awash in the purest form of white light that I had ever seen, had become a moth that ventured too close to a flame.

Judging by the barge's maneuvering, it was clear Jaeger and his men knew they were being hunted. Also it was obvious that the Stratford-Upon-Avon wanted to be anywhere but here. But try as she might, she could not escape the Nautilus' relentless pursuit.

Holmes stared intently out the viewing window. His facial muscles hardened, as his eyes locked onto something that I couldn't see. Suddenly, inside the Nautilus, it went dark. The beam of light that had locked onto the barge fluctuated in intensity.

"Watson, did you see that?"

"Of course, I see that the lights have gone out!" I answered. "What's going on? Are we in danger?" I couldn't help but feel ill at ease after all we'd been through.

"The ship is charging," said Miss Verne, with a touch of sadness in her voice. The lights returned to their normal, soft glow. I briefly considered asking her about the dead seafarer with the gold in his gut, but this didn't seem to be the right time. Holmes had stiffened, almost like a pointer coming to an alert. Miss Verne's lower lip trembled as though she might burst into tears at any second.

But I did not understand what was happening. I asked, "What do you mean charging? We're barely moving."

"*Non!* Not moving!" she said with a raspy edge to her voice.

"My sister means that the weapons system is charging," said Monsieur Verne, entering the observation area. Holmes stood up, spun on his heel, and strode determinedly towards the inventor.

"Monsieur Verne, what else is there that I should know about the barge?" Holmes' words were spoken acidly, and I got up and joined him in an act of solidarity.

"Ah, Monsieur Holmes," Verne replied, his eyes darkening, "there is much to the barge that you do not know. Though you are recognised as a man of brilliant reasoning, of course, there are many things you do not understand."

"It would be wise," said my friend, balling his hand into a fist, "that you do not pursue such a patronizing tone with me."

"What is it, Holmes? What did you see?" I asked anxiously.

Miss Verne burst into noisy sobs. Her brother stared at Holmes contemptuously but said nothing.

"Watson? Please take Miss Verne to her quarters and make her comfortable. Come back here as soon as you're through," Holmes said. He turned and walked back to the window, as I led the sobbing woman to her cabin. She sank down onto her bed, covering her face with her hands.

I couldn't help myself, and so I asked, "Was there ever a Mr. Morel?"

"No," she said.

"Who was that man? The body with the tattoo? Why did you send us to see him?"

She sniffled. "That was Jaeger's doing. He wanted Sherlock Holmes to believe the rumours we were spreading about the Queen using the gold to set up Munshi. If the great Sherlock Holmes believed it, then all of England would, too. Or so he thought."

"But that poor man!" I stopped and stared at the woman I'd found so attractive previously. "Forcing him to swallow all of that gold! He'd been tortured! And killed!"

All she could do was nod at me. I realised then that her sympathy was limited. Yes, when death was occurring before her eyes, she could quiver and quake and cry with the best of them. But when the poor tortured fellow was unknown to her, when she was far removed from the scene of misery, whenever she could turn a blind eye, she would. In short, when it came to the sufferings of others, she could care less.

I carefully measured out a dose of laudanum and she

happily swallowed it. Rather than return it to her bedside table, I slipped the bottle into my pocket.

"Good-bye, Madame," I said.

Yes, she was beautiful. True, she could give a good performance. But like her brother, she lacked an essential human kindness and that lack rotted her from the inside out.

55

A few minutes later, I rejoined Holmes. "I gave her a dose of that sedative that I found in her nightstand. She'll be fine. What did you see, Holmes?"

My friend stood alone in front of the observation window and gazed out at the blackness. Suddenly, the giant beam of light flashed on. It was seeking out the barge once again. Holmes' eyes lit up in horror. He turned on his heel to run out of the cabin. I started to follow, but something caught my eye.

"Holmes!" I cried as I came to a jarring halt. I stared out the huge expanse of glass. I felt rather than saw Holmes' return to my side. We watched as two torpedoes ploughed through the water from somewhere below us.

"That first light," he said. "I believe that it was searching for the exact placement of the barge. Like a bat using its high pitched cries to find its way in the dark."

Holmes' eyes filled with sadness as we stood transfixed whilst the weapons of death sought their target. The torpedoes continued their deadly mission, disappearing as their distance from us grew. For a few seconds more, we stared blankly into the light. Our eyes were looking for the torpedoes, but we saw nothing.

"They missed!" I exclaimed.

"Brace yourself," Holmes warned.

The first torpedo struck. An instant later, the second one found its target.

When the first torpedo detonated, a single fireball lit up the water. Then came a second blazing ball of light. Curiously, the barge seemed to shrink into itself—and then it blew apart as the concealed explosives were set off.

The flash from the explosions, combined with the debris of the twisted wreckage, rolled lazily outward, confined by the weight of the water. This wave of detritus continued for several seconds. I thought we'd seen all there was to see, but astonishingly, a white wall made its way towards us.

Shards of wood and metal were captured in its feathery roll when the first wave hit the Nautilus. The submarine listed to one side and nearly flipped over. The second wave hit us an instant later. Holmes and I were sent sprawling. I feared that the observation window would shatter under such a powerful force and we would die a horrible death. Thankfully, Monsieur Verne had built the Nautilus to withstand even greater forces.

Slowly, the ship righted herself, even though the lesser shock waves rolled across and over our hull. The lights in the Nautilus went out again. In flickering fits and starts, they struggled to come back on. I had no idea where Holmes had gone and called out to him. "Holmes, where are you? Are you hurt?"

I saw my friend rising to his knees from behind the divan—a trickle of blood ran down his chin. "Knocked to my knees but not seriously hurt. What about you?"

"As well as can be expected," I replied, rubbing a tender bump on my head.

Holmes walked to the observation window. There he stood

and silently watched as the wreckage fell to the bottom. "The murderous fool!" Holmes howled, watching the last of the debris settle.

"I'd be careful of your words, Monsieur Holmes," said Monsieur Verne upon entering. "Those men out there—they're the murderers. I meted out justice—nothing more."

Holmes never turned round. He merely tensed, as he watched the reflections of Verne and his men draw near.

"Steady, Holmes," I whispered. "They've pistols drawn."

With a jerk of his head, Verne motioned for two men to come and guard us. I felt a pistol being pressed into the small of my back. A crew member behind Holmes did the same to my friend.

"Look! Do you see who the real murderers are?" Verne gestured, demanding that we look towards the surface of the water. "Your Queen's precious Fleet!"

The Nautilus shuddered as report after report of explosions from the Queen's Fleet sent tons of water moving around us. Verne whispered something to one of his men and sent him running aft. Seconds later, the submarine sprang to life. The Nautilus slowly backed away from the carnage happening on the surface above us. One by one, portions of the pirate vessels slipped beneath the surface. Their broken hulls and masts groaned in protest, as they drifted down through the murky water.

Pieces of shattered masts and stray decking boards fell through the water. Although their impact was cushioned, they still bounced noisily off the submarine. Slowly, the poor, tortured bodies of the men rained down. One victim, his right arm torn off cleanly, slid down the observation window. His face seemed surprised in death. His head lolled lazily, as it bobbled from side to side and eventually bounced against the glass.

Long after this case was concluded, I learned that the mysterious, green ooze that dripped down on the observation windows in molten globs was actually blood! At the depth we were, light could not penetrate, and thus, blood would seem to be black-green in colour. However, I didn't know that at the time. Instead, I found the ethereal droplets of greenish liquid to be morbidly fascinating. I could not tear my eyes from the carnage. The corpse of a tattered sailor drifted past and continued floating down to its final resting place. The beam of light flickered at last, and the scene was bathed in merciful blackness.

Monsieur Verne sneered at my friend. "Well, Monsieur Holmes, what do you think of your compassionate Queen and your patriotic brother now? Surely, you of all people, understand that what I did was proper."

"Proper?" Holmes said. He half-turned and glanced at the divan.

"Excuse my manners, gentlemen. Of course, by all means, sit," Verne said. We did as we were invited. As soon as we were seated, Verne's men pounced on us. Before we could resist, they had bound us hand and foot.

"What is the meaning of this?" I demanded.

Monsieur Verne sneered. "A necessary precaution. Wouldn't you agree, Monsieur Holmes?"

Verne continued, "I am sorry that you do not see the wisdom in all of this. The Stratford-Upon-Avon and the Nautilus were not designed as weapons of terror. I only took money from your brother because I could not secure the funding any other way. I had hoped he and the Queen would come to realise ships like these should act as benevolent protectors—mediators of nations and their petty squabbles. Scientific explorers of the first order. And do not forget the advances that could be made, as these ships embark on the greatest expeditions ever conceived. Our purpose is to explore the proper use of this planet's dwindling natural resources. That is what this ship is designed for—for the common good!"

"Oh, I see!" Holmes laughed sarcastically. "If I understand you correctly, each captain of his own submarine would be a... Let's see how did you explain it? Ah, yes. Now I recall, a benevolent protector for the common good?"

"Yes! You do see it!" nodded Verne, enthusiastically. He chose to ignore my friend's obvious disdain. But just as quickly, Holmes made his censure obvious by saying, "Common good for whom? You and your private navy? Who decides what is best for the citizens?"

"Perhaps that is a question you should put to your brother," said Verne. Shaking his head, the inventor remarked sadly, "There is no point in my trying to convince you, then?"

"None."

"I see. Very well. *Tant pis.*" Monsieur Verne glowered at us, muttering beneath his breath in French. Cocking his head to one side, he gave a nod to the men standing behind us. Immediately, I felt the prick of the needle, as its tip penetrated my neck. A quick glance at Holmes told me that he, too, had suffered the same fate.

I found myself going limp. My last thought was the realisation that I could no longer hold my head erect, as my chin fell heavily against my chest.

56

I awoke with a start and was surprised to find myself in my own bed at 221B Baker Street. It was nighttime. The streetlamps glowed softly outside my window.

In the chair at my bedside sprawled my friend, Sherlock Holmes. With his fingers laced together and chin resting on the shelf formed by his hands, he stared at me through troubled eyes. However, upon seeing me stirring, his face lit up. "So there you are, good fellow! I was beginning to worry."

He patted my shoulder roughly.

"Holmes," I rasped, my throat raw.

"Quiet, Watson. There's time enough to talk later. Get some rest. You can join me in the parlour when you're ready."

Though I had many questions, I was thankful for his consideration. I burrowed deeper into my bed, pulling the covers up to my chin. Holmes rose from the chair and smiled down at me. He was walking away when I called to him, "Holmes, tell me, is it over?"

"Let's just say that we're out of it," he replied, shutting the door. "For now, at least."

I slept for the rest of the day.

THE SUN SHINING INTO MY ROOM THE NEXT MORNING, AWAKENED ME. My pocket watch on the bedside table said it was gone ten. Blinking back the sleep, my eyes played over the walls of my room. Taking in the various souvenirs and trophies that I had accumulated over the years during my association with Holmes, I caught sight of an unfamiliar looking carton on top of my dresser.

Tossing off the covers, I rolled out of bed and jammed my feet into my slippers. Pulling the sash of my robe tight round my waist, I shuffled over to the mysterious box. Before my hands reached the package, Holmes knocked on my door and pushed it open. His smiling face stared in at me. "Excellent! I thought I heard you rustling around. How are you feeling?"

"Fine. What's this all about?" I asked, pointing to the carton.

"Open it. I thought you might wish to have a keepsake of our adventure on the Nautilus."

Placing the carton back on the dresser's surface, I struggled with the cord that held it closed. Holmes tossed me his pocketknife, and I cut into it with anticipation. Folding back the flaps, I peered at the carton's contents.

Inside was a beautifully crafted shadow box made out of polished cherry mahogany. Encased in glass and resting on an emerald green crushed velvet backdrop sat a cocked pistol crossbow. A *fléchette* rested next to it. There was also the modified band quiver with its darts. On the bottom portion of the frame, centered and tacked into the mahogany wood, was an engraved brass plate. The inscription read:

The Pistol Crossbow used by
Dr. John H. Watson

with remarkable results.
From a very grateful
Sherlock Holmes

I smiled at my companion of these many years. "I don't know what to say, Holmes. Thank you."

"No, old friend. It is I who should thank you. Never has a man performed so brilliantly. You saved my life. Numerous times."

An awkward silence filled the room.

"Don't bother getting dressed," he said. "I suggest we lounge about the apartment like carefree bachelors for the rest of the day. We'll browse the papers, though I have already done so. We'll discuss precisely what this case was all about. I'll have Mrs. Hudson send up some breakfast."

True to his word, that was how we spent the rest of the day. Occasionally, we were interrupted by an arriving telegram, which Holmes would read before tossing angrily into the fireplace.

"Nothing!" he groaned. "It's a disgrace! How does our government ever get anything done? No mention of the young Prince being returned to Prussia. Nothing about the pirate fleet! There are no signs of the Vernes or the Nautilus!"

The name of the submarine jarred me to ask the question that was gnawing at the back of my mind. "Holmes, how did we get here? I mean, the last thing I recall was being tied to a chair and feeling the needle. What happened in between then and now?"

He faced me. "I don't know for sure," he answered, pressing his lips together, not accustomed to be lacking answers. "I recall coming to at the very spot where we first encountered Ezekiel Emeritus Marder. There down by the dock. A carriage driver helped me get you into the growler. Obviously, it wasn't in Monsieur Verne's plans to have us killed. He simply cast us off as so much excess baggage."

"But why?" I countered. "Do you think he was mad?"

"Most definitely. He was very cross with us."

"You know very well that is not what I meant!" I cried, in frustration.

"Oh, Watson, of course I know what you mean. Is he insane? No, I think not. As his sister explained, he's misguided. All he sees is the science and the horizons and none of the politics or misuse of his creations. As Tom Brown at Oxford puts it, *He continued to behold towers and quadrangles, and chapels, through rose-colored spectacles.* Verne is undeniably naïve when it comes to matters of world dominance. As brilliant as he is, he doesn't understand the destruction and chaos that his devilish inventions will bring upon the world. Maybe not now, but in the future, as his inventions will become far more deadly than even we can imagine."

"How so?"

Holmes stared into space, attempting to breach the misty veil of the future. He shuddered, as a sudden chill ran through his body.

"I don't know," he answered, "I can't say exactly, but I can tell you this. In the wrong hands, that submarine ..." Again he shivered. "Let's just say that a nation's sovereignty will become meaningless."

"Being a bit melodramatic aren't we, Holmes?"

A knock interrupted further conversation. I got up and opened the door impatiently. A very startled Mrs. Hudson stood in the entrance. "The evening papers, Doctor," she said, handing me the voluminous pile. "And, oh yes, there's a telegram for Mr. Holmes."

Before I could reach for the telegram, Holmes ran to the

door and snatched it out of the bewildered landlady's hand. "Thank you, Mrs. Hudson. That will be all."

Holmes kicked the door shut.

"Holmes, really!" I whined, taking pity on our poor landlady. "Some day, we're going to return to the flat, only to find our belongings tossed out into the street."

But my friend didn't hear me. He was already deep into the reading of the telegram. It was a query from another would-be client, a man who needed help with a missing daughter or some such quandary.

TWO YEARS HAVE PASSED SINCE OUR ADVENTURE ON THE NAUTILUS, and the notes from the case have been gathering dust in a box on the shelf. One day when Holmes was taking a walk and I was reading the morning papers, a tiny mention caught my eye. A Monsieur Jules Verne, the well-known author, survived a madman's bullet but would be crippled for the rest of his life.

The possibility that Jaeger or Zeke Marder had their revenge prompted me to recall the events of that fantastic adventure, and I have finally put the case to pen and paper.

~THE END~

OUR GIFT TO YOU

Dr. John H. Watson has written a background report on the famous Diogenes Club. If you are interested in all aspects of Sherlock Holmes' world, this is a must-read! To claim your copy, go here —

https://BookHip.com/TNQTC.

BOOKS IN THE SHERLOCK HOLMES FANTASY THRILLER SERIES, CONCEIVED BY C.J. LUTTON—

Sherlock Holmes and the Giant Sumatran Rat (Book #1) * Concept by C.J. Lutton. Written by Joanna Campbell Slan.

Sherlock Holmes and the Father of Lies (Book #2) * Written by C.J. Lutton

Sherlock Holmes and the Nefarious Seafarers (Book #3) * Written by C.J. Lutton.

Sherlock Holmes and the Time Machine (Book #4) * Written by C.J. Lutton.

For more information and purchase links, go to: https://www.thesherlockstories.com

Or contact us at sherlock1277@gmail.com

ABOUT C.J. LUTTON...

C.J. Lutton was born in North Bergen, New Jersey. He lived his life with great curiosity. He spent four years in the United States Army, and after being honorably discharged, he traveled and explored Europe, Alaska, and the continental United States. He was, for the most part, a man of thought, honesty, and giving. He had a great imagination and love of words – reading the dictionary was a passion of his. He read and wrote. I bring to you one of his favorites – Sherlock Holmes – from The Confidential Files of John H. Watson.

I hope that you will love his imagination, and his gift to tell a great story.

Roberta Lutton (Mrs. C.J. Lutton)

ABOUT JOANNA CAMPBELL SLAN—

Joanna is a *New York Times, USA Today,* and Amazon bestselling author of 80 books. She's edited many more. Her historical fiction — *Death of a Schoolgirl: The Jane Eyre Chronicles* — won the Daphne du Maurier Award for Literary Excellence. Her first book – *Paper Scissors Death: Book #1 in the Kiki Lowenstein Mystery Series* — was a finalist for the Agatha Award. Learn more at linktr.ee/jcslan

www.ingramcontent.com/pod-product-compliance
Lightning Source LLC
Chambersburg PA
CBHW060810310726
48980CB00002B/298

* 9 7 8 0 9 6 6 4 7 0 7 3 4 *